UNDER
THE FLAMBOYANT TREE

BY

RICK TUCKER

Under the Flamboyant Tree

Copyright © 2021: Rick Tucker

First Printed in United Kingdom 2021

Published by Conscious Dreams Publishing
www.consciousdreamspublishing.com

Edited by Elise Abram

Illustrated by John Ashton

Typeset by Oksana Kosovan

ISBN: 978-1-913674-82-3

IN MEMORIAM

This book is dedicated to much loved members of my Trinidadian family and friends who are no longer with us: Pa, Doo Doo, Tiny, Karl, Branny, Joey, Smiley, Myrtle, Sunny Jones, Ben, and Methi.

'Au milieu de l'hiver, j'ai découvert en moi un invincible été.'

– Albert Camus

'When I think of where I'm coming from
Looking back at where the journey began
I really haffi say that I'm strong, I'm strong...'

– Lila Iké, 'Where I'm Coming From'

AUTHOR'S NOTE

All characters and events portrayed in this book are fictional. Some place names are real. Although the village of Muga in Trinidad does not exist, it is typical. Many people in Trinidad and Tobago are known by their nicknames, and some of these are more widespread than others. The nicknames used in this book are either ones I created myself or ones I have come across, but none of them refers to anyone I have met or know. Like many places in the world, Trinidad has its problems, but it remains a beautiful country, where I have much loved friends and family.

CONTENTS

~ CHAPTER 1 ~

CAMILLE MOVED LIKE a welcome breeze through the streets near her home as she hurried to and from work at the École Henri IV just a few winding streets away. She knew most of the shop and café workers on the adjacent rue Saint-Jacques well enough to stop and talk or wave and shout, *'Ça va?'* Some days, it was as though everybody knew her. They always greeted her with a smile and warmth that demonstrated much about the way local communities went about life and survival in large cities. If you had somewhere to live and enough money to eat and drink, then you were a part of a dynamic community, a group who could afford, however humbly, to turn their faces towards the world and open up their arms.

Times were certainly harder than they had been for years, and the conversations now more often turned to grumblings about politics, the economy, some new piece of infuriating bureaucracy, or restrictive regulation, but the familiar faces and well-worn attitudes provided the constancy everyone needed in these uncertain times, and Camille was one such familiar face in her local community. No one ever had a bad word to say about the bright, warm woman who waved, smiled, and asked after her neighbours' health, the progress of their children at school, or when their babies were due.

The young women working at the Patisserie Richard always chatted excitedly with her whenever she called in to buy *un croissant aux amandes* for a breakfast treat, which was usually two or three times a week. It was a busy, bustling, noisy neighbourhood, its narrow streets funnelling the icy blasts of winter or providing welcome relief from the smells and heat of a Parisian summer. Camille loved the streets where she lived with all their local characters. It was a diverse and crowded neighbourhood, where people of different ages, religions, skin tones, and sexual orientations mixed in intricate and muddled harmony. She relished the time spent with her immediate neighbours in the apartment block where she lived. There was Auguste, the waiter who lived across the hall, a young Lyonais who entertained a variety of young men and listened to choral music; Eugène and Marie, who lived below with their two teenage children; and Sylvie, the magnificent, painted lady and ageing courtesan who claimed to have known every artist or writer that was ever associated with Paris – not that anyone really believed her – and who still had some regular customers despite being well into her seventies. 'If a man knows how to make love,' she had told Camille, 'and is willing to pay me for the pleasure, then why should I retire?'

Camille enjoyed her work, for the most part, teaching French to English-speaking professionals, most of whom were businessmen and women in their fifties and sixties who offered her an intellectuality and enthusiasm that allowed her to view the world through a different, more multi-coloured window. She both craved and valued that stimulus because the only part of Camille's situation that didn't offer her any warmth was the life she shared increasingly less with Philippe, her husband of twenty-four years, the father of her grown and departed sons. Philippe ran a small arts cinema in the Latin Quarter, worked unsocial hours, drank to an unhealthy level, and had a disproportionately inflated view of his own importance. He was an embittered failure of an artist who had never had the character to realise his literary and cinematic aspirations – which Camille had come to view as pretensions – and who took his frustrations out on Camille with aggressive silences, sharp critical carping remarks, and rough, short-lived sex.

Having family in Trinidad, her mother's country of origin, was an increasing source of wonder for her, something that accentuated her restlessness and dissatisfaction of late. She remembered the stories her mother would tell of her homeland, how exotic and warm it all sounded, and how those tales had fuelled Camille's desire to find out more about her roots.

As a mixed-race girl – and now as a woman – she considered herself non-white, and she always sought reassurance and identity with other non-whites or those who felt they didn't fit in with conventional white society. Marriage and motherhood had been a way to ignore the call of her ancestry, but the restlessness it provoked remained somewhere inside her, and now that call was becoming ever more urgent and shrill. Her sons, Eric and Fred, both in their early twenties, had long ago left home, and the drudgery of domestic life and the alienation she felt in the confines of her marriage in their small apartment had led her to become less cautious, or at times, she believed, reckless.

Two years previously, she had engaged in a clandestine relationship with an older Irish man she had met at work. He was balding, a little overweight, and as far from physically attractive, vain, and arrogant as Philippe could be. But he was intelligent and kind – not an artist in any way – whose ageing body fascinated her more than attracted her, and in whose arms she felt, although briefly, a sense of being nurtured and cared for. She didn't mind his old hands on her or inside her or his heavy body collapsing upon hers because it didn't frighten or oppress her. Philippe was still a child, she realised, trapped inside the forsaken body of a cynical alcoholic, whereas Liam was a mature man who had seen the world, and although too opinionated for her liking, offered her something different, the least of which was unqualified attention. Maybe one day, she would find someone near enough her age who was safe, sensible, and sexually arousing, with whom she could laugh, link arms, curl up on a sofa, travel, and make love without feeling she was doing something wrong.

Liam lived in Dublin, worked for an international bank, and only came to Paris four times a year, each time for a few weeks. During his visits, they arranged to meet at one of their favourite places – by the bookstalls on Quai St Michel or in one of the expensive restaurants on Montparnasse or Place Joffre. From there, they would stroll through Parc du Sonny de Mars and look at one of the world's most familiar constructions and its queues of tourists, African vendors of miniature Eiffel Tower replicas hustling passersby to look at their wares neatly arranged on mats on the ground, or the sharp-tongued, armed, padded gendarmes and security personnel.

If there was time, they would go to his hotel room or apartment, depending on what his company was willing to pay, and he would ask her to undress him, which she did with the curiosity of a virgin before undressing in front of him and watching his sixty-seven-year-old penis stir to life beneath his outsize belly. When they were close to coitus, his arousal would diminish, which would anger him, but it did not concern her at all. She was happy to satisfy him by other means. In fact, she preferred his tongue and fingers penetrating her to any other part of him. She didn't really see this as sex at all – it was just caring companionship. Whenever he told her he loved her and wanted to leave his wife of forty years for her, she reminded him that his son and daughter, for whom he'd expressed so much love, would never forgive him. 'Anyway, she needs you,' she would tell him, 'and you're too honourable to abandon her.'

'But I want only you,' he would plead.

'Shhh...don't spoil it,' she would say, and that would be that.

Whenever he returned to Ireland, she would miss him for a while, and she wondered if it was actually love she was experiencing. She certainly cared for him, and he made her smile whenever they'd meet, but she couldn't tolerate his jealousy and possessiveness. It was impossible to be objective about him. She knew he was an old man who naturally enjoyed the company and feel of a younger woman. She knew he confused his ensuing arousal with love, and she knew she was probably his last roll of the dice when it came to an exciting sex life. It was this to which he was addicted, mistakenly thinking of it and describing it as love, but she still missed him. They would text in secret, but that was most unsatisfactory as it often led to misunderstanding and misinterpretation. If she appeared distant or non-committal, he would be quick to anger, and that anger would strengthen her resolve to remain distant and non-committal, all the time reassuring him – falsely – that, of course, she wasn't.

Meanwhile, her marriage to Philippe grew colder, the chasm in their marital bed ever-widening, the hours he spent away from home ever-increasing. She was trapped and going nowhere. She often asked herself if life was meant to be like that. Was that the only reason she missed Liam? Once, when in Liam's company, she had flirted with a waiter, a good-looking younger man with a smooth patter and an irresistible glint in his eyes, provoking Liam to become audibly angry, unable to calm himself despite her taking his hand and telling him not to be silly.

He'd walked out on her without paying the bill – something he always insisted on doing – so she'd stayed and invited, non-verbally, the waiter to make the first move. The end result was an apparently passionate – but in reality, just rough – kiss in the locked unisex toilet where he'd grabbed her breast, she'd grabbed his cock, and he'd put his hand up her skirt. At that point, she'd pushed him away, winked, and walked out. As she meandered up the rue des Écoles she found both Liam and the waiter's desirous behaviours amusing and curious. This made her realise that she needed to leave, to go away for a while and do something different. Maybe now was the time to travel to find out about her long-lost family in Trinidad. Philippe wouldn't care, and Liam knew such a trip was on the cards one day. She would find her mother's people and let the Caribbean sun warm her body and reenergise her. She would be able to think, do what she liked, and no one would be there to disapprove. Then, serendipity played its fickle hand, and she met Fingal Reid.

~ CHAPTER 2 ~

S HE LOOKED AT Philippe, slouched there on the sofa in track bottoms and a crumpled sweater, barefoot, a whisky in one hand, the remote control in the other, unshaven for days, hair lank and greasy, the skin on his face dry and red with inflamed patches on his forehead and either side of his nose, a faraway look in his eyes as he watched the screen with the sound turned down so low as to be barely audible, nothing more than an irritating, inconsistent hum in the background. It was the evening of their twenty-fifth wedding anniversary, and while she had only just remembered, he hadn't said a word, so maybe he'd forgotten too, she thought, or he just couldn't bear to mention it. She couldn't either. Life was about choices, after all, and the ones you make, even when you're sixteen and pregnant, lead you down a path where, as life goes on, it becomes impossible to retrace the steps you've already taken.

There were times they had been functional, happy, even. They had sailed together out of the storm that had ended her innocence, accompanied the early years of parenthood and the subsequent marriage to a man her parents – especially her father – did not like. In those days, Philippe – seven years her senior – had appeared worldly, confident they would get on in the world. He had connections, he had talent, and he assured her he would make more than enough money for them to live comfortably without compromising their free-spirited values. He had seemed so mature when emotionally, she now realised, he was really only a boy, troubled by his background and upbringing in a dysfunctional bourgeois family in the suburbs of Paris, alienated from his parents and older siblings as soon as he'd left home to go to art school. 'To hell with them,' he'd often said. 'We don't need them.'

Eighteen quick, busy, tiring months after Eric had been born, his younger brother, Fred, followed, and then there were the four of them, living in a cramped apartment in Belleville, struggling each month to pay the rent and bills as each plan for earning a real income had fallen apart. She was nineteen, and the handsome romantic with whom she had fallen in love began to lose some of the light from his eyes.

Now, twenty-six years on from their first meeting, the boys had gone, Philippe was a barely functioning alcoholic nearly fifty years of age, and she was beginning to yearn for something else, but what? It was Eric's departure for Madrid and Fred's to South America a few months later that had brought all of this into sharp focus. As she looked out of her kitchen window down upon the cars queued at the traffic lights in the rain, the reds, greens, whites, and ambers of the lights converging in an insentient, alienating haze, she felt completely isolated. People disappear, she thought, they abandon you, leaving you feeling alone, and then you realise no one ever rides to the rescue.

Some aspects of her relationship with her father had recovered, especially after her mother's death a few years before, when they seemed to rediscover something of the joy they had both experienced when she was young. That feeling of closeness had remained trapped somewhere under the surface of both their exteriors since her early teens. Her father, Yves, had distanced himself from her and Philippe for many years, leaving her mother, Elma, to be the main point of contact, and thereby, a conduit for communication between father and daughter. As Eric and Fred grew, Yves softened, and he started to enjoy the company of his grandsons, but he could never fully accept Philippe, who he saw as flawed, weak, and immoral. His beautiful precious daughter, their only child, had been taken from him by this man who was, at best, an impractical dreamer, and at worst, a hopeless, lazy, little shit.

For Camille, a woman yet to discover who she really was in terms of her talents, abilities, strengths, weaknesses, and even her likes and dislikes, life had suddenly begun to look different, as though everything that had gone before was illusory, made-up, a pretence constructed to avoid the possibility that underneath it all, she was a viable individual with a life of her own to lead. As Philippe had retreated into his fog of drunken resentment and her father had aged, she instinctively, but quietly, began to explore life in a way she had not done before. This included trying to find out more about her Caribbean-Indian roots. Who were the people her mother had told her about? Would she ever find them? She imagined the Caribbean Islands in much the same way a tourist would – white sands, turquoise seas, coconut palms, blue skies – but she also imagined the sense of freedom Trinidad might offer her – less neurosis, wearing fewer clothes, not worrying about make-up or fashion or politics or art or work or anything that filled her thoughts when in Paris. Going to Trinidad could be the start of her experiencing her true self, helping her to become more self-reliant and more discerning about what she shared with others. It would be a fresh page, filled in only by her as and when she chose.

She had, of course, embarked on a strange affair with an older man. That, too, she reflected, was a part of her seeing the world in a new light. An experiment, perhaps, in which Liam was a willing participant, but maybe he wouldn't have been had he understood how she really viewed their relationship. The trouble with forming new relationships of any kind at that stage of life, she realised, was that it would lead those with whom she engaged to have raised expectations of how she might behave towards them, and understandably so. When it came to the chemistry of her relationship with Liam, she felt more like a laboratory technician examining cultures and microbes: detached, rarely excited, but nevertheless intrigued by what was going on in the Petri dish.

Liam often said he believed their closeness and physical intimacy to mean she should leave Philippe, and he should leave his wife, and although, sometimes, it was an attractive thought, even comforting to her, she would always push it – and him –

away. She didn't want to live with him. He was wealthy enough and would look after her, no doubt, but he was, for the most part, a welcome curiosity whom she admired and respected but for whom she would never feel strongly enough to live with. That would carry with it all the baggage of their marriage break-ups and having to tell and deal with their families and friends. She liked him, his old body didn't threaten her, and she liked to please him, but it was a relationship of convenience for her, a harbour where she could shelter from both the turmoil of her storms and the inanity of the subsequent calms.

It was the same with the women in her limited social circle; she observed their behaviour at work or on nights out with a detached curiosity. Their chatter about men, sex, clothes, television programmes, children, politics, art, culture, and travel all left her cold, if not a little amused. She would join in with them, but she never felt a part of them, neither superior nor inferior to them, just different. This led to a desperate feeling of alienation and being alone, heightened each time she left their company and returned home to either an empty space or one filled by Philippe's halitosis, short-temper, and increasingly mean spirit. Only Mireille – her gentle friend, suffering her secondaries and trying to survive with a ready smile and one breast – had enough depth and intelligence to understand her feelings. She only ever confided in Mireille, though sparingly.

Then, she met Fingal, and she was aroused by him and by his arousal for her. He was a Janus who looked in one direction with the eyes of an innocent, sensitive artist and the other with those of a traumatised war veteran. Fingal Reid, the passionate, wounded singer and harmonica player for whom music was as essential as breath, who often infuriated her by being so damn non-judgemental and reasonable, so *non*-possessive and *non*-jealous she would accuse him of indifference, to which he would respond with saint-like patience, telling her he accepted her without condition, and that he acknowledged, with nothing but positive regard for her, all that she was and all of the life she had led up to that moment. That he did so with such obviously genuine and honourable feelings for her didn't stop her dismissing his love, telling him he was a fool and that he didn't know what love was. In fact, the more he did so, the more dismissive she became.

She told him she didn't want him to be her lover, that she didn't have the space for another man in her life, that it was difficult for her to ditch Liam, that she still loved Philippe and didn't want to hurt him despite often being hurt by him, but that also – paradoxically, she admitted – whenever she parted from Fingal, perhaps after a long weekend in London, Lyon, Lille, or Bruges – wherever they'd managed to meet – she felt inexplicable anguish.

'It must be love,' he'd say.

'Must it? Do you think I'm in love with you?'

'Only you can answer that. I know how I feel.'

'How can you be so sure?'

'Because I know how I feel, and I own my feelings, and you always want to negate or deny how I feel about you, so you do the same to yourself when it comes to what you're really feeling.'

She would taunt him, sometimes, after their love-making –
usually passionate and climactic for her in a way she had never
experienced – telling him it had nothing to do with love, that
it was just sex, and that, of course, he enjoyed the physical
excitement, but that's all it was, something physical and base
with no metaphysical connection between them at all. This would
hurt him, and he would tell her so, but he would also assert, time
and again, that he loved her and wouldn't go along with her
game of self-doubt and faux morality in order either to give her
the attention for which she was looking or to confirm for her
that she was some kind of flawed alien who was impossible to
live with and not worth loving. He gave her attention because
she deserved it, he'd said, because she was interesting, because
they got on well, because when they walked arm in arm, they fit
together easily. She quickly came to trust him. It was instinctive,
not unnatural at all, but without doubt, a new experience for her
as he accessed the most private areas of her body and mind with
his eyes, his words, his silent gestures, his hands, his tongue,
and his lips, always sensitive and responsive to her reactions.

He had also been the only one in her triumvirate of lovers
astute enough to question her about her relationship with her
father and understand its importance, something from which
Philippe had always shied away. It was obvious enough, she had
come to see, that her search to be loved by a man without being
able to commit, afraid of being judged and that the negative
judgement would somehow confirm the negative view she had
of herself was a disposition that must have its roots in her
relationship with the first man she had ever known. Her father,

Yves, was a taciturn, seemingly unemotional man who, she felt, always judged her too harshly, loved her so much but was only able to express that love through trying to micromanage her life, and when he failed to do so, he made his disapproval disproportionately apparent.

There were so many ways in which she and Fingal had become intimate – why couldn't she commit to reciprocating his feelings for her? Why, whenever she drove him away, did she go looking for him again? Why did she feel more in control of her life when lying in Liam's flabby arms than when in Fingal's all-enveloping arms and mind? It was as though she dared not allow all of her real self to emerge in case she was unable to control whatever would follow. Instead of allowing the river of her life to flow, she rather imagined – and therefore, feared – it would burst the dam of her well-defended psyche and drown her, and the fear always won.

Then, one day, all of a sudden – and she should have seen it coming – the long-suffering Fingal declared he had had enough of her prevarications and inconsistencies, had told her he would always love her, that she was the love of his life but he must – for his own good – leave her behind. He had sounded wretched and sad. Alone in a cottage in Scotland, he often disappeared and communicated only by text because whenever they tried to speak, the signal failed. Fine, she thought at first. It's over. It's for the best. But she had thought this before, and he had always come back. However, that time, he had sounded so nihilistic, embittered, and angry. She hadn't deleted the texts, and she re-read them every so often.

– there's nothing so good for the soul as arousing the indifference of someone you love ffs! I can't do this anymore it's too one-sided and I have to protect myself

– what do you mean?

– I love you more than I can say but that's not enough for you. I have to accept that so I have to move on

– is there someone else?

– ffs Camille if I was lying on my death bed and God asked me who was the greatest love of my life I would tell him it was you – of course there's no one else!!! Fuck this! Fuck life!

– please don't say that Fingal please

There was a gap in their exchange, which had lasted for over an hour before she'd received his final text: *goodbye Camille*

The dark mood of his worried her, and she tried to contact him a few hours later to see if he was all right, but he never replied. Her number blocked, she was stunned he could just walk away and turn it all off like a switch, but he had. He had really gone. What would she do now? It was time for Trinidad, she'd decided.

~ CHAPTER 3 ~

CAMILLE HAD TAKEN the train to London, where she would stay one night before flying out from Gatwick the following morning. The easy journey from Gare du Nord to St. Pancras inevitably made her think of the times she'd travelled the same route to see Fingal. This time, she knew she wouldn't be seeing him, although the fantasy that they might meet by chance was one that intruded upon her quieter moments during the journey.

She checked into the Anselma Hotel on Argyle Street, just a few minutes' walk from King's Cross, a small, terraced establishment worthy of its three stars, cushioned in a quietness that seemed to be from a bygone age. Her compact, tidy room with its box-like en-suite, a window that looked out on a small garden, and an old wooden dresser with two drawers was comfortable and welcoming. It had an air of aloneness about it, though, and alone was exactly how she felt. She laid back on the bed with its brilliantly white, stiff sheet folded over a blue blanket so neat and tight as to suggest the housekeeping staff were watched over by an old-fashioned matron on a hospital ward who might discipline them if the folds and corners were not just so. The pillow was large, soft, and cool, and her head sank into it as she laid looking up at the ceiling or at the small, switched-off flat-screen television attached to the wall with an adjustable bracket. It wasn't the most comfortable of feelings, but it wasn't the worst either. She had left Paris to travel alone for the first time in her life, acknowledging that the journey was not just about travel – at least, not in the physical sense. She decided she would rest for an hour or so and then go out for a walk to see where her steps might lead.

Camille had told no one she was leaving other than Mireille. She had stood in the doorway of the sitting room with her coat on, her suitcase and backpack at her feet, and said to Philippe, 'I'm going now.'

He was lying on the sofa, watching television, and he didn't look up when he responded, 'We need some milk.'

The smile on her face as she descended the stairs was one of grim satisfaction, as though she had been presented with the proof of something she had always suspected but often doubted: their marriage was over. The once charming and handsome man she had fallen in love with was now so locked into his own existence that he could no longer see the world clearly. He worked hard – his business was apparently doing well – he earned good money – although she worried he was jeopardising even this – and he drank to excess every day now. She recalled asking him once, 'Why do you drink?'

'Because I want a gentler way than a bullet to quieten the world,' he'd said.

'Does it work?'

'To a degree. It puts up a barrier, a shield all around me, but no, it doesn't quieten my head. That's still mad as fuck.'

She remembered the day he'd signed the lease for the cinema and how excited he'd been when he'd come home like a small boy who had just been picked for the school team and was now compelled to show off and get the praise he so pathologically needed to affirm his worthiness. This would be the end to all of their worries, he had asserted, the end of financial insecurity; the boys would want for nothing, and they would all be free and happy and fulfilled. And so, it proved to be for a while, until the boys were teenagers and started showing the archetypal signs of children everywhere at that age: answering back, sullenness, secrecy, and not wanting to be in their parents' company. Philippe had struggled to accept this even though he had so obviously – and more extremely than his own boys – reacted to his parents in the same way. He'd found it incurably disappointing that his determination to have a close friendship with his sons in which he was an experienced guide and encouraging catalyst or facilitator for them to experience the world, the very opposite of his relationship with his own father, was misspent energy. They would find their own ways in life, and even though he knew this to be right, it was still hard to take the fact that they now only needed their parents to provide a stable home life and regular monetary hand-outs.

Her approach had been the opposite, more hands-off and respectful of their privacy, and the boys had turned to her in their own ways throughout those years. It was she who'd advised the more worldly but still naïve Eric about how respecting his girlfriend's honour and choices was a much better way to have a more satisfying relationship with her. Camille hadn't flinched from talking to him about sex, the importance of being responsible when it came to sexual health, and the risks of pregnancy. Fred, on the other hand, wide-eyed at his elder brother's exploits or the cleavages and legs of his girlfriends, needed the biology of sexual relationships explained in almost clinical detail, all of which he'd accepted like some unworldly professor being read a piece of complicated research. There were times she'd express anger at one or the other of them or both for various misdemeanours – she never stopped being a parent – but her relationships with them and theirs with each other was, for the most part, openly warm and loving, full of hugs, laughter, and the enjoyment of any time spent together, whereas the increasingly isolated Philippe had looked on with green and bloodshot eyes, a growing resentment, and a sense of estrangement, which she'd tried, to no avail, to dispel him of.

The nature of his work at the cinema meant he was often not home for evening meals, managing to see his sons in passing only. He would then try to force an issue, and more often than not, over-compensate. Typical of teenage boys, they had no time or sufficient experience in the ways of the adult world to respond to the vagaries of parental behaviour with anything other than finding a quick and easy way to avoid them altogether.

It was during those years Philippe began staying out more, and when at home, drinking more. It hadn't been the boys' fault, nor had it been hers, although she often tried to blame herself. It was as though a demon, dormant since they'd met, had reasserted itself within him, a demon they'd both believed to have been tamed; she had only glimpsed the darkness within him occasionally, and he'd known it had never gone away and that his whole mission in life was to keep it at bay. Like a cancer, it was soon in control, and she could do nothing to halt its malevolent progress. The grossly abnormal had become normal: the long silences or irritated responses, or the way the smallest of frustrations seemed to trigger an explosion of self-loathing and subsequent anger, which was then directed at her. The way he would provoke – even consciously construct – an argument to have an excuse to erupt and then punish her for being witness to it by staying silent, sometimes ignoring her for days at a time. She wondered if she could have tried harder, but having to constantly face down his bitterness and the self-destructive way he'd dealt with it was exhausting and demanded a greater capacity for patience and forgiveness than she'd had or even wanted to have.

It wasn't only the alienation he'd felt from his sons. Philippe was a creative man, a gifted photographer and filmmaker who, despite top class qualifications and a portfolio full of original, technically brilliant work, had not managed to secure an exhibition of any note or any backing for his art-house films. He refused to compromise his artistic integrity by becoming a jobbing photographer – weddings, catalogues, cheesy family portraits – despite the financial security it offered them. So, when he had the idea of running his own cinema, one that would showcase new filmmakers as well as show classic art films, it seemed an honourable compromise. Inevitably, the demands of running his own business meant his art was constantly shelved as he waited for the energy, space, and time to commit to it. There never seemed to be enough of any of them, so he drank and allowed the resentment to seethe within him, feeding his demon and its malignant influence on them all.

Despite the inward and downward trajectory of his spirit, there were times the bright, boyish Philippe resurfaced. He'd brought her a cup of coffee in bed one autumn morning, and as he drew the curtains, said to her, 'When you wake up in the morning, do you see how the breeze moves the branches in the trees? Do you watch how the leaves loosen their grip and fall? Can you hear the birds sing, Camille? Let's have coffee on the balcony together the way we used to and feel the sun upon our faces. Let's look forward again to how our day might unfold.'

They'd walked that lunchtime through Les Jardins du Luxembourg, arm in arm, light-hearted and comfortable in each other's company, but she'd known it would be short-lived, and the darkness would return, and so had he.

A tear formed in her eye as she laid on her bed in the Anselma Hotel. She let it work its way unhindered out of her eye and down her cheek, over her lip and into her mouth where she tasted it, and a silent sob shuddered through her body.

~ CHAPTER 4 ~

AFTER A SHOWER and a change of clothes, she phoned Mireille, who was full of questions as to how she was – *'Je vais bien.'*

She replied with where she was – *'Un petit hôtel confortable'*; how the journey was – *'Très facile'*; what Philippe had been like when she'd left – *'Il n'a pas compris que je le quittais'*; and whether or not she had told her boys yet – *'Non, mais bientôt.'*

She asked Mireille how the latest round of chemotherapy had gone. *'Très amusant,'* she replied full of sarcasm; was she in pain? – *'Un peu'*; and how things were at home – *'J'ai un cancer. Je n'ai pas d'amant et mon mari est un connard.'*

'Tout va bien alors,' Camille said, and they both laughed. Camille promised to text every day once she was in Trinidad and to phone at least once a week.

Cheered by Mireille's black humour, strength, and concern for her, Camille set about emailing Eric and Fred, deciding that was the best way to communicate big news without getting embroiled in a long-distance phone conversation or exchange of text messages. Wherever they were, they would pick up their emails and have time to digest the news before being able to speak to her. She told them she had decided to travel alone because she needed time to herself and a breather from life at home, trusting they would read between the lines. She had always been honest with her boys but had rarely commented on the state of her relationship with their father or his difficult behaviour. She trusted they would have seen much of this for themselves and drawn their own conclusions.

There were missed calls and texts from Philippe, none of which she returned or replied to. She had texted him from the train saying much the same as she had told Eric and Fred, that she needed a break, had decided to travel alone (she hadn't told him where she was going), and that she would be in touch when she knew she was returning to Paris, adding that, in the meantime, he was to take care of himself and hopefully find some time to reflect on why she had done this. She didn't expect him to understand immediately, but if he was honest with himself, then maybe he would. She then deleted his messages and texts and blocked his number.

She stepped out into the summer streets of London with a lightness of being and plenty of daylight hours remaining for her to wander wherever she wanted, knowing she would find herself in the dappled shade of memory lane at some point. She saw some petals swirling around on the pavement beneath some hanging baskets before being blown up into the air, and she imagined they were her worries and stressors – the burdens she carried that had weighed down her spirit for so long – being scattered to the wind. It was that easy, she told herself. All you have to do is take a step in the right direction and find your true pathway, the path with heart, and there – you've changed the world.

As she walked down Hunter Street and Bernard Street into Russell Square, it was as though the world was bathed in a new light, one that allowed her to see it with a much sharper focus, the people, the traffic, the architecture, the shops and bars, all teeming with life. Instead of being overwhelmed or frightened of its enormity, she felt a part of it. Even though she was a French woman alone in a foreign city, she was embraced by humanity and taken into its fold.

She found herself walking past the British Museum and recalled when Fingal had taken her there for the first time, and they'd headed straight to the upper floor and the galleries dedicated to Ancient Egypt. How strange and exciting it had been to look at all those artefacts – the mummies, the intricate jewellery, and household items that had been stolen from the pyramids – and how privileged she'd felt to bear witness to the sophistication of Egyptian art and society from five thousand years ago. Fingal had demonstrated a surprising amount of knowledge, and when she'd commented on this, he'd laughed and told her how he had once plucked up the courage to ask a particular woman – after whom he had lusted for weeks – out for a date. She had been the girlfriend of a famous pop star, and they had met at a party where the pop star had also been in attendance. Unsure as to whether her friendliness had signified genuine interest in him, he decided to find out by asking her if she'd like to meet again. Amazed when she'd agreed, he'd suggested meeting by the mummies in the British Museum. He had arrived early, feeling nervous and unsure of how to greet her or what to say to break the ice, but she didn't show, and he'd spent two hours or more wandering around the Egyptian galleries, hoping she was just late and was still coming. In that time, he learned a lot about Ancient Egypt and had since developed a passion for ancient history as a direct result of the misadventure.

Camille was tempted to go into the museum to see if he was there, but then she chastised herself for such a foolish thought. Then she acknowledged how wonderful it would be to see him if she did meet him by chance while there in London. Then again, he might be in another relationship now. What if she saw him with someone else? How would she feel? She laughed at herself but conceded that she had actually loved him, something she found hard to admit or accept, let alone tell him when they were seeing each other.

She walked on towards Tottenham Court Road and realised she was heading towards another part of London they had often frequented, so she decided to trust her unconscious guide, letting it lead her back to Soho. She crossed Soho Square and approached the Toucan Pub on Carlisle Street. It was a warm evening, and there was a happy, vibrant crowd drinking on the pavement outside, all talking in loud voices, laughing and smoking. It was where she had first taken cocaine courtesy of Fingal, and the two of them had joined the people outside with their pints of Guinness while she'd felt the first effects of the cocaine and started talking quickly and enthusiastically while he smoked and laughed and every now and again, leaned forward to kiss or hug her. It was a good memory, she decided, so she went in and ordered a pint.

Afterwards, she strolled down Frith Street and saw Ronnie Scott's Jazz Club with its neon sign lit up in red and green letters with a blue saxophone flickering alongside them: *ronnie scott's 6.30-3 am open nightly*. She looked at the poster outside to see who was playing, wondering if it might be Fingal Reid and the The Long Neck Bottle Band, but it was a band of which she hadn't heard. Nevertheless, she pondered paying for a seat and going in to revisit a place they had visited together a few times, including once to watch his band perform, but the sign outside said: *House Full*.

Feeling hungry and ready for another drink, she wondered if she could find the tapas bar they had once gone to. Camille remembered it was on a street with a French-sounding name, so she doubled back, turned down the next left, and reached Dean Street, remembering the strange little passageway running off it called St. Anne's Court, with its Chinese restaurants and massage parlours. One shop front advertised all manner of herbal medicine and physical therapies including reiki, shiatsu, acupuncture, and reflexology, where a young woman in a skin-tight top, red leather miniskirt, and thigh-length, leather boots stood in its doorway, smiling, beckoning with a single finger to any passers-by to come inside. It was still light, and after the busy streets from where she had just come, it was suddenly quiet.

Two men, who stood smoking in a doorway, looked Camille up and down unashamedly as she passed by them, staring straight ahead. She reached Wardour Street and knew she must be near the tapas bar. Then, she saw the sign: D'Arblay Street – that was it! Sure enough, there it was, the Spanish restaurant, *La Cazuela*.

It was busy. Couples or small groups of friends filled the communal tables and the air with their chatter and laughter. Feeling completely self-contained, she sat on one of the high stools at the window where she could watch the endless movement of the people of Soho going past to a soundtrack of flamenco guitar and handclaps from the speaker above her head. She ordered a cold beer and a plate of ham, cheese, and bread and slowly savoured every sip and bite.

It was there that Fingal had ordered a bottle of red wine called Muga. She'd said it was the name of a village in Trinidad near where her mother had come from and how one day, she wanted to go there. Fingal said he'd been to the Caribbean, having performed at the Tobago Jazz Festival a few years before, and he encouraged her to go, saying he would love to accompany her, but it was probably a journey of discovery best undertaken by herself. 'Shake off those shackles, Camille. Life is such a short, bittersweet journey, and you? You deserve to travel the length and breadth of this world if you want to.' She had never experienced anyone, especially a man, encouraging her to do anything other than to be dutiful and responsible. She looked at him, narrowing her eyes and tilting her head slightly to one side, a look that questioned whether or not he was for real. He looked straight back at her, confirming without any shadow of a doubt that he was.

She cast her mind back to the first time they had met, at the Club Jazz de la Lune, in Paris. She had since dissociated from so much of that time, but now, in Fingal's home town, they had spent so many happy days together that the memory of their first encounter came flooding back to the fore of her consciousness, drowning out the chatter of her fellow diners.

~ CHAPTER 5 ~

THE SMALL AUDIENCE cheered, whooped and applauded as Fingal led the band back on stage for the encore. It had gone well despite using a local rhythm section with whom they'd had barely enough time to run through the songs. It had originally been a gig just for Fingal and his guitarist, Goose, and then they'd been surprised by Thabo Brown, a UK jazz musician, alto sax player, and rapper, joining them on stage uninvited to freestyle and solo on their penultimate number. Old friends – they had met at the Tobago Jazz Festival – Thabo and Fingal embraced each other warmly, despite the surprise of seeing him there at the side of the stage. Musicians don't usually care for someone joining them without first being asked, but Thabo was different. The crowd had loved it. Parisian audiences were some of the best when it came to jazz and blues. Always have been.

Goose counted them in slowly, warning the drummer and bass player to keep it light before launching into a slow blues in E minor. The crowd hushed, and Goose started the number with a twenty-four bar solo that was as edgy and raw as he had ever played. Fingal stepped up to the microphone, and the lights dimmed further as a blue and red aura surrounded his body.

It was a great gig. She remembered how he had told her that when the relationship with the audience was so strong as to be coalescent, it affirmed much of why he did this, their enthusiasm and encouragement giving him the high he always craved but didn't always attain. That night was one such occasion, and he rewarded them with a memorable vocal performance. He sang from his soul as if conjuring up the spirits from long ago, channelling the forces of the music's history and roots, letting his unconscious mind take over the controls for the way he pitched, timed, and delivered the lyrics.

If only I could hold you now,
I'd never hold you so tight.
If I could feel your breath,
I might just sleep tonight.
Oh, I want you –
Do you want me, too?

If I could see the dawn break
With you by my side,
I may not feel
so restless inside.
Oh, I want you –
Do you want me, too?

Then, he launched into his harp solo, an unplanned, forty-eight bars of gut-wrenching, note-bending blues harmonica, his left foot bouncing off the stage, the veins in his neck so proud they looked like they might burst as he put everything into it, cupping the mic in his hands, his eyes closed, his body swaying. At the solo's climax, the crowd clapped and cheered when Goose quietly started his next solo with a light-fingered touch that belied the force of the music. He built the tension slowly, the fingers of his left hand moving in different tempos smoothly up and down the frets, climaxing with some of the dirtiest, earthy bass notes he could find. The crowd was on their feet. Fingal stepped back up to the mic, his voice now dry and hoarse:

If only I could see my world
Reflected in your eyes,
And if only I could kiss you hello
Instead of waving you goodbye.
Oh, I want you –
Do you want me, too?

If only you could hear me calling
to you across the sky,
I just may not feel
Like I'm dying inside.
Oh, I want you –
Do you want me, too?

If I could see you standing
Framed in my door,
I'd ask you one question:
Who loves you more?
Oh, I want you –
Do you want me, too?

The last line was repeated and drawn out, slowed right down as the band finished the song in a swirling, noisy climax of crashing cymbals, rumbling bass lines, power chords, and wailing harmonica. Drenched in sweat, their arms around each other, the whole band took several bows before waving to the crowd and exiting at the side of the stage through the door marked *Artistes*.

Within a few minutes, Fingal was sitting at the bar where only performers and their guest list were allowed, sipping a negroni. Camille walked past on her way to the cloakroom. He looked at her, she smiled and walked on. On her way back, he asked her if she wanted a drink. 'I'm with friends,' she said.

'Have one with me, then ask them over to join us,' he said.

'Negroni.' She smiled.

'My drink, too.'

That had been the start of their relationship. He did not return to London other than for a couple of shows, choosing to stay in Paris to see her as often as possible. Sometimes, it was for just a half-hour, other times for half a day or an evening spent walking, talking, eating, drinking, or making love. She was totally open with him, telling him of her marriage and her affair, all of which he seemed to accept without judgement or opinion. When she told him of her roots, he described his experiences in Trinidad and Tobago, having played the jazz festival there a few times. She wanted to know more about her mother's country, and he encouraged her to find out for herself.

'I'm serious about you,' he said one evening as they laid in bed.

'Well, don't be.'

'There's no one else in my life. It's up to you, but with me, you can leave all those others behind. I'll take you for exactly who you are.'

'I don't even know exactly who I am, so I don't see how you possibly can.'

'You're something – someone – waiting to be released.'

'Maybe.'

'I want you.'

'Maybe.'

'It must be love,' he said, smiling.

'What *is* love?' she asked, turning away from him, pulling the sheets aside and getting out of bed. 'I have to go. Philippe will be wondering.'

There followed a period of separation. At her instigation, there had been minimal contact. He expressed anger and hurt at her, suddenly distancing herself from him, telling her he'd nurse the wounds by writing songs, gigging, and drinking, but couldn't get her off his mind. She was under his skin, and he hated allowing that to happen. He persisted, nevertheless, because, apart from anything else, he enjoyed her company, was always open with her, and found her to be the softest, most comforting and beautiful person to whom he had ever been close.

At first, he had bombarded her with text messages, voicemails, and emails, demanding to know where she had gone and what was happening, asking if she was having great sex with her old man lover, repeatedly telling her that he loved her, and she needed to break free. Then, he felt he was making a fool of himself and stopped. The silence between them became an abyss, deep and endless, where they both stood on the edge, though on opposite sides.

Then, unable to resist any more, she texted him: *tu me manques tellement.* His French wasn't good enough to understand, so he looked it up using an online translator, expecting the worst but smiling with relief when he read, *I miss you so much.*

He sent her the date of his next gig at *Jazz de la Lune,* and ten days later, there she was. When he joined her at the bar, they embraced, holding each other for a few minutes as though they would never let go. He kissed the top of her head, breathing in her scent, while she rested her head above his heart. They were in a crowded bar, but it was as though no one else was there. The reconciliation was bitter-sweet, hard-edged and soft at the same time, as though they were either on the verge of a catastrophe or about to escape it.

~ CHAPTER 6 ~

THAT NIGHT, THEY had stayed in his hotel room. In the morning, as they sat up in bed, she looked at his sinewy body, taught, defined muscles, and the tattoo that stretched across his shoulder and down his left arm to the wrist in grey-blue, depicting a sailing ship in stormy seas surrounded by mermaids on rocks. On his forearm was the fantastical figure of a yellow-eyed panther with giant, bat-like wings staring out at whoever might be observing the scene. Despite the intricate inkwork, she saw a series of thin scars patterning his wrist and forearm in random crisscrosses and straight lines.

She had enjoyed the sex – he was an attentive and responsive lover with whom she felt no inhibitions – but she felt more curious than satisfied as if still discovering things about herself and her body for the first time. Was it because of Fingal? Could other men – maybe even women – make her feel like this or even better? Was it because, as Fingal had insisted, he was expressing genuine heartfelt love for her and that loving intimacy was alchemic in the way two bodies and souls combined? It seemed too good to be true.

She put her head on his chest and thought how different he was from anyone she had ever met. Camille didn't have much experience with men, she realised, other than those who had dominated her life. There was her father, Yves, who had always told her how she must commit to whatever she was doing until she could do it well, and who would chastise her verbally whenever he believed she was failing. Then, there was Philippe, who had never appreciated how committed she had been to their mutual cause, who had taken her for granted and never accepted her point of view unless it was in agreement with his, who had abused her in a non-physical way, undermining her confidence and treating her much like a housekeeper with whom he had sex only when *he* was in the mood. Thankfully, it was an intimacy she had been spared in recent years as a result of his drunkenness and their subsequently aggravated disunion.

As for Liam, he actually demanded her commitment to him in a way that was more and more self-centred, domineering, and manipulative, having accused her of indifference (the worst of all behaviours, he insisted pompously) if she dared express uncertainty about their future relationship or didn't pay him the attention he believed he merited. He was old, set in his ways, used to dominating the women in his life, and his pomposity, which she had once mistaken for confidence and maturity, had begun to bore her.

Then, there was Fingal – dear, sweet, Fingal – who never asked her to commit to him at all, telling her instead to commit to herself. 'Only then, maybe your life will find room for me,' he had told her, 'and if it doesn't, so be it, but at least you – beautiful you – will be free.'

All the other men had wanted to possess her, control her, and mould her in their image of how they thought she should be to suit themselves and their needs, as though she should be grateful for it and rest forever in their patronising, suffocating arms. Even her father, who adored her without doubt, had wanted her to be the way he wanted her – settled, mature, safe, and preferably married to someone who was also settled, mature and safe – but he had been so disapproving and unsympathetic towards her marriage that it had created a schism between father and daughter that nearly destroyed their relationship completely. If not for her mother – doggedly diplomatic and determined to hold the family together – they wouldn't have a relationship now, even though her mother's death had forced them to reassess each other and their needs regarding their future relationship.

Fingal was so *non*-possessive and inured to the behaviour of men that he could impart such wise and mature observations about them. He helped her realise there was more to the world, even though his defiant, non-possessiveness was irritating and controlling in its own way. Whenever they spoke about what the future might hold, he often described her as keeping him at arm's length while all the time, she observed, he kept a vital part of himself, his inner core, hidden from her. She had pointed this out to him several times, and he had said that some things were best kept from view, but that didn't mean he didn't love her because he most certainly did.

So, was it her reticence and rejection of his love for her – the not believing anyone knew what they were talking about when they spoke of love – or was it his holding back something of his real self that meant they were eventually doomed to separate? She struggled with this dichotomy. She felt good with him. Everything was natural and easy. He accepted her for who she was, and she, as she peeled back his outer defensive layers, accepted him and enjoyed the new dimensions he brought to her life, though helping her to understand her potential was still far from fulfilled.

She looked at Fingal's face again: a few scars, laughter lines, and long eyelashes behind which, looking like they belonged to somebody ancient, were his sad eyes. She tapped him on the chest and said, 'There's hurt in there somewhere.'

'There's hurt in everyone, isn't there?' he replied.

'Maybe, but perhaps you could do with telling someone about yours.'

'I've had therapy. I've worked things out. I don't think you can cure some hurts by talking about them just because someone wants to find out about you, but you can learn to carry them, accept them as part of you, and that's what I do.'

'Will you tell me?'

He leaned over to the bedside table, took a cigarette from its packet, lit it, leaned back against the headboard, and sighed as he slowly exhaled.

'Go on,' she persisted. It's safe here.'

Rick Tucker

After a few moments, he said, 'No, I don't want to,' and then got up from the bed, picked up his guitar, and sat down on a stool before putting a harmonica in a neck holder and placing it around his neck. He finger-picked a country-style, mid-tempo blues and sang:

'Well, I can't drink no more whisky
And I've done my time with pills
Yeah, I've had enough of whisky
And I've done my time with pills
But now I'm doing time
With these bone-rattlin' chills.

The sun comes up over the mountain
Each and every day
The sun comes up over the mountain
Each and every day
But it's light just ain't enough
To burn these chills away.'

He played four bars of harmonica, repeating the walk down, and then continued:

You know I love my woman
Just the sweetest I've ever known
You know I love my woman
Just the kindest I've ever known

But when she heard my bones rattle
She was down the road and gone

He played a twelve-bar harmonica solo this time before singing the last verse:

Somewhere deep into the night
I hear the rattlin' of their tunes
Somewhere in the dark old night
I hear them rattlin' out their tunes
And I know they're telling me
They'll be no more rattlin' soon.'

'Why do you always sing blues songs?' she asked.

He affected a mock Southern United States drawl. 'Weeeell, I ain't a for-real musician, ma'am, and dems three chords is all this po' little lighty boy can play.'

It made her laugh.

'Lighty?' she asked.

'Mixed. Mixed race.'

'I thought you were white, actually.'

'I'm mixed. One more mix down the line than you, I guess. Mother mixed white and African, and my father Caucasian through and through as far as I know.'

'So, how do you define yourself?'

'I don't define myself, not by skin tone, anyway, but I would describe myself as non-white. If a barricade went up with whites on one side and non-whites on the other, then I would be on the other, but I get that most people think of me as white – maybe southern European – but white people mostly know there's something not quite white about me.' He smiled, and they sat in silence for a few moments.

She asked him again about the blues.

'Well, like I was saying, I'm a musician and songwriter, but I'm not a brilliant musician. I understand music, rhythm, timing, different beats, and so on, and I also feel music instinctively, deeply, and the blues provides a framework for me, which I can sing and play in, express myself. I get it, though. Like I listen to a lot of jazz, how they use the chords but then stretch the number of bars you play those chords for, or how the likes of Miles Davis and John Coltrane sometimes did away with chords altogether, losing the structure, discarding the framework because it was too restrictive – modal jazz, they called it – but they never lost sight of the origin, and that origin was the blues.'

He was animated, gesticulating and becoming more passionate and urgent about the subject, seemingly delighted to be able to talk to her about it. 'But because I can't play like them, I have to find some other way to channel whatever it is I want to express, so when I play the blues, I stick mostly to its original framework because I find I can channel something into it. It provides a...a – '

'A safe zone?' she suggested, and he thought for a moment.

'Yes, you're right, but also a discipline or structure, one that keeps me from disappearing or getting lost because if I am in the right place, the right frame of mind, if the band are, too, then something happens. Something comes up from the depths. It's almost like archaeology mixed with alchemy – archaeology of the soul if you like. The topsoil is the present where everything is going on – crowding out your mind and senses; then, the subsoil is like your subconscious – what's there beneath the surface, scratching away, trying to get out; and then, there are the different layers and strata that take you all the way down to the depths, beyond history or time, even, down to the spirit or the soul, and that's intrinsically connected to something otherworldly – the deep, *deep* past, something universal, the universe itself, other artists. All great artists get there. It's like how Rothko or Mondrian got there with their pure abstraction or Matisse with his cut-outs or with that painting of his, one of my favourite paintings of all time: *The Dance*. They could get into that place of universality, of the truth, through the way they worked and thought and lived, and lived and worked, and worked and worked.'

'I don't know that Matisse painting,' she said.

'Oh, Camille, it's wonderful. You'd love it. I saw it in New York once. There's a version in St. Petersburg, too. We should go. Let's go to New York – how about it?'

'Tell me about it.'

'What? New York?'

'No, the painting. The Matisse one.'

'It's simple. Simple colours. Five naked figures, all a kind of terracotta colour. Men and women holding hands in a circle on top of a green hill in front of a dark blue sky, and dancing with the life force bursting through them. They have found the secret of life or of the universe, and it's propelling them to dance, and in the foreground, one of the dancers, a female, has either slipped from the grip of the man to her left – his back is to us, and he's arched like a ballet dancer or a bullfighter; beautiful, beautiful lines – or she is trying desperately to reach his hand. For me, it's perfect. Will she reach him? Can he slow down enough to allow her to catch up, or will the fervour and momentum of the dance mean they will never connect? Will the dance – can the dance – ever end?'

'Have you experienced that?' she asked after a few moments of silence in which she wondered at how animated he had become when talking about music and art. Camille had never seen him so open before. She had never seen a *man* so open before.

'Experienced what?'

'Not being able to reach someone, or them not being able to reach you?'

'It's a universal phenomenon, isn't it?'

'I don't know.'

He took off the neck holder, and propped his guitar against the wall. 'Yeah, I've experienced it,' he said, getting back into bed.

She had since learned something of how such an experience felt, and as she wandered back through Soho, she put their last ever communication somewhere to the back of her mind, that awful day when he had severed contact with her. It felt better to leave it there rather than relive it as she had done so many times before. What was the point? It was old ground, and she could never tread it again even if she wanted to. He had made his decision, and no matter how many times she wished he would reverse it and make contact with her, he hadn't done so. She had put it to bed too often now, only to shake it awake during times when she felt alone or sad or cold. It never made her feel any better.

As she neared Ronnie Scott's again, she heard music coming from the bar upstairs. There was a blues band playing live. The doorman ushered her in with a smile, advising her to pay at the top of the stairs, and before she had time to talk herself out of it, she was pushing her way through the noisy crowd towards the playing area at the back, but it wasn't the Long Neck Bottle Band. Pushing away a persistent reveller who wanted her to dance, she went back down the stairs and onto the street.

'Goodnight, madam,' said the doorman as she walked towards Oxford Street, where she hailed a cab to take her back to the hotel.

~ CHAPTER 7 ~

'*MAMAN! MAMAN!...T'ES OÙ?*' she shouted from the bottom of the stairs, looking up with a mixture of irritation and entitlement. Her mother should be on hand *immediately*.

'In the kitchen,' came the response, 'and speak English, please!'

'*Comment?*'

'You understand, Camille.'

'Speak English, please...speak English, please,' Camille mimicked as she ran up the stairs. She reached the kitchen, threw down her bag, and peered into the pot her mother was stirring. '*Qu'est-ce que c'est, maman?*'

'Fish broth with okra, ground provision, and dumpling.'

Camille screwed up her nose. 'What is broff? What is grown proffi*shon?*'

'Broth is soup, a big, thick soup with cassava, sweet potato, and eddoes. Dem is ground provision,' said her mother, slipping into her natural accent rather than the one she affected when trying to encourage Camille to be bilingual. She lifted a spoonful of eddoes out of the pot to show her.

'Broff is soup, a big, thick soup,' Camille repeated with an exaggerated English accent.

'With a beautiful fish.'

'Maman, le poisson me regarde!' she said, looking at the head of a snapper peeking out from under the grey liquid and its array of strange-looking contents.

'Mummy, the fish is looking at me,' corrected her mother.

'I am not *your* mummy – you are *my* mummy.'

'Oui chérie.'

'Maman! S'il te plaît parle anglais. Tu n'es pas gentille!' Satisfied she had got one over on her mother, Camille ran out of the kitchen towards her bedroom.

Her mother shouted after her, 'Shower! *Maintenant!'*

Camille smiled at the memory as she put her head back and tried to get comfortable. Well, Maman, she thought, here I am on my way to the country of your birth, and I wish you were with me. You used to tell me so many stories about Trinidad, and I never went there with you those times you had to go back, but I have remembered much of what you told me, and so here I am, going to find something of you and hopefully something of myself, too. I love you, Maman, and miss you every day.

The past was something Elma Constantine had rarely chosen to talk about with Camille, but there had come a time when she thought she should know more. It wasn't that she was ashamed of her roots but that she had learned to be cautious from an early age. Being a pretty, mixed-race, African-Indian daughter of a single mother named Naomi, who was bright at school, meant she had to endure jibes and judgement, not only from her peer group but also from her neighbours. It wasn't as if she was the only *doogla* in the village, but she was the only one with a single mother, a mother who had conceived her and given birth to her out of wedlock, a mother who mostly chose to isolate herself in order to avoid the gossip, hostile looks, and unfriendliness she encountered all too frequently. Not only was she a black woman in a mainly Indian community, but she had had an affair with a prominent Indian man from their village who was married and popular. Her increased tendency towards isolation and self-sufficiency only fuelled the fires of vindictive gossip, including that she practised the dark arts of *obeah*.

The routine of their home life together, tending the crops in the garden, going to market to sell and buy, cooking and cleaning, was rarely interrupted by the welcome stimulus of a friendly visitor. Elma was devoted to her mother, proud and defiant in the face of the villagers' small-mindedness, and she was happy not to dispel any rumours of obeah being practiced in her house because it meant people feared her mother's retribution if she chose to call upon her apparent familiarity with the spirits of darkness. This was something that was confirmed in many people's minds by the occasional visit of her mother's youngest sister, Tanty Jo. Everybody believed Tanty Jo to be an obeah woman, one who several of the villagers had turned to themselves when looking to place a curse on a neighbour or lover or to cure an illness or painful condition in the absence of an easily accessed or affordable doctor.

Despite the aspersions cast upon them, Elma and her mother attended church most Sundays and sat together near the back. A few members of the congregation were friendly to a degree, but most ignored them at best. At worst, they made their disapproval obvious. One Sunday, the priest warned in his sermon of the dangers and sinfulness of dabbling in the dark arts, and even though many of the people there had themselves sometimes paid for obeah spells to be cast or lifted, everyone seemed to turn to look at her mother. The hypocrisy was clear to see. Elma had been thirteen years old, and neither she nor her mother ever went to church again.

Elma had studied hard and got good grades, but opportunities for employment as she reached her late teens were few. She had worked for a while in San Fernando as a so-called clerical assistant for a Chinese businessman, which, in reality, meant she had just run errands, tidied up his chaotic office, and put up with his bad moods and wandering hands. Even though it was Trinidad's second-largest city, it didn't feel big enough for her. She wanted to leave the smallness of her village – and even her island – but she always felt she couldn't leave her mother alone. Then, one day, at the age of nineteen, her life changed forever when her mother suddenly died, having suffered a ruptured brain aneurysm. Having had no time to prepare for such change and full of grief for her departed mother, she moved to La Brea and into Tanty Jo's comforting arms.

Tanty Jo had nursed her through her grief with kindness and sensitivity, offering her much in the way of insight as to the ways of the world but sharing nothing of her obeah secrets.

Sometimes, Elma would see Tanty Jo mixing powders and herbs in a mortar or occasionally hanging charms from the branches of the trees in her garden, but she never asked for an explanation as she was just happy to have been embraced by the loving and eccentric woman who was the only extended family she had ever known.

One morning, when Elma had been there a few months, Tanty Jo handed her a purse in which was two thousand Trinidad and Tobago dollars. She told her to go to Port of Spain to find work, that she shouldn't waste her life and her intellect living there anymore, and that she must go out into the world to find her destiny.

Tanty Jo had told Elma how she had dreamed of a winged spirit, an angel of sorts, who, from birth, had never been able to fly but who had been given the gift of flight by a giant bird who had taken pity on her and who had witnessed the purity of her spirit through her devotional behaviour and lack of sin. It was a sign from the spirits, Tanty Jo had said, that Elma needed to leave, that she couldn't keep her there any longer, as much as she would have liked to do so. There was a cousin in Port of Spain who could find her work, but she should only view that as a stepping-stone on her journey. There would be more to come.

The cousin ran a cleaning company, and soon, Elma had found herself working as a cleaner at the French Embassy in the district of St. Clair. She had never been in such a building before. It was as though she had stepped back in time: all the grandeur and splendour of the colonial past with its steep, downward-curving roofs, tall, narrow windows, white steps leading up to the front door, itself set back within a gallery of a polished, dark wooden floor and elaborate fencing. The garden alone, with its variety of mature trees, flowering shrubs, and manicured lawn, was enough to make her feel she had arrived in a different world.

The first time she had walked through the front door, she saw a large sign on the wall with the words *Liberté Égalité Fraternité* written in large letters above the smaller logo, which read: *République Française. Ambassade de France à Trinité et Tobago.* Despite the obvious wealth and sophistication on display, Elma had felt more a sense of excitement and fascination with her new place of work, and it didn't take long before she had met Yves.

Yves Sauveterre, a bespectacled, slightly balding and studious-looking tall man in his mid-twenties was the *Sécretaire des systèmes d'information et de communication*, and he found the life of a junior diplomat boring, despite its privileges. It didn't take him long to start talking in his immaculate English to the pretty, young woman who cleaned and tidied his office every day. He was surprised by her erudition and intelligence, much to his shame at his own arrogance. She could even speak some conversational French that she had learned in school. It hadn't taken long before they began to see each other outside of work, and despite his loathing for the island, they were soon in love.

When trying to impress his friends or Elma herself, Yves would often reference the history of the French in Trinidad, saying that not even in the late eighteenth century, when Republicans and Royalists alike fled to the island in the aftermath of the French Revolution from the neighbouring French colonies of Martinique, Grenada, St. Lucia and St. Dominique at the invitation of the Spanish and brought with them their slaves and disproportionate wealth, did French people really want to be there. When the British invaded in 1797, the Spanish gave in without a fight, meaning the island became a British colony with Spanish laws and a French-speaking population, which included the majority of its slaves. This demonstrated, as far as Yves was concerned, that no one had ever known what to do with the island and that only the British, with their obsessive sense of their own entitlement and superiority, had decided it was worth keeping.

Elma had tried to dispel him of his bias, pointing out how beautiful the island was, how its society was so enriched by being this melting pot of so many cultures, how peaceful and friendly its people were, and how abundant and unique it was in natural resources, including its spectacular flora and fauna. Whenever he persisted in being critical of her country, she had accused him of displaying a typical colonial arrogance, telling him his hypothesis about her country was erroneous, racist, and an affectation that did him no favours. His pomposity exposed and punctured by her integrity, Yves was happy to eat the necessary amount of humble pie for their relationship to flourish. When he was posted back to Paris via a short stint in Caracas, she had no hesitation in accepting his invitation to go with him. Soon after their arrival in France, they had married in the art nouveau *L'Église Protestante Du Foyer De L'Âme on rue du Pasteur-Wagner*, close to *Place de la Bastille*. Yves's father had walked her down the aisle.

So, there you were, Maman, twenty-one years old and in a strange world, stranger than you could have ever imagined, having to deal with the language, the food, the cold – how did you survive your first winter there? I hope Papa treated you well and took care of you. Where did you find ground provision in those days? So many things I would ask you now. I will look for you when I get to Trinidad, the land of the hummingbird, you told me. I will hear your voice in the breeze, maybe feel your warmth in the sun that is bound to be shining. I will remember all those strange words you told me about, like *doogla, obeah, soucouyant, jagabat, badozee,* and so many more. I will look for Tanty Jo, who I hope is still alive and living near that place you told me about called the Pitch Lake. Do you remember telling me, Maman? You used to read that poem to me, the one called *Legend of La Brea,* where an ancient tribe offended the gods by feasting on hummingbirds – who were the spirits of their ancestors – and the gods were so angry they made the ground upon which the tribe lived open up and then summoned a great lake of pitch to drown the whole tribe and its village as punishment. I still remember some lines from the poem:

Down beside the loathly Pitch Lake,
In the stately Morichal,
Sat an ancient Spanish Indian,
Peering through the columns tall.

Rick Tucker

Watching vainly for the flashing
Of the jewelled colibris;
Listening vainly for their humming
Round the honey-blossomed trees…

I can't remember the rest other than: *Fish I sent you, sent you turtle, Chip-chip, conch, flamingo red* and that part when it describes how the *cursed ground* of the village *boiled with pitch*. You had to explain to me what *chip-chip* were and how you and your maman would go with her maman and papa to Manzanilla Beach, carrying buckets and shovels to dig for the chip-chip, which you would find burrowing into the sand as the tide went out, and then, when you reached home again, how you would have to rinse them a few times before they were ready to cook in a curry sauce. You told me that even though you had come to love oysters in Paris, for you, nothing could taste sweeter than your grandmother's curry chip-chip.

Maman, you told me all about the Pitch Lake, too, how it was a wonder of the world, a sight to behold, and how you used to swim in its strangely coloured sulphur pools, which are meant to have healing properties. What a strange place it must truly be. I can't imagine it at all, but I will make sure I go there, Maman, and I will bathe in its healing pools and think of you.

~ CHAPTER 8 ~

TANTY JO WAS sweeping her front gallery. She saw the ghost of her long-dead, long-haired German Shepherd as he stretched the chain that tethered him to the fence so he could come the whole way round the house to be close to her. He lay back down in the shade and yawned, scratched behind his ear with his hind leg, and cocked his head, looking at her as though he wanted to say something but not wanting to interrupt. As she swept, she talked, perhaps to him or perhaps to herself. 'Yuh smell anyting in de air? I smellin' some *ting*.' A small, dismembered plastic doll was on the porch table. A piece of string had been threaded through one of its eyes. 'I must hang dat on de tree by de track,' she said.

She looked over to the pen where she kept her fowl. Two hens pecked at each other's beaks, and she stopped her sweeping to study them. 'Boy,' she said to the dog, 'de fowl sayin' we gettin' visitors sometime soon...me eh know who dat go be nah.'

A pod of a hundred or more pelicans, high and black against the unclouded blue sky, flew over, heading south. 'Huh. Whey dem sea-duck goin', Rocky boy?' she said, addressing the dog directly. 'Yuh see dem? Some*ting* happenin' wi' dem.'

It was five days since Camille's arrival, since she had nursed her great-niece gradually back into the real world, watching over her as she drifted in and out of consciousness for the first forty-eight hours, fearing her medicine and prayers might not be enough and that she would have to summon a doctor as Camille writhed and perspired and cried out. She had lit six white candles and placed them around the sofa upon which Camille laid. She had chanted incantations and burned sage, wafting the smoke over Camille's closed eyes and under her nose. She had waved an ancient charm, a small stick with a chicken's skull attached to one end and chicken feathers attached to the other, up and down Camille's body while repeating the healing prayer to St. Lazarus: 'Oh, mighty God, Father, Son, and Holy Spirit, in worship and undivided Trinity – look tenderly upon thy servant, Camille, held in disease. Forgive her and all her sins. Heal her from the illness the unworthy have inflicted upon her. Bring back her health and strength and give her peace and thine blessings so that she will bring gratefulness in prayer to thee. My God, heal thy servant, Camille, and let all thy saints and angels pray for she.'

Camille eventually came round, wild-eyed and scared at first, confused and exhausted, full of questions that Tanty Jo answered with gentle reassurance and compassion, and unable to control the torrents of tears that burst from her as though she had taken a purge to rid her of her deepest levels of grief.

Three days of sipping broth and drinking water, mostly with Tanty Jo at her side, followed. She stayed on the sofa, only getting up to use the toilet, and return exhausted each time to sleep some more. On the fifth day, Camille asked to take a shower, and she wanted to get dressed in fresh clothes. She was hungry again and asked for food. She said she felt better, and a relieved Tanty Jo could maybe now find out what had happened to her surprise visitor and the chain of events that had brought her there.

Her first morning of feeling normal again had, nevertheless, been strange as she began to take in and notice her surroundings. Still not thinking as sharply as she would have liked, she did, nevertheless, feel safe and secure, despite the other-worldliness of Tanty Jo's house. Camille got up from the old sofa where she had slept and looked around her. The house consisted of one large room which contained the sofa and a couple of armchairs, some floor cushions scattered randomly, and one wall filled with shelves, in the middle of which there appeared to be a small altar. The kitchen area – consisting of a hob set into a long worktop – was on the other side of the room. It was as though she had stepped back in time but not to a place she had learned of or seen before. This was completely different. The altar's centrepiece was a faded iconic portrait of the Black Madonna, who held a dagger in her right hand that pointed to the sky. Resting on her left arm lay a disproportionately small African child, whose head was encircled in gold and whose eyes were completely black. The Madonna herself stared straight outwards with mournful dark eyes, the whites of which were blue, and she wore a chain around her neck from which hung a red, heart-shaped pendant pierced by a sword. Her head was covered in a dark blue shawl adorned with golden stars, and a halo shaped like a golden sun filled the background. She bore tribal scars on her right cheek. Written in faded red ink (or was it blood? Camille wondered) upon the wooden surface in front of the icon were the words: *guide us through our darkness*. On either side, a scented candle burned, emitting a black and acrid-smelling smoke.

The shelves were filled with sealed glass jars, some of which were labelled, others were not. Camille read the words out loud with a hushed sense of wonder: worm weed, jumbie beads, duppy basil, bald bush, gully root, shine bush, plumbago, angel's trumpet, trumpet tree, lis rouge, mouron blanc, love vine, patate bord la mer, patate sauvage, manchineel, lavender, cedarwood, pimento, sawdust, castor oil...there were so many – too many – to comprehend.

Otherwise, the house was plain, simply furnished, and sparsely decorated. The board walls were dry and cracked. There was no television, radio, or telephone as far as she could see, and the exotic smell of fish and spices from the kitchen area filled the house. Outside the back door, she could see and smell the sea. It sparkled in the sun, and the calls of seabirds and the sound of turning waves reached up towards her. She saw a path leading down and decided to explore.

Tanty Jo looked over at the next house, a crudely converted shipping container, where the young black Spanish woman, the one from Dominica, lived, and who was now outside, barefoot, wearing a skin-tight black singlet that barely reached below her breasts, her hair in green and yellow curlers, and the curve of her slight belly showing between her shorts and top. She was carrying a plastic washing basket of wet clothes. She waved to Tanty Jo, who called out to her, 'Lola! Yuh see she?' Lola put the washing down, walked to the small gallery protruding over the cliff face, and looked down. *'En la playa,'* she said. 'She come.'

Carelessly barefoot through the water's edge, Camille, with her head down and the sun at her back, a northerly breeze cooling her face as she walked into it, looked up to see Lola high above her, leaning over the gallery, waving. Pelicans in a long thin line flew southwards, and she wondered where they might be going. It was as though an important pelican conference had been arranged somewhere farther south, and they were all heading there with great urgency. A few stragglers sat on the jetty, beating their wings before flying off to join the rest, so laboriously at first, you would think they were weighted down until they'd reached the required thermal and become at one with the air in an effortless beating of their wings.

A group of vultures – corbeau, they called them there; she mused at another example of French words used in the local language – hopped and pranced around a scattering of small, dead fish washed up on the shoreline, discarded from a fishing boat, glinting in the sun like shards of silver, the gentle retraction of the waves making them flicker as though they were still alive and gasping for breath.

Before long, she would have to make a decision as to when and if, and if so, how, she would go back to France. She wasn't sure she felt at all safe, although Tanty Jo's house was probably as safe a haven as any, not in the least because her reputation as an obeah priestess would no doubt be enough to deter most uninvited visitors. But, she realised, there was a precariousness about life there, existence was threatened by all manner of things: the extremes of weather, the lack of infrastructure when compared to the relative sophistication of Europe – health, law, and transport for instance – aspects of life the first world took for granted and barely considered. If uncertain about such things, then life felt more fragile in a way she wasn't accustomed to, and she needed some reassuring evidence that she was at ease enough to remain. After all, people did live there, and many of them seemed to flourish. However, equally as many lived on the edge, often not realising that was where they were. The edge was all they knew. It was normal. They had a different frame of reference, that was all.

So, the search for her roots was not going to be a romantic homecoming or a reunion with the land, people, and culture that were a part of her genetic code. No, it was more challenging, more about her gaining an insight into something more complex, and at the same time, completely unromantic. So that was her reality for the time being, her mother's land under a harsh, relentless blue sky, a gentle ocean, the call of seabirds, the detritus of plastic, wood, and weed in a long arc around the bay, a path back up the cliff to a house protected from the dark spirits by an array of totems hanging from branches or attached to the tops of poles secured in the ground at various junctures around the house, a pretty young woman with laughing eyes and an easy smile who always walked barefoot and who lived in a shipping container next door. There was fresh mango to eat in the morning, fresh coconut water whenever she wanted it, and Tanty Jo's heartening fare – broth, bhaji, and fish – cooked in every way imaginable. Maman, how easy and difficult it was to be there, she concluded with tears.

When Camille walked back to the garden, Tanty Jo didn't look up as she asked her, 'Yuh see all a dem sea duck flyin' south?'

'Yes, Tanty,' replied Camille.

'An' two fowl peckin' dey beaks this mornin' – someting in de air. I tell Rocky jus' now. Someting.'

Camille looked around. 'Who is Rocky?'

'De dog. He gone long time, but he does still sit right dey.' She pointed to the long chain attached to one of the posts supporting the fence, at the end of which was a large metal clip attached to nothing.

'Come, help me feed de fowl,' said Tanty Jo, resting her broom against the front gallery rail.

Camille followed her to the side of the house, down a small path, and through a row of yellow and red hibiscus bushes leading to an enclosed pen in which a dozen chickens squawked and fussed at their approach. Tanty Jo opened the mesh door and went inside, scattering feed as she went, aiming gentle kicks at any chickens that encroached too enthusiastically. A

73

jet-black cockerel sat on top of the hutch, eyeing them with disdain, its comb and wattles blood red. Tanty Jo collected a handful of eggs from inside the hutch, ignoring the cockerel as she did, and put them in the pockets of her dress.

They walked back in silence to the front of the house. Tanty Jo picked up the broom and made as if to sweep the gallery some more but then thought better of it. She leaned on her broom and looked Camille in the eyes. 'Wh'appen to yuh, child?' she asked. 'Someting happen. I can see dat. Yuh go tell me when yuh ready.'

~ CHAPTER 9 ~

THAT EVENING, CAMILLE stood on Lola's gallery. The sea beneath the western sky changed from turquoise to indigo, and the horizon throbbed with the colours of a gigantic fire coming to life. Two long belts of illuminated orange stretched across space, sandwiching an expanse of yellow too brilliant for the human gaze to settle upon, while above it all, the black clouds of a gathering storm rolled and billowed with the menace of an erupting volcano somewhere far away in the nightmare realms of her imagination.

Camille stared into the sunset as though it was a mesmeric jewel, shining its unearthly light directly at her, drawing her towards its core where she felt she could easily disappear in sweet, helpless surrender. However deep its beauty, this really was nature untamed, and it was unconcerned, dismissive of what Camille now perceived to be her minuscule sense of being, her lost way, and her vulnerability. As the blinding heat of the colour she looked upon amplified her insignificance, the gathering storm became a portent too imperative, too discarnate to withstand. Her strength dissipated. Her sense of freedom and independence gone, she called herself a fool.

She looked down to see the last few corbeau hop and patter along the shore, hissing like snakes while the rest of them flew into the trees to start their roost. As common as the European crow, these black vultures were ugly birds, scavengers, defiant survivors who saw the demise and misfortune of others as cruel opportunity. The featherless head – grey and wrinkled – looked like the wig of some diabolical judge about to pass a sentence of death.

The wind picked up, and Tanty Jo came silently to her side with feather light steps, placing her hand gently on the small of Camille's back. 'Wh'appen, chil'? Yuh go tell me?' she whispered.

Camille looked at the kind-eyed, old woman, stooped but strong like a piece of living wood, the lines of her face crisscrossed and deep, jowls carved into her clay-like flesh by the elements of life, a stranger, yet also familiar. She didn't hesitate to rest her head upon her aunt's shoulder. 'How did I get here?' she asked.

'Two police bring yuh. Dey find yuh staggerin' on de road in de night, an' dey ask yuh whey yuh goin', an' yuh tell dem La Brea, to Tanty Jo. Yuh lucky, girl. Yuh meet good police. Not all a dem good so.'

'They know you?'

'Plenty people know me.'

'I don't remember.'

'Let we go back by me,' said Tanty Jo, linking her arm around Camille's, leading her back to her house, 'an' tell me what yuh can remember.'

The old woman rocked on her chair and looked at Camille sitting on the small faux-chenille sofa, twisting a strand of hair in her fingers and thinking back to her arrival.

Slowly, Camille started to unravel the knot of her memories. She had stepped from the plane into a wall of heat. Dry and breath-taking, it drew her in and didn't relent as she walked down the steps and across the tarmac. Unprepared and over-dressed, suddenly alienated from her surroundings, her perspiration flowed as she collected her luggage from the carousel and waited in the queue at immigration until the uniformed officer had, politely but sternly, asked why she was visiting Trinidad and Tobago. Her reservation at the Hilton Hotel in Port of Spain had seemed to reassure him; the fact that she had an open return less so. When she explained she intended to travel south to La Brea, he'd raised his eyebrows.

'You alone?' he asked.

'Yes. I will hire a car.'

'Be careful, madam,' he advised, before stamping her passport and snapping it shut. 'An' doh take a drop from de touts outside.'

'The hotel is sending a driver.'

He'd nodded with a slight grimace before saying, 'Enjoy yuh stay.'

Her driver was a tall, young black man called Gus who was dressed in an immaculately ironed white short-sleeved shirt, black trousers, and white trainers. He took her luggage and walked ahead of her to the car, a black Mercedes-Benz C-class saloon with tinted windows. As she luxuriated in the backseat, she saw him looking at her in the rear-view mirror. He'd smiled warmly and asked, 'First time in Trinidad?'

'Yes,' she'd replied, adding, 'my mother was from here. I have family in the south.' She hoped it would give her added credibility.

He nodded as though absorbing a piece of complicated information. 'I eh know de south too good,' he'd said before saying something she thought incongruous, 'Sweet, sweet, T and T – plenty to see.'

'It's a small island – do you ever go to the south?'

'Nah. If yuh from north, yuh wouldn' really go south unless yuh have to. I went dey to play cricket – Point Fortin', all around dat side – but people from de north think it better up here, an' people in de south, dey think it better dong dey. Me eh know. I would say more ting does happen in de north.'

It was half-past six in the evening and dark outside. She'd commented on that, and he'd explained how Trinidad had roughly a twelve-hour day and a twelve-hour night all through the year. 'We near de Equator,' he said.

'Of course,' she said, feeling foolish not to have thought of that.

She looked out of the window at the unfamiliar sights of the small town they'd been driving through. The street was lined with open-fronted shacks where all kinds of food, drink, and clothes seemed to be on sale. One vendor had strung up live crabs from the overhang of his shack's roof, purple and green

and swaying to and fro like puppets performing a macabre
dance. There were a lot of people on the street, and as the
traffic moved slowly, she was able to observe them all. There
was not a white person in sight, but otherwise, she saw Indians,
Afro-Caribbeans, mixed-race, and Chinese going about their
various businesses or just standing on corners in small groups,
laughing and joking. Her mother had told her that when groups
of people got together, wherever they were, and whatever they
were doing, they called it *liming*.

'Are they liming?' she'd asked.

Gus laughed and nodded. 'That's what Trinis do for real,'
he said.

Car-horns and loud bursts of Indian music, soca, and reggae
provided an amorphous soundtrack. 'Dis might take a li'l while,'
he said, 'it have traffic on de highway, de Churchill-Roosevelt
Highway, so we have to pass through Kelly Village, but it seem
like everybody have de same idea, so anyhow yuh take it, we go
meet a li'l traffic.' He laughed, and she saw his warm smile again
in the mirror.

Once through the village, she noticed the road was flanked
on either side by unfamiliar vegetation, tall and dense with grey
spindly trunks and bursts of green sword-shaped leaves at the
top. 'What's that growing there?' she asked.

He looked surprised at her ignorance. 'Yuh never see cane
before?'

'Cane?'

'Sugar. Sugar cane.'

'Of course,' she said, feeling foolish again.

When he pulled up in front of the Trinidad Hilton Hotel and Conference Centre, he told her how the hotel had been built on the side of a hill and that its bedrooms were below the reception areas, bars, and swimming pool, so unlike most hotels, you had to take the elevator *down* to your room. 'Dey call it de upside-down hotel,' he said, laughing as he hauled her suitcase and backpack from the car's boot.

She fumbled in her handbag for her purse, but he waved her away and told her it had been a pleasure to meet her and that she was to have a nice stay. He carried her luggage to the reception desk and gave a slight bow before saying goodbye. She suddenly felt alone. She would have liked Gus to have been her guide and protector in the coming days.

The next morning, despite the cloudless sky, the mango and pawpaw she'd eaten for breakfast and the seductive luxury of the poolside loungers and waiter service made her feel ill at ease. Travel had been the easy part. It hadn't been difficult to switch off and ignore reality within the confines of a long-haul flight, but now, there she was, a stranger alone with nothing but a vague notion of finding something of her roots and a member of the family she had never met who might not even be alive. It would have been easy to book the next available flight back to Paris. Paris, where it would soon be summer's end and where Philippe would be angry and cold and where she really couldn't face returning. Not yet, anyway. So, she would have to stay to see this through one way or another. If all else failed, she could just have a holiday. Maybe go to Tobago and lie on a beach or visit one of the other islands.

The assistant manager was called Gabriel, a short Indian man in a blue suit, white shirt, and green tie, who wore his hair plastered down with so much product that it reflected the spotlights in the ceiling, his hair so stiff, it wouldn't have been disturbed in a hurricane. He also had an affected English accent that sounded incongruous, pompous, and comical. 'Good morning, *marm*,' he said with a fawning smile as he glanced her up and down with just a hint of disapproval, 'and how can I help mad*arm* today?'

She told him she'd intended to travel to La Brea the next day and wanted to know about transport options and hotels in the south where she could stay. Gabriel's eyes widened in surprise. 'Is mad*arm* considering staying in the south?' he'd asked.

'Yes. For a few days. Should I hire a car?'

'Mad*arm* intends to drive?' His eyebrows had raised even higher.

'Yes. Unless – '

'Has mad*arm* ever driven in Trinidad before?'

'No.'

'I would suggest mad*arm* considers a driver, which we, of course, would be happy to arrange.'

'I don't know where I'm going to yet.'

'Might I respectfully advise mad*arm* that it would be wise to have somewhere to stay before she ventures to the...er... *south*?' His smile was that of someone who had just been served something foul to eat but didn't want to offend his host.

'Perhaps you could help me to find a hotel?'

'In de *south*?' he asked with incredulity, momentarily allowing his forced English accent to slip.

'Yes.'

'There will be a few...es*tab*lishments, but not of the standard that mad*arm* probably expects.' He winced. 'Most of them will have rooms that have an...ahem...an *hourly* rate.' He winced again. 'If mad*arm* gets my meaning.'

She was perplexed for a few moments before understanding what he was saying. 'Are those the only kind of es*tab*lishments in the south? Surely not.'

'Allow me to enquire for you,' said Gabriel with one last wince before turning to the computer on the reception desk. She could practically see her reflection in the hair on the top of his head.

After several minutes, he looked up from the screen. 'Hmm. We have three choices, one in the centre of San Fernando. It has a pool but is in the centre of town. Another is near the Gulf City Mall, which is only twelve miles from La Brea. There's also one a mile or so farther south on the Main Trunk Road, about ten miles from La Brea. It's called The Diamond Suites. None are particularly well-reviewed, you understand.'

'There's nowhere near La Brea?'

'There really are very few establishments that cater to tourists, you see. There is a guest house in Dow Village called *Paulie's*, very close to La Brea, but – '

'Oh, good.'

'No, mad*arm*. Not so good. An hourly room rate. I wouldn't imagine mad*arm* would get a...ahem...*restful* night there.'

'The other one nearest La Brea – how would I get transport from there?'

'The hotel will arrange taxis for that, I'm sure.'

'Please, book me in there for two nights, and arrange for your driver, Gus, to take me there.'

'If mad*arm* is sure.'

'Yes. Please, go ahead.'

She sat by the pool and ordered shark and bake with a cold beer. I'll give it two days, she told herself, and then I can always come back here for a while before deciding where to go next. A few other guests joined her poolside – white couples, mostly Americans – and a group of men in suits who looked and sounded Chinese. One of them, wearing aviator shades, looked at her from time to time while she ate. She stared back at him, forcing him to avert his gaze but only temporarily as she continued to draw his interest. She ordered another beer and moved to a table where he would have to turn his head to look at her.

~ CHAPTER 10 ~

THE LIGHTS FLICKERED. The night was still and soundless. A mosquito coil smoked beneath the louvre windows as they sat on the threadbare sofa in silence. A harsh, rhythmic thrum started somewhere close to the house, increasing in volume and intensity, and Tanty Jo glanced up when the dog barked once. Camille looked to Tanty Jo for reassurance. '*Crapaud,*' she said with a smile, 'big frog.'

'Toads?'

'Yeah. Big frog.'

Camille resettled her head on the old woman's bosom and calmed when she felt her head being caressed. 'Tell me, chil',' said Tanty Jo in a whispering voice. Camille sighed and continued with her story.

She arrived at the Diamond Suites Hotel near Mosquito Creek in the late afternoon sunlight. Gus carried her luggage into the reception area, said goodbye, and flashed her a smile, telling her he hoped they would meet again 'real soon'. They had talked together throughout the two-hour journey, his calmness at the wheel and the softness of his slightly lisping voice welcome distractions from the madness on the highway, where every kind of vehicle imaginable seemed to compete for space, crisscrossing lanes, braking, and sounding horns in a chaotic carnival of composition the likes of which she had never seen. She was glad to have heeded the advice not to drive herself and felt fortunate to have Gus as her driver and companion. He had been a reassuring presence, one that helped her to start feeling at ease in this strange country. When she pressed a generous tip into his hand, she looked him in the eye and said she would see him again and that she was looking forward to it. The young man appeared suddenly awkward, but his return smile conveyed to her that the promise of an intimate encounter with him would be easy to realise. She hugged him and held on for the extra seconds necessary to convey her attraction to him.

The air-conditioning in the lobby was up so high it had brought goosebumps to the surface of her skin. A tall Indian man in smart clothes was leaning on the reception desk talking to a black man wearing the hotel uniform of a maroon short-sleeved shirt and beige slacks and a badge on his chest that read *Benjamin. Asst. Manager.* The two men laughed together before high-fiving after Benjamin had alerted his friend with a flicker of his eyes towards Camille, indicating he had to get back to work. The Indian man turned around to see Camille, and he looked her up and down, his glance resting on the unbuttoned top of her blouse. 'Excuse me,' he said to her.

She gave him an amused smile before turning to Benjamin so she could start checking in. The Indian man walked away, and she watched as he entered the adjacent bar and sat down with three other men.

Her room looked out over a bay and a semi-circular coastline that faced towards the west. She could see small fishing boats with outboard motors moving slowly through the green-grey waters, trailing lines behind them. Pelicans dived vertically and at sudden speed, piercing the surface like stilettos through flesh. In the distance, an oil tanker moved impassively across the horizon, heading north.

She showered in cold water and then, feeling hungry and curious, dressed without applying make-up, closed her bedroom door, went down a single flight of stairs and then through the lobby to the bar, where she sat on a high stool and ordered a beer and a plate of chicken wings. The barman, a tall melancholy-looking black man, dressed in a white tunic, attended to her, moving with the grace of a ballet dancer, even though he was built more like a basketball player.

The Indian man she had seen in the reception area was sitting with the three men she had seen him with earlier. Two of them looked Hispanic – Venezuelan, she surmised – and spoke very little. The other had been a short, chubby Indian man in a suit with a white open-necked shirt, his eyes hidden behind tinted glasses. Much of their conversation was in hushed tones, and the short man, evidently the boss, had done most of the talking. As he emphasised some point or other, he'd wagged his finger or pointed at the younger man, while the two Hispanics nodded in agreement at every point the older man made.

The pepper sauce on the chicken wings agitated her mouth so much that she felt as if she had been chewing a hot and spicy cactus. So intense was the tingling on her tongue and lips, she ordered another beer. 'Pepper hot,' the barman said with a chuckle. 'Next time, ask for *slight* pepper because we serve dat with *plenty* pepper.'

The short man and his two companions stood up to leave. There were no handshakes or smiles towards the younger man, and they left without a backward glance, the boss wiping his forehead with a paper napkin as he waddled towards the lobby. The younger man remained seated for a few moments, one of his knees bouncing up and down like that of a drummer working his high-hat. He'd seen Camille looking at him, so he got up, moved over to the bar, and introduced himself. 'Rajan,' he said.

'Camille,' she'd replied, fingering the neck of her beer bottle and looking away from him.

'Mind if I join yuh?'

'Not at all.'

'I like yuh accent.'

There then followed a series of questions from him, asking where she was from, where she was going, what she was doing there, and who she was with. She tried to convey confidence in her responses without giving too much away. He was quite handsome, she thought, but something about his demeanour – childlike, over-familiar – had turned her off. She felt relieved she didn't find him attractive. Whenever she turned the tables and asked him to tell her about himself, he was vague, but at the same time, tried to make an impression that he was wealthy, a businessman of sorts. He ordered a bottle of Champagne and two glasses without checking if she'd wanted any.

As was her way, Camille tried to look past the veneer, the persona he'd adopted in order to impress her. He was a charmer, no doubt, but when he wasn't talking, she detected something in the way he struggled to hold her gaze – not in a shifty or suspicious way, but shyer, the way a child might look upon someone or something they coveted but knew was beyond them ever to possess. Just as she started to warm to him and enjoy the distraction he provided from her aloneness, he would say something that reminded her that her initial instincts and her subsequent wariness were valid.

'You're very beautiful,' he said.

She didn't smile or say thank you. She just looked at him without expression, conscious she didn't want to give him any sign he might misinterpret as encouragement.

He continued, 'De women here in Trinidad doh really have class, yuh know? Dey all kinda dotish, but *you*, yuh have someting more about yuh. Yuh smart. An' yuh beautiful.'

She continued to say nothing, but she looked away from him and sipped her Champagne.

'Yuh like me?' he asked. Camille turned to face him, giving him the sort of look a mother might give an errant child who had disappointed her.

'Look...Rajan, is it? I – '

'Call me Raj. Da'is how my friends does call me.' He gave her a wide, toothy grin.

'It's been nice to meet you. I'm very tired. I've been travelling an'...well, you know. I'm very busy tomorrow.'

'Oh, Chenille,' he said, misremembering her name, 'at least stay an' finish yuh drink. Yuh can tell me all about de plans yuh have for tomorrow. Maybe we could meet up. I can drive yuh anywhere yuh wah go.'

'It's okay. I have people to meet,' she lied.

'Yuh like me, eh?' he asked again, this time more insistently.

She smiled weakly as she'd stepped down from the barstool and put her bag over her shoulder. 'Goodnight,' she said.

Rajan sucked his teeth. 'Stay an' finish yuh drink nah, man. I buy we Champagne. De best in de house.'

'Goodnight,' she repeated before making her way out of the bar and into the lobby where Benjamin was sitting with his feet on the desk, reading a newspaper. She read its headline: *CHURCH SHAME Bikini fashion at Holy Trinity deemed scandalous and disgusting*.

She felt tired, and as she climbed the stairs, decided to go straight to bed. She could shower in the morning. She unlocked the bedroom door, and just as she was about to step inside, a violent shove from behind propelled her without control into the room. The door was slammed shut behind her, and she turned around to see Rajan standing a few feet away. She opened her mouth to scream, but before she could coordinate her intentions with any action, he backhanded her across the face with such force she was knocked to the floor.

90

'Fuckin' bitch,' he said. 'Doh make a fuckin' sound or I gonna tie yuh up like a fuckin' crab an' I go fuckin' kill yuh.' An image came to her mind of the live crabs hanging by strings from the roofs of stalls she had seen on the journey between the airport and the Hilton. She started to pass out but unscrambled her senses enough to realise he had ripped open her blouse and was pawing at her breasts. Then he undid her jeans and attempted to pull them down. As he tried to mount her, she'd poked him in the eye with her middle finger. Again, she felt herself on the verge of losing consciousness. Why had it been so difficult to keep her eyes open? She forced herself to look at him.

He was standing over her, and despite his frenzied attempts at self-arousal, he stayed limp, his socks and shoes still on, his trousers and underpants at his ankles. She thought he looked absurd and wanted to laugh. Humiliated and enraged, he spat at her, hitting her on the cheek before kneeling on her chest, and pushing himself towards her face. She punched him in the ribs and then, mustering as much strength and concentration as possible, punched him again, aiming for his eye and finding her intended target. Then she grabbed his flaccid cock and yanked it as hard as she could. He screamed, and she sat up, even though he was still sitting across her. She elbowed him in the mouth, and he fell off her. She staggered to her feet, leaning on the wall to steady herself as the room seemed to swirl around her.

He was lying on his back, cupping his hand over his cock and balls like a codpiece and sobbing. 'Yuh fuckin' bitch,' he said, defeated, as she opened the door and fled, trying to run down the corridor towards the stairs while pulling up her jeans, bouncing off the walls and into a table, knocking over a vase.

When she reached reception, she saw Benjamin. He looked at her in both fear and surprise but settled his gaze on her exposed chest. She had hoped to be safe there but remembered he was possibly Rajan's friend and so was immediately terrified. She ran out of the hotel, down its sloping driveway to the main road, barely able to stay upright, and then across the road into the darkness of the beach and a copse of coconut palms.

'Dat is whey dey find yuh,' said Tanty Jo, 'on de sand under de trees.'

'Who?' She lifted her head off Tanty Jo's breast and looked up at her.

'De police. That night, they was lookin' out for boats comin' in de creek. Smugglers. Dey tink yuh tight at first, but den dey realise someting happen to yuh, but yuh could hardly speak. Yuh couldn't make sense. Yuh keep sayin' Tanty Jo, Tanty Jo, Tanty Jo by de Pitch Lake.'

'So, they brought me here?'

'Yes chil'. Dey bring yuh here, but dem eh know me. Dey just ask around. Plenty people know me, so somebody must be tell dem where to find me.'

'So, am I safe here?'

'Yes chil'. Yuh lucky dey good police, but dey wah know more about wh'appen to yuh, so dey say dey comin' back.'

'You must have got such a surprise.'

'I shock, girl – Lord, I shock – but I kinda expectin' someting, yuh know? De signs, dey all day – two fowl peckin' each other beaks, bird feather on de ground – but chil', yes. I real surprise to see yuh.'

She smiled at Camille with a warmth and compassion that brought tears to Camille's eyes. The tears became a torrent of sobs, deep guttural yawps as she released what felt like a lifetime's worth of grief. Tanty Jo held her and let her cry.

~ CHAPTER 11 ~

THABO BROWN LAY back on the sofa in Fingal's sitting-room, his long locks hanging over the armrest and nearly touching the floor, his silver saxophone resting on his body, still attached to the strap around his neck. He let out a long sigh. Fingal and Goose both laughed. 'You're exasperated,' said Fingal.

'No, man – I just can't explain myself properly.'

'I get it,' said Goose, 'and I like the idea.'

'I nearly get it,' said Fingal, 'but I couldn't explain it.'

The three of them had been talking about how they could collaborate, and Thabo, a classically trained musician, was patiently trying to explain how he saw them proceeding. 'Look,' he said, 'most of your songs are either eight or twelve-bar basic blues, right?' Fingal and Goose nodded. 'So, what I'm saying is we just stretch some of them during the instrumental sections where we all solo. You know when you walk down back to the tonic chord? Well, instead of heading straight back to the tonic chord, just repeat the walk down a couple of times, and then you, Goose, play an altered chord. If we were playing in E, say, you could play something like a B7 sharp5 flat9. Then, just improvise some more chords before soloing, then letting me or Kieran have some bars.'

'Speak of the devil,' said Goose as there was a knock on the front door. Fingal opened it and greeted his occasional bass player, Kieran Kelly, who walked in with a mile-wide grin on his face and shook hands, brother-style, with all of them.

'Bobby's on his way. Shit traffic,' he said.

'We're just thinking how best to proceed with Thabo,' said Fingal.

'Cool. Do I get a bass solo?'

'Yeah, man,' said Thabo. 'We all get to solo. I reckon even Fingal could freestyle on his harp.'

'One thing I'm not sure about,' said Fingal, 'is how we keep the rhythm going. It will be down to Goose and Bobby if KK solos.'

'Look,' said Thabo, 'it should be cool. I know you guys are used to playing within the confines of a basic blues, but this won't be difficult. We will always come back to the tonic chord, and we will always count the bars. This is what Basie did all those years ago, what the beboppers took to another level. We won't go there, I know, but maybe, if we listen to some Basie, some Louis Armstrong, even, you might get the idea as to how it's really simple. The way jazz musicians stretched the blues – actually, Herbie Hancock for someone more modern. Try him, and you'll get what I mean.'

Fingal fingered through the vinyl on his shelf, selected Herbie Hancock's *Takin' Off*, and played *Watermelon Man*. Meanwhile, Goose had answered the door to Bobby Lewis, their drummer, who, on seeing the concentrated and studious looks of his friends, leaned up against the wall, stayed quiet, and nodded his head in time until near the end of the track.

They all listened until the trumpet solo had finished, and Thabo said, 'Now, listen to the sax. They keep to a strict bar structure, though. I think we could freestyle some more.'

Bobby interjected, 'Play *Three Bags Full* off that album. That's more what Thabo means, I think.' Goose looked at him. 'I didn't know you like Herbie Hancock.' Bobby looked at Goose with mock incredulity. 'That's Billy Higgins, man. He knew how to let everyone else *play*!'

'You play like him?' asked Thabo.

Bobby laughed. 'No, man. If I live to be a million years, I couldn't play that good, *but* I understand what he was always trying to do, and I can keep it going for you guys if that's what you want.'

'Let's try it,' said Goose, and they all looked to Fingal as de facto leader of the band.

'I'm in,' he responded, 'and we have a gig tomorrow. Could be perfect as it's a pub. No fee, just a bucket passed round. It won't matter so much if we fuck up here and there, so let's go run through some of the songs. Thabo?'

'I'm cool. Where's the gig?'

'Great little pub in High Wycombe called the Belle Vue. Tight. Compact. Great landlord and bar manager. Good crowd usually.'

'And then there's the tour,' said Kieran.

'Where y'all going?' asked Thabo.

'We got about eight UK dates,' said Fingal, 'and a few in Europe. Interested?'

'Where in Europe?'

'We're playing Paris, then Spain, Bilbao, Madrid, Seville, then up to the Netherlands, Rotterdam, and Amsterdam.'

'Dates?'

'Early new year. Here.' Fingal handed him a flyer.

'I'm not promising, but that could work.'

Fingal felt more motivated than he had for some time. This collaboration could be fantastic, he thought. We could go on to record something really new, a different sound, something original but with real credibility. It will be good for us all.

Before they'd left for the rehearsal studio, he telephoned Pav, the bar manager at the Belle Vue, to tell her the news. She was delighted and said she would update their Facebook page and website and message the regulars. Then, he went online to change the listings on their website to advertise that the higher-profile Thabo Brown – a rising star in the burgeoning London jazz scene – was playing with them at the Belle Vue. They now advertised the gig now as *The Long Neck Bottle Band featuring Fingal Reid and with special guest on the saxophone: Thabo Brown!*

He sent the link to Pav, and after doing so, checked to see if there were any messages on the band's website. There was only one, but it made him gasp audibly: *Attention Fingal – I think C is in trouble. She left Philippe, went to Trinidad alone. No word from her for three days now when she said she would contact every day. She doesn't answer her phone or my texts. I've tried messenger, WhatsApp, everything. I know something is wrong. I'm so worried, Fingal, please help. Mireille.*

'Shit,' he said. 'Fuck.'

'What's up?' asked Kieran.

'It's Camille.'

'You still seeing her?'

'No, I'm not,' he spoke slowly, 'but it seems she might be in some kind of trouble. I need to make a call. You all go on to the studio. I'll be there soon.'

When they had all gone, he hovered over his phone, weighing up his options. If he called Mireille, he would open a door, and he would have to accept whatever came through it. If the situation was serious, it would prey on his mind unless he got involved. On another level, as well as beginning to fret about Camille, he was already thinking about flights to Trinidad and whether it was the right time of day to call his only real contact there, Israel Taylor. What if something terrible had happened? What if she couldn't be found? There was always the possibility she was fine and had just settled in with her family there. Nevertheless, Mireille had seemed certain something was wrong.

He pictured Camille, allowing suppressed memories of her to come to the fore of his mind, and he admitted to himself, as a knot tightened in his guts, that she had, as well as being the love of his life, served as some kind of muse for him, albeit a fiercely independent one. It wasn't something he cared to admit, but there was no denying that when they were seeing each other often, spending long intimate periods of time together, he had written more, sung with more passion, and played his harmonica as though his whole soul was being dragged through those notes. She had acted as a reference point, a patient listener, and critic, with her recognition of him as someone who always needed approval and who, as an artist, never felt good enough. She had given him something of the affirmation he had always needed to validate himself. Even the bitterness and aloneness he'd felt after he had severed contact with her had given him a rich source of emotion from which he could draw, and he'd subsequently written some of the most painful lyrics he ever had. He had walked away, tried to draw a line under it all, told his closest friends he had moved on, but he always knew, even though he tried to deny it, that she was still there under his skin, her soft eyes looking at him, the skin of her hands soft as she held his; her honesty and beauty. The hole in his spirit she had once filled had been empty ever since that rain-drenched day in Scotland when he had stopped responding to her calls and texts. All the rationale he summoned to persuade himself not to go to find her was to no avail. On some visceral level, he knew he was going. He had no choice. She had to be safe, or his ensuing grief would be unbearable. He found Mireille on Messenger and called her.

The band took it well, if not enthusiastically. 'I'll be back soon enough,' he said, 'so we'll play tomorrow's gig at the Belle Vue and then make plans for after I get back.'

'The tour, man,' said Bobby. 'What about the tour?'

'I'll be back in plenty of time. I'll only go for a week or so, two weeks, tops.'

'You sure, man?' asked Kieran. 'You sure you ain't confusing a soulmate with a hard life lesson? She hurt you, man.'

'No choice,' he replied. 'Really, I've got no choice.'

~ CHAPTER 12 ~

THE WESTERN HORIZON looked aflame with the setting sun, and Fingal Reid was thinking about love. He looked towards the vast sky turning from blue to black, the billowing clouds resting upon the edge of the world, and the brilliant burning orange of the sun making its way to the other side of the Earth. He knew the signs and symptoms so well, bearing the scars as he did from a few, but not many, previous romances. This one was different, though, and he had felt so from the start. How he had once obsessed over the object of his desires, betraying all the normal traits of the lovesick. How he'd checked his phone several times a day (and sometimes night) for messages, texts, and emails via all the various forms of modern-day communications, the fretted-over misunderstandings brought about by the one-dimensional nature of words conveyed only by text, words without body language or tone of voice, humour mistaken for sarcasm, the economy of language mistaken for abruptness, mild frustration interpreted as disproportionate anger. It had resulted in too many late-night, angst-driven attempts at reparation, lying awake at night wondering or lusting, lying in bed in the morning, yearning for her arms, recalling vividly the times they were in each other's company. How they laughed, cried, ate, drank, slept, and made love in such apparent calm, harmony, and passion so strong he had once believed that in her he had found everything he had ever looked for. And then he had shut down.

Weary of the inconsistency and uncertainty, suddenly vulnerable when once he had felt so safe. Shutting down something that had taken so much effort to open up hadn't been easy, pushing it all back in, cramming it back into that confined space deep within his psyche; it had taken its toll. He thought he had left her behind and moved on, so what was he doing there?

Camille Brossard, the beautiful French-Trinidadian woman of his dreams, was a few years younger than him. The daughter of a diplomat and a woman from a different social class to his, she had the maturity and insight of someone who had survived some of life's more difficult battles, as well as the intelligence, humility, and sensitivity of someone who had travelled, lived in different cultures, and learned about life and the ways of the world. It had perplexed him at first and ultimately angered him that she'd always seemed to doubt his love or dismissed his expression of it with reactions like 'What does love mean?' or 'I don't want anyone to love me,' and it deeply troubled and frustrated him that she would suddenly withdraw from all communication, sometimes lasting for days.

There was a time when he had no doubt that he wanted to live with her, but maybe due to the physical distance between them (he was based in London, she in Paris), she had always been cautious or doubtful. These feelings were not at all evident during the best of times spent together when she was warm, open, generous, attentive, and lustful. She claimed never to have had sex as intense and satisfying as she'd had with him, and he had never wanted anyone physically or emotionally as much as he had wanted her. However, the contradictory, inconsistent way she behaved towards him was so exasperating it sometimes formed a knot of anxiety in his gut so severe he would go for days without eating or sleeping until their communications had settled down again. When they did, he would bathe in the warmth and glory of their relationship with such ease and familiarity that he could rationalise the preceding torture as being worthwhile. She had often asked him why he put up with her, and he would tell her the same thing every time: 'Because you're worth it.'

He couldn't remember exactly when she started to withdraw more extremely than she'd ever done before, not answering messages for days, not answering phone calls or emails and then suddenly instigating contact, sounding anxious, depressed, or determinedly negative. – 'You mustn't love me anymore, Fingal. I will only hurt you.' – but it made him suspect she had either found someone else or something was wrong with her. Or both. These possibilities induced such intense desperation that the relationship had begun to damage his health and play havoc with his emotional equilibrium, yet he still couldn't abandon his feelings for her.

Once, when there had been no contact with her for a whole month, Fingal had given up and texted Camille to tell her he couldn't take it anymore. He'd tried to find the rationale needed to put her behind him. She was married for a start, he'd told himself, and even though she was unhappy in her marriage, she still professed to love her husband despite his coldness towards her and his heavy drinking.

Then, there was the older man she was having an affair with, whom she'd sometimes said she loved, needed, and cared for, who, despite being possessive and self-centred, seemed to have a hold over her. To Fingal's mind, she needed to clear her decks of both husband and lover and be with him, but if she didn't want that or couldn't decide what she wanted, he had to stop laying his heart open to her. After his text, there was one particularly emotional and hurtful telephone conversation with her, after which he'd decided enough was enough.

A year and a half or so had passed since then, and there had been no one else in that time with whom he had shared any intimacy. He had concentrated on his music, playing live with the band – they accepted gigs all over the country – or writing songs and recording demos in his home studio. He did, however, remain on the lookout for someone else to fill the gap in his life, the emptiness that, if he let it, induced a deep sense of grief to shudder to the surface. He'd met no one who'd come close to her, so he'd learned to bury the loss, although he now realised it was in nothing more than a shallow and transparent tomb.

Then, out of the blue, he'd received the message on the band's website. Within three days, Fingal arrived at Piarco Airport near Port of Spain, where he was met by Israel, the Rasta, whom he had met and befriended at the Tobago Jazz Festival. Israel agreed to help, but he was wary and asked Fingal why he was doing this. 'For love,' was his straightforward reply, 'and she might be in trouble.' The wise and weathered Rasta shook his head in perplexity at Fingal's obsession and determination and said, 'Man, she must be something special.'

'Yep,' Fingal replied. 'The best I've known.'

~ CHAPTER 13 ~

H E THOUGHT RURAL Trinidad was as close to paradise as he had ever experienced. The colours, the dazzling lights, the apparently simple agrarian way of life reminiscent of southern Europe but with coconut palms and countless other extravagant displays of flora everywhere you looked, all so vibrant and fresh, had quickly seduced him into such a feeling of resonance and calm that he started thinking it was somewhere he could start afresh, turn his back on his long but vain quest for recognition, see it for the illusion it was, and find the peace of mind and space to lead a more honest existence. Why do musicians seek that acclaim? he wondered. Addicted to the high of live performances, crushed by the come-downs – for him, being a musician was like being an addict. Maybe it was time to break the habit.

Trinidad was showing him something he hadn't expected, that when you stripped life bare of its adornments, all the things the first world strives for in terms of materialism and status, the really important stuff – your true self – remained. If you couldn't come to terms with that, be at peace with that, then what was the point of it all? If you were strong enough to look upon your naked self and feel comfortable, then maybe you had cracked it.

On his previous visits to the islands, he had only been to the capital, Port of Spain, and Tobago to perform at the jazz festival. Port of Spain was a noisy, bustling city with enough no-go areas to keep a stranger mostly confined to his hotel complex. When he ventured out, he felt uncertain and wary, finding the people either indifferent or hostile, depending on where he dared to go. Tobago, mostly beautiful to behold, was more commercialised, and so, more apparently first-world, with its numerous hotels, restaurants, bars, and tourist attractions. Pigeon Point, where the jazz festival had taken place, although obviously once the archetypal white-sanded, turquoise-sea, coconut-palm stereotype of an idyllic West Indian beach, was heaving with festival-goers, musicians, road crews, cameras, police, and tourists when he'd been there. Where he was now, in the sparsely populated south of Trinidad, it could be a different country altogether.

It was a little after six in the morning. The sky was cloudless and powder blue, a gentle breeze was blowing, and the ubiquitous song of the kiskadee was the only sound in the air other than a distant car horn or Israel splashing his body as he washed himself standing in front of an old oil barrel filled with water. A hibiscus with its blood-red flowers like trumpets grew defiantly from a rough patch of ground in front of the house, encircled by an old tyre. A hummingbird, only about four inches long, its head and throat an iridescent green, its back like polished copper scales shimmering in the sunlight, hovered as though suspended by the gods, wings a blur of shimmering indigo, in front of the flower's cavity.

They had arrived there in the dark of the previous night, and the strangeness of the surroundings and night-time sounds had initially made Fingal feel the uncertainty of someone a long way out of his comfort zone. They'd sat around a fire, eating rotis filled with curried channa while sipping rum. 'Where are we?' he had asked Israel.

'About a half-mile from Muga village. It have a beach down de road. Point Carlos.'

The next day, Israel drove Fingal around the area so he could get his bearings. Where they were staying looked so different in the harsh, bright light of daytime. Just outside of Muga on the road to Cedros was a turning with a sign reading *Point Carlos Trace*, and a few hundred yards down that road, they turned inland following another road sign which read *Trace Off Point Carlos Trace*. A short way down the trace were two buildings about twenty feet apart, one a house abandoned to the bush many years before, judging by the extent of the overgrowth and the amount of rust on the doorless, tyreless car sitting alongside it. The other was the house Israel had borrowed from 'someone in me fraternity' for the two of them to stay in for however long their strange mission lasted.

It was basic, to say the least, but it had two foam mattresses in separate bedrooms, a large water tank at the side of the house, and a latrine fifty yards or so along the road in a barren field. Other than that, there was a fire pit, a washboard, an old oil drum in which to wash, and a parking bay with a galvanised iron roof to shield cars from the beating sun.

The bush was all around them, a lush rainforest full of exotically coloured fruit and unfamiliar sounding birds, and if the strange sounds were anything to go by, numerous wild animals. A mango tree and two coconut palms grew in the makeshift garden area at the back of the house, where two hammocks were attached to support struts holding up a galvanised iron roof over the porch. To Fingal, it was the wilds. To Israel, it was a typical dwelling in that part of the country, otherwise normal if not a little old-fashioned and in need of modern conveniences.

As Fingal watched Israel wash his lithe, sinewy body, burned the darkest black by years in the tropical sun, his long, matted, grey locks reaching past his waist until he tied them up in a bird's nest arrangement above his head, he recalled their first meeting.

The band had finished their set soaked in sweat and high after the gig and the enthusiastic reception they had received. Fingal went to collect their payment and was talking heatedly to the promoter in the green room bar, which was situated in a marquee backing onto the sands behind the main stage. They were arguing over money, Fingal accusing the man of not paying what had been agreed. In the end, the promoter handed over a roll of cash, and Fingal then downed his beer and walked out onto the sands to take some air and calm down. He looked up at the clarity of the constellations in the unpolluted night sky and became aware of someone approaching him from behind. As he turned, he had his arms yanked back and held by someone telling him to *shhh*. A second, boyish-looking man then held a cutlass to Fingal's face and told him not to move as he started to go through Fingal's pockets, all too easily finding the roll of notes. Shaking with fear and with little choice but to do so, Fingal obeyed. The man behind him loosened his grip, and the man with the cutlass started to walk away, and then Fingal heard a shout and a string of swear words as two other men appeared and started to attack the robbers, knocking the one with the cutlass to the ground and kicking him several times in the stomach and groin. The other one ran away. Fingal didn't know whether he was being rescued or if the two new figures were also robbers, perhaps more violent than the first ones.

One of the men approached Fingal and patted him on the shoulder. 'Yuh okay, bruddah?'

Fingal stammered a reply of, 'Yes, thanks,' as the second one, a tall, older man wearing a Rasta hat, picked up the roll of notes and handed it to Fingal.

'Should be all dey,' he'd said.

'Thanks,' said Fingal, still wary of who the men might be.

'We security. Doh worry – we work for de festival,' said the Rasta, understanding Fingal's disquiet.

'Wow. Thanks,' said Fingal, still shaking and unable to think of anything sensible to add.

'Yuh welcome, bruddah,' said the Rasta's companion.

'Let me give you something,' said Fingal, fingering the notes, beginning to peel off a few from the roll but unable to see in the dark how much he was about to hand over.

'Nah, man,' said the Rasta, 'Yuh earn it wi' yuh music. We jus' doin' we job. Sorry, we eh see de muddacunts before dey reach you. Dem eh comin' back no time soon, so doh worry. Leh we take yuh back to de green room.'

When they reached the marquee, Fingal insisted on buying them a drink. The Rasta accepted, but his colleague said he was going back to the side of the stage where the next band had just started playing. They introduced themselves. 'Israel Taylor,' said the Rasta with a grin and a handshake. 'If any further assistance is needed, leh me know.'

It wasn't exactly an instant friendship, but the two of them drank a few beers and rums before parting and promising to look out for each other over the next couple of days. Israel later told him he'd thought Fingal a different kind of white man, more at ease with black people than usual, a lover of reggae music too, so he'd seemed cool enough.

The two of them spent more time together over the following days, between Israel's working and Fingal and his band playing a further couple of sets. During the downtime of their last day, Israel had taken Fingal out on a boat ride to Buccoo Reef and afterwards, the Nylon Pool, where Israel anchored the boat, and the two of them swam in the clear, shallow waters, diving for fragments of coral, getting better acquainted all the time. They had more in common than either of them would have expected: hatred of hypocrisy, arrogance, racism, and politics to start;

a love of cricket and football (Israel supported Arsenal and thought Dennis Bergkamp the greatest player to ever have worn the shirt); and a distrust of materialistic people and their values, both preferring the simpler things in life such as food, drink, friends, and family, none of which needed riches to enjoy. Then, there was reggae, and Israel had been impressed by Fingal's knowledge and genuine appreciation of the music, listening attentively to his stories of London, its flourishing reggae, jazz, and hip-hop scenes, and the places he had first heard steel pan and calypso as a young musician playing the circuit.

The band went home ahead of Fingal, who stayed on with Israel at the home of a friend of his – another Rasta called Cecil – who lived with his wife, Sandra, in a humble wooden house above Mount Irvine Bay. Israel explained that Cecil and Sandra were true Rastas, unlike him. 'Me nah strict Rasta, yuh know? I does eat ital but sometimes a li'l chicken an' fish. I doh eat nothin' de pig. Yuh know, dey say Rasta is a levity, a way a life, so I jus' follow some of de ways a Rasta an' try to live humble an' peaceful an' cool, but yuh know, sometimes in life, it cah be all peace an' love. An' I like de ladies an' a li'l rum now and again,' he added with a wink.

During the time they spent together, their friendship cemented into something real, which they both appreciated. When Fingal couldn't delay his departure any longer, Israel accompanied him on the ferry back to Port of Spain and then on to Piarco Airport before bear-hugging his new friend in a fond farewell, both of them promising to stay in touch, but neither knowing when they would see each other again. A few weeks later, an Arsenal shirt with the name BERGKAMP and the number ten across its back had arrived in the post at Israel's home in Williamsville.

Israel was sharpening two cutlasses, honing them on a stone with practised, rhythmical strokes in time with the reggae playing loudly from somewhere in the house, appropriately enough, Peter Tosh's *Steppin' Razor*. He tested the blades on some old coconuts, which they sliced through with ease. Satisfied, Israel wiped the cutlasses and placed them on the table. Fingal watched his friend, realising, perhaps for the first time, that he was a very hard man, weathered, scarred, lean, and strong. No one dared mess with him unless they really didn't have a choice.

Fingal looked down the road and noticed the tattered, faded flags attached to bamboo poles fluttering in front of the abandoned house fifty yards away. 'What are those flags for? he asked. 'I see them everywhere.'

'Dey is *jhandee*. A Hindu ting.'

'Meaning what?'

'Hindu plant dem after dey pooja. Have some kinda ceremony an' prayer in dey house. Is like a covenant wi dey gods, so you plant a jhandee for, seh, if yuh wan' yuh children to make a good education, or if yuh wan' be a successful head a de house, or for yuh business to do well. All kinda ting dey plant a jhandee for. It maybe like goin' church so yuh can show yuh neighbours how upright an' holy yuh is. De bamboo stick symbolise yuh upright an' strong an' dey plant dem wi' milk pour in de hole, too. Symbolise purity a thought.' He laughed.

When Israel finished sharpening the cutlasses, he handed one to Fingal. 'Dis one yours,' he said.

'I've never used one.'

'Jah willin' yuh won' have to, but it easy, man. It have a sharp blade, and yuh jus' chop at anyone who come at yuh.' He laughed again.

Fingal stood up, and holding the first weapon he'd ever held in his life, made a few sweeping arcs through the air.

Israel smiled, gold teeth twinkling in the bright light. 'I need to show yuh someting,' he said, pointing to the road's dead end.

The two of them started walking to where, it appeared to Fingal, there was a wall of impenetrable vegetation, rich, verdant, shining plants with large leaves, all at about shoulder height.

'Dasheen bush,' said Israel, chopping at some of it with his cutlass to reveal a narrow track leading farther into the untamed bush where occasional, intensely-coloured flowers somehow managed to grow and flourish. 'Look here,' said Israel. 'Dis track go up to de flamboyant tree opposite de bar in de village, de one dey call Neighbour's. It maybe a half-mile, an' yuh might have to chop some a dis out de way, but is a route between here an' dey dat nobody seem to use. Watch out for snake, an' if mosquito bite, doh slap yuh skin cos de sound will travel. Jus' bein' extra cautious, cah yuh never know, eh.'

Walking back to the house, they contingency-planned, agreeing that if anybody asked, Fingal was a writer, there to research a travel book, and Israel was his guide to the local flora and fauna. Since Fingal didn't know anyone in Trinidad, any casual enquiries about Camille's whereabouts would be conducted by Israel. He could move about less conspicuously than Fingal even though he was an apparent stranger in those parts. He said that he had a contact nearby, a friend of a friend, one of his 'fraternity', and soon, when the time was right, he would make himself known to him. Meanwhile, they wouldn't do too much lest they drew unwanted attention. Appearing normal was, nevertheless, important, so the odd drive through the village, even stopping for a beer at the bar, would probably avoid any of the villagers becoming too suspicious. They could shop at the local store for provisions, buy hop rolls at the parlour, even watch the people going to church. 'Be familiar,' said Israel, 'but not conspicuous.'

Fingal queried whether the secrecy and caution were absolutely necessary, but Israel's view was that if anything bad had happened to Camille, it was important they considered anyone involved in her disappearance was likely a criminal, or at least involved in the kind of business that no one asked questions about, so caution was paramount. If in doubt, retreat, was their agreed-upon mantra for the mission. Nevertheless, Israel thought it wouldn't be a bad idea for Fingal to be seen in the village so people got used to him being around.

Israel sat on the steps of the front door and started to clean his gun, a handgun of some kind, the make and calibre of which was a mystery to Fingal. He watched as Israel practised releasing and replacing the magazine several times until it was as smooth and seamless an action as he could attain. Fingal observed all of this with mixed feelings, not least of which was a slight alarm that Israel's preparedness signified a potential for violence and danger. However, he also felt a sense of security and trust in his friend, who was a reassuring presence in what was, he was now undoubtedly beginning to sense, a volatile country.

That lunchtime, as Israel cooked plantain and roti over a fire, he said to Fingal, I go help yuh find she, but it have tings I need to find out. Tell me more.'

'What do you want to know?'

'Everyting yuh could tink of about she. Every li'l detail so I can make a picture in my mind: who she is, wha' she like, an' how she look, speak, dress...yuh know – everyting.'

Fingal described her as best he could, smiling at the memory of her beauty, making Israel chuckle. 'Man, yuh real mad for she,' he said. Then he stood up. 'Now, me have to go see some a mi bredren. Yuh be cool here. It safe, man. Take a walk to de village, get to know de place, jus' be a li'l careful, yuh know?'

~ CHAPTER 14 ~

THE MAN THEY call Hero was the first to see him. Walking home along Moncoeur Road, a cutlass in the scabbard attached to his belt, and a planting-hoe resting on his shoulder like a rifle, Hero's sleeveless jersey was stained with sweat, his skin burnished like brass and shining, his work done for the week. He had planted one thousand pakchoy seedlings that day, having started just before sunrise. Like the best of gardeners and farmers, he'd planted according to the cycles of the moon: upward-growing plants three days before the full moon, ground provision any time after. If the moon's gravity wasn't able to pull the plants upwards, they wouldn't grow so well, wouldn't grow tall and look healthy, and wouldn't fetch the best price at market. He had hurried to get the planting done in time, even though it was actually four days before the full moon, as he didn't want to work over the weekend and had decided a day earlier would worry neither plant nor moon.

He had made ten furrows, then a hundred indentations in each one before walking between the rows and throwing the seedlings like darts to land perfectly, roots-down in their individual beds. That had taken most of the morning, and before he could call it a day, he'd secured the plants in the ground by pressing down the earth around them with his hands. He had no doubt about climate change; it was as hot as hell, and that was now the norm. Every day he hoped for rain.

Villagers sitting in the shade of their porches or underneath their houses waved hello to him or called out as he passed by, his familiar figure a reassurance the old ways still prevailed. It seemed to many that he had always been there, but sometimes he wondered, as he accepted his lot in life, if anyone would miss him were he not there. He would have liked to have gone away. There were places in the world he had seen on television or heard about from neighbours and friends where he might like to go. Canada, for instance, where he had a sister, somewhere in England where he had an aunt or that place in Scotland where the monster lived. He would like to have seen all these places, but he had never left Trinidad; he hadn't even travelled to Tobago. Now, in his fifties, he couldn't imagine ever being able to afford the journey to one of those far-off places. He needed some work done on his teeth, and for now, what little he made from his job would have to go towards that. He hoped he could save enough before all of his teeth had fallen out. Anyway, he had never gone hungry, always had the means to make a little money, and he'd kept his friends.

Rick Tucker

The one time a neighbour gave him bad-eye and all his crops failed, he didn't have, as he'd put it, a black cent to his name, but his friends had helped him out, letting him share food and drink until he was back on his feet. The neighbour who had put the curse on him had been ostracised for a while, but it hadn't taken long for everything to be forgotten and for life to carry on as normal. Bad-eye – *maljo*, as it was known, after the Spanish phrase *mal de ojo* – something he had learned from one of the Venezuelans who had come into the local bar — was just a part of life. People there sometimes tried to settle their disputes by placing curses. On that occasion, it was because the neighbour had suspected Hero of coveting his wife when, in fact, she had been carrying on with someone else. It was a drama everyone but her husband knew about, and the easiest way to take care of it was to give someone *maljo*, look at them a certain way, and strike the fear of evil into them.

Such are our ways, he mused, and although he accepted he was a simple, uneducated man who had preferred to work in the fields with his father and grandfather planting lettuce or bodi or cutting cane on the plantation down the road than go to school. He also favoured the soft comfort of rubber boots over the smart-but-too-tight school shoes his mother had bought him the one time (but never again); he had nevertheless tried to educate himself. He liked to watch documentaries on television, especially about the natural world, and he liked to hear the way people from different countries spoke, their accents, and the strange words they used. But when the time came for him to meet his maker, he knew all he would be able to say he did well was gardening. He planted, he watered, he studied the moon and the weather, and he harvested. He lived alone, simply and honestly, not causing anybody any harm, trusting that the arrangement with the universe was a reciprocal one.

He was so hot and weary from his labours and the walk home, he decided to call in at Neighbour's Bar, have a beer to slake his thirst, and maybe even a shot of overproof rum to revive his spirits. He would sit under the flamboyant tree on the opposite side of the road and smoke a cigarette or two in the cooling breeze. Maybe his friends, Larry, Champs, Birdy, or Clock would be there.

He came round the bend and looked towards the tree, screwing up his eyes to focus against the glare of the sun. To his surprise, he saw a stranger there, sitting with his legs crossed, wearing jeans and a polo shirt, and smoking a cigarette calmly. A white man in a hat, slim, middle-aged with a red face, long, greying sideburns, and pink tattooed arms.

As he neared the bar, Hero studied him. Upon entering its open front, he saw Larry and Clock sitting there. Neighbour was behind the grille, leaning on the counter, her head resting on her arms. She didn't look up. 'Whey boy,' said Larry upon seeing his old friend and offering his open palm for what you could only describe as a low-five. Clock offered him a high one.

'Who dah man dey?' asked Hero, jerking his chin in the direction of the flamboyant tree.

'Who dah man whey?' replied Larry.

'De man dey.'

'Wha' man whey?'

'De man *dey*!'

'Whey you talkin' 'bout?' asked Clock.

Hero pointed over the road. '*Dah* man dey, under de tree.'

Neighbour raised her head up from her folded arms, looking sleepy.

Larry and Clock walked to the front of the barroom and looked across the road.

'Wha' man?' asked Larry.

'Whey?' asked Clock.

Hero had sat down, and Neighbour was getting him a beer but he got to his feet again and walked to where his friends were standing. Before looking over the road, he raised his voice in exasperation. 'De man *dey*. De *white* man under de tree! All yuh blin' or what?'

'Boy, eh nobody dey!' shouted Clock, equally exasperated.

Hero looked, and sure enough, the bench under the flamboyant tree was empty. 'Huhm. Boy, I tellin' allyuh it had a man dey, a *white* man wid he face an' arms all red an' pink from de sun. Not like Syrian white, but like a white man who never see de sun before. He was dey, I tellin' yuh.'

'Boy, yuh tink if it had a white man in de village we wouldn' know?' said Larry. 'Neighbour, yuh see a white man here?'

'Yuh mean Paul de artist fellah?' asked Neighbour.

'No, man,' said Hero. 'Paul here long time now. I tellin' yuh, dis was a *new* white man. He had on a longpants, in *dis* weather, too. Pinky skin white man wi' plenty tattoo all up he hand. Wearin' a hat. One a dem hats.'

125

'Wha' kinda hat?' asked Clock.

'Like a Panama, but not a Panama. One a dem hats. A *federer*, maybe? A grey hat ting wi' a black ribbon.'

His friends all cackled with glee, but Hero would not be deterred. 'An' he have a little moustache, tin tin, like a line above he lip. An' a goatee. An' he have tattoo an' a earring in he ear.'

'Whey else he have a earring?' laughed Larry. 'It bound to be in he ear!'

'Well, some fellahs like to have one in dey nose or dey lips or dey eyebrow,' said Clock.

'An' some,' Larry paused for effect, 'like one in dey peepee!' They all laughed, even Hero.

'So,' said Neighbour, 'if he had on a hat, how yuh see he face was pink?'

'He hand pink an' he neck,' replied Hero, getting frustrated. 'How de hell do I know? I only see him for a few seconds, but I tellin' yuh, he was *right* dey.'

'Boy, yuh sure you eh seein' tings or mistakenin' him for somebody?' asked Larry.

'No, boy. I see a white man me eh ever see before. I tellin' yuh, sittin' dey, smokin' a cigarette.' He went back to the bar, took a shot of rum, picked up his beer, and walked over the road. Larry and Clock followed him.

All three sat on the bench and lit cigarettes. Hero started studying the ground. 'Wha' yuh lookin' for, boy?' asked Clock, laughing. 'Lookin' for he footprints?'

Larry laughed. 'Yuh get too much sun,' he said. 'Makin' yuh see tings.'

'I lookin' for he cigarette butt,' Hero said softly. 'See if is ah English or American brand.' His friends laughed at him again, and Hero began to wonder and question his own truth, but he didn't want to lose face. Maybe he hadn't seen what he thought he had. The sun was in his eyes after all, and he was tired, but he was sure. 'No, man. I see him right here. On my life.'

~ CHAPTER 15 ~

LESS THAN A half-mile down the road from Neighbour's Bar, in the house the locals referred to as De Pink Palace, Kajri Ramkissoon was getting ready to go to the mall, looking in the mirror, deciding what to wear. She had put on her tightest three-quarter length jeans and high heels, taking time to twist and twirl so she could look at her backside and assess whether what she thought of as one of her greatest assets was, indeed, looking at its best. She decided it was. Then, she put on her underwire bra, cupped her breasts with her hands to accentuate her cleavage, pouted in disappointment at herself in the mirror, and wished she had a little bit more up top. Then, she put a diamond stud in her pierced belly button before choosing a checked blouse that she tied in a bow above her waist to show off her flat belly, and more importantly, the jewel itself. False eyelashes applied, hair tied tightly at the back to make her temples and cheekbones look more pronounced, her waist-length ponytail perfectly groomed and shining, she was ready to go. She went downstairs, anticipating and rehearsing her part in the forthcoming exchange with her father when she would ask him for money.

Faith Ramkissoon, also known as Angel, was in the sitting-room, watching an American soap opera with the sound turned down when Kajri walked in wearing a smile so big and fake, she hoped Faith wouldn't realise it was a ruse to hide the fact she had already spent that month's allowance. 'Ma, why yuh have yuh show on quiet so?' she asked.

'He on de gallery restin', so doh upset de man nah.' At which point, Radhesh Ramkissoon, known to his wife as Baba, walked barefoot into the room, dressed in a stained singlet and a pair of raggedy shorts.

'It have stew?' he asked, looking towards his wife, who ignored him. 'Angel, my darling,' he continued in a sarcastic tone, 'me little light of me life – please, tell me...it have any stew for me lunch?'

'Baba, all yuh have to do is walk in de kitchen and see to yuhself,' she replied.

'It have eddoes?'

'No. Green fig and Irish potato.'

He looked towards his daughter, who was leaning against the doorframe, smiling at him. 'Sit down, Papa an' let me fix up for yuh,' she said.

'An' where de hell yuh goin' dressed like dat?' he asked, looking her up and down.

'Just to de mall.'

'Just to de mall,' he mimicked in a high-pitched voice. 'Well, why de ass yuh have to go *just* to de mall wearin' *just* near nothin' at all?'

Kajri smiled at him coyly as though she were a baby doll. 'Yuh doh tink I look nice?'

'Sweet Jesus.'

'No need to blaspheme,' said Faith.

'How could it be blaspheme when I is a Hindu?' he retorted.

'Wi' a Christian wife an' a Christian mother-in-law.'

'I callin' Jesus sweet anyway.' He looked at his daughter again.

'Yuh need money?' She gave him her baby-doll smile and he pulled a money clip from his pocket and counted out five hundred dollars. 'An' doh drink and drive...police will hold yuh an' carry yuh out de road...dey hot by the crossing yuh know.'

'Tanks, Papa,' she said, taking the money and turning to leave.

'Eh!' he shouted at her, 'Yuh fixin' me something to eat?'

'All yuh have to do is walk in de kitchen an' see to yuhself,' she said laughing, and then she was gone.

'Baba, yuh does spoil de girl,' said Faith.

A bowl of stew on the coffee table in front of him, Radhesh Ramkissoon sat down on the sofa and joined his wife of thirty-one years to watch the silent soap. He coughed unproductively, turned to tell her he thought he might be catching a cold, and saw she had fallen asleep, her mouth wide open, and her glasses askew on top of her nose. He studied her. 'She belly now bigger than she breast,' he mused, 'an' she have more chin now than when we first meet. She have dem big old veins at de back of she calves, an' she hair is a mess, but she still my Angel, my rock.

131

I jus' wish she didn't eat so an' didn't spend so much damn time sittin' on de sofa watchin' dis bullshit American foolishness. Den again, she give birth to de three children, all a dem healthy, an' she do her damndest to raise dem up good, even though de boy too wild an' Kajri like she interested in too much foolishness, an' we lose one in de birth before she, so tank God for our eldest, Khalisha, my precious one so quiet an' sweet an' reliable. She husband, Ranesh, make some money, too, wi' he tailorin', an' she work hard in we shop. Angel also have to look after Bee Bee, she mother, de old she-goat, but is she mother an' she does do a good job dey, too. I worry about she diabetes, but she managin' dat, even if she drink too much a sweet drink. She does keep we place lookin' nice, an' I know people does call it de Pink Palace, but dey only bad-eye with dey envy. Dey jus' talkin' and maccoin', but my hard work pay for it, and Angel, she *always* keepin' it jus' so. Dis damn stew real good, too. So I cah complain. I guess we blessed. Hindu or Christian, we blessed.'

He heard the electronic gates open and a vehicle drive into the carport below the house. He guessed it was Rajan. Why he home so early? he wondered. Their only son, now twenty-nine years old, was married to Alicia, ten years his junior, whom he had made pregnant a year and a while ago, was Radhesh's only real worry in life, other than the usual stresses and strains of being a businessman, all of which he could cope with. He could manage his staff, most of his suppliers and customers, keep a good cash flow, manage the accounts, and pay at least some tax, but his son was another thing altogether.

Radhesh needed the boy to take over the business one day, and he had set about preparing him for the role a few years previously, but Rajan's waywardness and weaknesses for drink, drugs, and women had presented Radhesh with some unanticipated challenges. Rajan had his own ideas about how to make savings for the business, often involving deals with people who traded illegally, importing all manner of goods and supplies by motorboat from Venezuela and some of the other islands. Much to his regret, Radhesh had gone along with the early plans when he'd seen how much cash could be saved and made, but he had always felt a certain disquiet about it, confirmed when he'd met some of the men with whom his son was associated. Radhesh understood that many people in their country were poor and that Trinidadians were too often obsessed with making an extra dollar here or there, so he didn't object on moral grounds that there were people involved in illegal imports. That cocaine and guns often accompanied the farm equipment, car parts, white goods, corn flour, rice, chicken feed, or the caged wild birds was something he opportunistically ignored, but that disquiet scratched away at his insides from time to time, often keeping him awake.

It was Faith who had nicknamed their son Raja or Raj, the king, as a shortening of his birth name, believing him to be a handsome, prince-like character who would grow up to be a powerful and respected man. He was their second child, and they thought their last until Angel had become pregnant with Kajri eleven years later. Suddenly usurped of his role as the youngest and most special one, Rajan had reacted jealously to the arrival of his sister, who, as she had grown, had mercilessly played on this insecurity. Nowadays, the two siblings barely spoke, and when they did, it was cursory at best, screaming insults at worst. Rajan had once taken his hand to his younger sister when she was fifteen, blackening her eye, accusing her of behaving inappropriately with an older boy in the village and bringing shame on the family. Radhesh – and not for the first time – had taken a belt to his son, even though he had then been a man of twenty-six, beating him until he'd bled and wept for mercy.

He took his bowl to the kitchen and was placing it in the sink as his son came in and threw his keys onto the marble-topped island. Radhesh didn't look up before starting to wash his face and rinse his mouth.

'Papa.'

'Yeah, boy.'

'Yuh have a problem wi' dem fellahs. De Spanish.'

'Wha' kinda problem?'

'Dey want more for de corn flour.'

'How much more?'

'Next seventy-five dollar a bag.'

'How many bags?'

'A hundred.'

'Why so?'

'Dey say some kinda trouble wi' de supplier, an' so it raise up de cost.'

Radhesh grimaced and shook his head. 'Seven an' a half thousand more...tell dem we eh need it again.'

'Papa, dem eh go like dat, dey lookin' to sell all quick-quick.'

Radhesh snorted in disgust. 'Boy, if yuh go sup wi' de devil den yuh mus' know how to deal wi' him.'

'But Papa – '

'I tellin' yuh, we eh need dey corn flour again.'

~ CHAPTER 16 ~

THE SHORT CLOUDBURST scared Fingal into wakefulness as the rain clattered on the galvanised iron roof of the carport outside his window in a cacophony of apocalyptic sound. It was dawn outside, and he reached in panic for the bedside lamp. It didn't work, so he got up, hurriedly pulling on a pair of shorts as he walked to the bedroom door and reached around its threshold to the light switch he knew was on the sitting room wall. That didn't work either. He called for Israel but got no reply. Then, the lights all came on at once, as did the kettle on the trestle table on the other side of the room. He remembered Israel had warned him the current often cut out suddenly, and you just had to wait for its return. His sleep had been restless, anyway, and now, at half-six in the morning, he felt tired and lost. He returned to the foam rubber mattress on the floor of the bedroom and pulled the single sheet over him. This was the most negative he had felt since his arrival in Trinidad. The feeling had come over him slowly like a wave, and he'd let it roll, then recede and then wash all over him again. What was he doing there? She was probably perfectly safe and having a good time. She would be shocked to see him, even if he did find her, and could so easily be annoyed at his presence in her life again.

He sat up, reached for his harmonica, and bent a few notes at the lower end of the register, making up lyrics between the bursts. *'Where you been, baby? Why you been gone so long? Where you been, baby, and why you been gone so long? I've been sitting here waiting, feeling so alone.'* He blew the harmonica for twelve bars and sang again: *'Where you been, baby? Who you been hanging round? I said, where you been, baby, and who you been hanging round? I been looking for you, baby, looking all round this town.'* He blew a few more notes and stopped. 'What *am* I doing here?' he asked himself again.

He thought back to the night when he had severed contact with her, when he had felt closer to the edge than he had been for many years, and he had determined never to go back there again because he now knew what it was like to stare into the abyss, realise there was no longer any reason to live, and that death would come easily to him, its siren call irresistible. Having to once more step back from such a place, he had no wish to ever return, so why was he risking his recovery and wellbeing by being there? Because that particular wound had never healed, he realised. So, why did he have to scratch at it, pick the scab, and risk the life force seeping from him again? What was that life force? It was pain, pure and simple, and he knew no other driver but had hoped to keep its malign influence at bay.

Rick Tucker

He looked at the mesh screen across his bedroom window. It was thick with dead insects, moths the size of his hand, beetles the size of golf balls, and hundreds of others – flies, wasps, stick insects, mantises, and grasshoppers – all different sizes and colours. One screen on one window had trapped all of this in one night. God only knew what the nearby rainforest contained.

He checked his phone, and there was a text message from Goose asking him how it was going. He replied with the minimum of detail that all was well. He thought about the band. That last gig at the Belle Vue had gone well, better than he expected with the small, packed crowd, whooping and hollering for two encores at the end of what had become a two-hour set. There was no doubting the added dimension Thabo had brought to their performance, and Fingal hoped his friend would be able to join them on the tour for at least some of the dates. For the first time in ages, Fingal felt the band was progressing, moving through the gears of blues and jazz to reach an altogether more sophisticated level of playing, always with an authenticity and proficiency which allowed them to attain a sound that was all their own, while still staying steeped in the blues tradition. Again, what was he doing there? He texted Goose once more: *'don't worry I'll be back in good time for rehearsals and tour'* and received an instant response: *'I should fucking well hope so! Good luck brother.'* Good old Goose, he thought, solid as a rock as usual.

Camille came back to the fore of his thoughts. That day in Scotland when he had written to her, when he had lain awake in the early hours, wondering whether or not he had the energy to do so, but he'd kept hearing her insistent voice: 'Tell me,

Fingal, tell me. You are hurt, and you need to tell someone. It's safe here. I am here for you. Tell me. Tell me. Tell me.' So, he decided that he'd write to her before going on a long walk. He got out of bed, made coffee and opened his laptop.

Dearest Camille,

You want to know what it is that is buried deep within me, that which I have never told anyone, that which I have learned to bear even though I can feel it gnawing away inside of me like some trapped and desperate rat. No one needs to know, least of all a lover, not the least because, with knowledge, judgement always follows, so I am trusting you with this. I don't know what you will think, but if you are the woman I think you are, the woman I love, then you will understand it and why I carry it and why I don't need anything from anyone in relation to it other than acceptance and affirmation of who I really am.

The first abandonment was my father leaving my mother when I was too young to remember. 'That white boy', she used to call him, that blond-haired, green-eyed devil who'd charmed her and wooed her and fucked her and left her. And left me. Left me alone with her as she – mixed-race and alone, a misfit in her own eyes – struggled to bring me up, living on an estate in west London, never feeling she fitted in, trying to write, working as a cleaner or shop assistant and drinking. Always drinking. She was the second one to abandon me, although I didn't know it at the time because I loved her. She once looked beautiful to me. She read to me, helped me with my schoolwork, encouraged my music and art. Two books of her poems were published, I realise now, to little or modest acclaim, but she had a talent, and some of the people who came into our lives were great characters, literary types, or painters or musicians, bohemians and layabouts and drunks and drug users. I remember being about thirteen and standing in the doorway of our sitting room and watching one of them with his arm around her, both of them obliterated with drink and drugs, and he put his hand on her breast and started squeezing, and she let him, looking away from him as she downed another gin, and on he went, squeezing her breast, stroking her leg, and trying to put his hand up her skirt. There were others there, too, but no one seemed to notice or care, let alone notice the boy on the threshold. But she looked up and saw me, tried to focus on me with her dead eyes before turning back to the man beside her and trying to kiss him before falling forward onto him and then onto the floor.

I wasn't important enough for her to stop drinking. The countless times she didn't come to collect me from school or would get on the bus with me drunk or didn't watch me play football or didn't come to parents' evenings or school pantomimes. The countless times I found her unconscious when I got home from school or that she just lay in bed for days, vomiting or begging me to pour her a drink. One day, I was sixteen, I came home and found her unconscious at the bottom of the stairs, blood seeping from a wound on her head, her dentures lying beside her face, her body contorted in an unnatural shape. And she was dead. Gone. If I hadn't understood this before – and maybe I did at an unconscious level – I now had it confirmed that life was totally arbitrary. There's neither rhyme nor reason to it. People disappear. Sooner or later, one way or another, they disappear.

Under the Flamboyant Tree

I left home and lived in a squat in Hammersmith with no running water or electricity and where people had written and drawn all over the walls using the smoke from candles. Many of my fellow squatters were heroin users, and I would try it from time to time, usually smoking it but mainlining on a few occasions. And it was there I started playing music with other people, eventually joining a band as the singer. I fell in love with Phoebe, the girlfriend of the band's drummer, but she stayed loyal to him despite breaking up a few times. She developed a heroin habit, and when she broke up with him for the last time, she moved in with me in my bed-sit in Shepherd's Bush. I had moved out of the squat and was working in the headquarters of a French geology company. It was my job to refill the drink machines and take in deliveries. I worked with a brother called William, and we used to hide in the store cupboards and smoke weed on our breaks. Anyway, Phoebe eventually got clean, but she was sick. Hepatitis C, and soon after, she found out she was HIV positive. She used to ride a motorbike, and one day, she lost control of it and hit an oncoming car and died, not of her injuries but of liver failure, the trauma of the crash too much for her compromised body. And then, she was gone. Another disappearance in this arbitrary life. She is buried just outside of Ullapool, way up on the west coast here, and I visit the grave whenever I can, not always on the exact date of her death, but at least once a year around that time. It's my favourite part of the world, raw and wild and beautiful, and I go there not just because of Phoebe, but because it's somewhere I can be alone and mostly at peace with myself. The solitude, the sound of the wind or the rain, the colours, the wildlife. The locals don't impose or intrude, but I'm happy to while away a few hours in the nearby bar if the mood takes me. She's buried in a beautiful graveyard in a remote spot where there is a ruined sandstone chapel and a surrounding dry stone dyke where you can hear cock pheasants call from the woods beyond and deer eat the flowers people leave for the dead. It's wild all year round, but in winter, it's bleak and empty and beautiful. I imagine, in spring, wildflowers grow all around where she lies, and I think she would love that.

So now, Camille, sweet Camille, you know. I have been abandoned three times. I have survived grief and anger so destructive it could have killed me or imprisoned me or both. I have faced suicidal despair and found somewhere within me a reason to live. I have pressed the self-destruct button so many times I couldn't count, but I somehow emerged from the wreckage each time. I am now as at one with myself as I ever have been and want to live and love and laugh and create. Being with you has helped me realise this even more. You are the great love of my life, Camille. It means the world to me that I have found you.

With love, ever, Fingal.

Her response had been quick and brief, and by text message: *I am humbled you shared your innermost self with me. U are a good and strong man. Please don't spoil what we have by saying u love me*

There followed a fateful exchange:

– but I do love you

– how do u know?

– because I know! I don't say it lightly it's real ffs!!

– u can't know it's real

– Camille please don't negate my reality, my truth

143

– *i just don't think u can know*

– *so all the times we spend together? when we lie together? do you not feel how connected we are, how beautiful it is to be so close??*

– *that's just sex*

– *????*

– *i know you want love but i don't want u to b my lover*

– *what am I to you then?*

– *fingal I care about u very much and love to be with u*

– *but you don't love me?*

– *i don't know what love is*

– *FFS!*

– *fingal please don't*

– *fuck this! fuck life!*

– *please don't say that*

– *after all we have shared you deny it's love, you negate the truth, you negate my reality, what I know to be real*

– *i don't know what is real*

– *i want you, Camille, in my life, my life companion*

– *u don't know that*

– *I can't take this anymore, every time we get close you back away, you play with me, let me in beside you then you push me away*

– *no*

– *yes*

– *i just am not ready for this*

– *then go back to your old fat lover and stay with your cunt of a husband*

– *fingal please*

– *fuck this, really fuck this*

~ CHAPTER 17 ~

THOSE WERE THE last words he had sent to her, and there had been no communication between them since her messages a few hours later, which he had read after he had come back down from walking angrily in the hills and when he'd decided to block her number. Now, there he was, a few thousand miles away from home, looking for her because he feared something had happened to her, that she might be in danger or worse. She really was under his skin, and all his strategies to keep his feelings about her suppressed had unravelled too quickly for comfort.

An unease simmered inside him. It made him restless. It made him consider abandoning the venture completely and returning to London. How would he feel when he got there? He knew he would feel dissatisfied at not knowing, dissatisfied with himself. It would be hard to bury such thoughts and just carry on from where he had left off. In fact, the whole trip was an opportunity to reach a conclusion, once and for all. If he found her, how would she react? She might be overjoyed to see him again and declare her boundless love for him. Or she might confirm that she didn't love him. Then, at least, he would know and could move on. He might need to see her just the one more time in order to be sure, to be able to go with a clear conscience, a clean slate, a line drawn. Or she might be dead. Or in prison. Or shacked up with someone there and happy to be so. The point was he had to find out. 'Damn,' he said to himself. He got up and made coffee. A kiskadee called persistently from somewhere on the roof, and the heat began to rise.

He closed his eyes, hoping that, by doing so, he would bring some order to the chaos of his thoughts. He concluded he had to leave by the next day or the day after at the latest. It was time to go, time to give up the pursuit of the unattainable, not just there but anywhere. This fruitless effort to secure a reality he had only ever glimpsed but never effected, one where he was not alone and where he could be held like a child in a mother's arms, a softer, kinder life that, for such a brief time, he had believed was actually possible and which had apparently been there for him to step into. It had been illusory, and it had been a grave mistake to consider it at all. It was as though he had looked upon something forbidden, something never meant for him, the way a homeless person looks into the warmth of a family evening through the undrawn curtains from a comfortless vantage point outside, that easiness between people who want to be with each other, the familiarity of comfort, the enveloping warmth of shared lives and mutual recognition. All illusion.

He had kept her last texts to him to which he had never responded, and read them once again:

Fingal, call me please

pourquoi tu réponds pas?

inquiète pour toi

At the time, he had told himself that he would never allow that to happen again. He could simply close the doors and never open them. It was time for self-sufficiency, to leave the past in its place and minimise his desires, to abandon hope. He had felt so strong and calm. It hadn't been her fault; she should live however she wanted to live. But until she'd worked out how to do that, he couldn't remain caught in that heart-wrenching limbo, that Never-Never Land of storms and inconsistencies, of doubt and hurt and overwhelming desire. He hated himself for having allowed it to happen. It had been a brutal lesson to learn, but he had learnt it.

In the soft dawn light, he followed Point Carlos Trace for a couple of hundred yards until it became a rough track lined with thick vegetation leading downwards towards the sea, a forest seemingly impenetrable, and one he wouldn't dare enter but which, nevertheless, held for him a fascination not just born of his curiosity about the flora and fauna but of how easy it would be to lose his bearings in it. In the same way, he was drawn to tall buildings or high bridges or walking up mountains because looking down made him feel mortal and reassured by the potential for falling, it gave him an option if he couldn't take any more. The dense rainforest held a similar attraction: somewhere to disappear, never to be found again.

Under the Flamboyant Tree

A small blue bird with a long beak curved to a fine point like a scimitar sat on a branch looking down at him, its bright yellow legs contrasting with flashes of black on its wings, under its chin, and across its eyes as though wearing a Zorro mask. A hummingbird no bigger than his hand, flashing emerald and crimson and indigo, hovered above a star-shaped flower from whose yellow and orange petals burst forth a group of long stamen the colour of saffron. The more he looked, the more he saw the intermixture of colour and life in exuberant profusion set against the *mise-en-scène* of a thousand different shades of green glistening in the sun and rustling in the breeze. His senses felt overloaded, as though he were connecting with the world as it existed in another dimension, primaeval yet timeless, something so sacred and powerful as to be beyond the reach of mortals.

He reached the beach – a shallow arc of narrow sands lined with coconut palms jutting out from the base of a terracotta-coloured cliff – and spotted two figures in the water. A black woman dressed in white robes and a turban was cradling another apparently topless woman, ducking her head repeatedly into the sea whilst incanting some indecipherable prayer-like chant. They hadn't yet seen Fingal, and he hid behind a tree at the bottom of the track as a large pod of pelicans, black against the sky, flew past, heading south.

Transfixed but afraid of what he was witnessing, he saw a path leading up into the forest and decided to head for it. From a vantage point at the top of the cliff, he looked upon the scene again with fearful fascination. He felt he was violating the ritual by his very presence, but he couldn't turn his head away from it. At times, the woman in white shouted and looked up to the sky with her eyes closed. Other times, he could barely hear her but the other woman screamed, groaned, and cried as though possessed by some unearthly entity. He pulled himself away and followed the path deeper into the forest, trusting his sense of direction would either lead him back to the road or the rough piece of land at the back of the house.

As he walked, the thought came to him that how – despite all of Western civilisation's influence on the island – within a short distance from there, you could find supermarkets, cars, bars, roads, concrete houses, schools, factories, billboards, electric lights, computers, and pharmacies – something of the ancient ways still flourished and centuries-old traditions with their roots in African and Indian religions and folklore were still practised and honoured. Underneath the surface of the island's society was a mixture of human culture so potent as to be both enriching and alarming to the unprepared.

He thought of Israel with his casual attitude towards weaponry and violence and breaking the law in order to lead the life he chose. He thought of the congregation gathering at the church in their Sunday best, the proliferation of Hindu jhandi flags outside houses or on the seashore, how the imam from the local mosque called the faithful to prayer five times a day, how traditional Rastafarians dropped out of conventional society to smoke their pipes in peace and live off the land. And he thought of how first-world people, in their condescension, dismissed this richness of culture as superstition and ignorance, a heterodoxy to be laughed at or even outlawed.

He saw Israel waving at him from the house, and he waved back, realising that his absence first thing in the morning may have caused some alarm. When Fingal reached there, he realised Israel was getting ready to make a move. 'Come nah, man, we goin' church,' he said with a grin.

'Church?'

'Yeah, let we see wha' de good people a Muga get up to.'

~ CHAPTER 18 ~

THE NEXT DAY was Sunday, and Faith's mother, Victoria Persad – known to all as Bee Bee – wanted to go to church, but she had her doubts. She wasn't sure if her knees would hold out, and even though it was acceptable for the injured or elderly to sit for the duration of the service, she didn't want the village to know she was suffering anything that might appear to be an infirmity. Then there was the new reverend. She didn't like him at all. She took an instinctive objection to something about him, although she knew that was very un-Christian of her, and she would have to ask for forgiveness the next time she prayed. He irritated her with his long, thin neck and pronounced Adam's apple that went up and down like a yoyo as he preached in that self-righteous, sanctimonious way of his. Then there was his stammer and preference for wearing scruffy trainers with his priestly black trousers and shirt. One time, she remembered with distaste, during the choir's out of tune rendition of *All Things Bright and Beautiful*, he'd even checked the messages on his phone and appeared to reply to at least one of them.

It would be nice, though, to see some of the old crowd, and if Dorothea Ramlash was there, the two of them could catch up afterwards over a sweet drink in the church hall. That was another thing she didn't like about the Right Reverend Kissoo. He had suggested to the church council that they start to charge for the sweet drinks and coffees the church provided every Sunday for their parishioners. They had been served for free ever since Bee Bee had been a girl.

She was very fond of Dorothea, even though she knew her to be a terrible gossip, and their friendship stretched back some seventy years to when they were at school. 'An' who knows how long we all have left?' she asked herself out loud as she picked out the red and white floral dress her sister Mary had bought for her in England, where she had lived for over forty years. Bee Bee liked to wear it because it looked so different, more sophisticated when compared to the dresses you could find at the mall. That dress had a touch of class to it, and people would think when they saw her wearing it that she, too, had some class. But which hat to wear with it? She called out for her daughter, Faith: 'Angel! Come nah.'

'Yes, Mummy,' came Faith's immediate reply, followed by her appearance seconds later in the doorway of her mother's bedroom.

Bee Bee jumped. 'Yuh give me a fright, girl. Spyin' on me or what?'

'Sorry, Mummy. Nah, I jus' washin' down de floor, so mind yuh doh slip an' fall.'

'Yuh is good girl, an' I eh know what I would do without yuh. Now, which hat I go' wear wi' de dress?'

Faith picked out a straw cloche hat adorned on one side with plastic hibiscus flowers and handed it to her mother with a smile.

'Yuh comin' to church wi' me?'

'Not today, Mummy. It makin' hot so, an' I feelin' a little sick. Sugar low, maybe. I'll get Raja to drop yuh, an' if nobody could bring yuh home, jus' call me.'

Faith walked to the bottom of the stairs and shouted, 'Raj boy, get up nah and take yuh granmother to de church.'

Rajan Ramkissoon had come home in the early hours of the morning, argued with his wife, Alicia, and woken their baby girl, Aisha. Mother and child had gone to sleep in one of the spare rooms, and Rajan had tried to sleep, but the drink and cocaine consumed the night before had made his mouth so dry he had to keep getting up to drink water from the bathroom tap. On top of that, his ribs and face hurt, and the bruise around his eye was darkening. If lucky, he would have had a couple of hours sleep, but now he was being asked to take the old woman to church, for fuck's sake. He tossed and turned a while, but he couldn't get comfortable and couldn't ignore his mother's repeated calls, telling him to get up. Eventually, she walked into his room without knocking. 'Raja,' she shouted, 'Haul yuh damn ass an' take yuh granmother to de church. *Now*, boy!'

'Why de hell?' he started but stopped when he saw the look on his mother's face as he peered out from under the sheet.

'I tellin' yuh, boy – do it. Make a change for yuh to do something for someone other dan yuh blasted self. I see yuh

153

upset yuh wife an' chil' again. De whole house an' all hear it. Yuh well stupid, boy. Too damn stupid.'

The quality of this particular family dynamic was something that had played out in similar ways countless times in the recent years and Rajan, despite his protestations and seething resentment of the way he perceived himself to be treated, always did what his parents asked or told him to do in the end. He got up, studied his blackened eye in the bathroom mirror, bathed, pulled on a pair of shorts and a jersey, tucked his gun behind his back, and went downstairs.

~ CHAPTER 19 ~

A S RAJAN DROVE past the flamboyant tree opposite Neighbour's Bar, his grandmother waved to Hero, who was sitting there, smoking a cigarette. Hero waved first and shouted 'Hoy,' as he always did to anyone who looked at all familiar, often mistaking total strangers for people he knew. Sometimes, he would get a shout back or a wave or a toot on the horn. Rajan thought Hero was a jackass and always ignored him.

He parked as near to the *Dar Es Salam Baptist Church* as possible, with so many others trying to do the same. The Right Reverend Kissoo, dressed in his black clerical clothes, white dog collar, and dirty white trainers, stood on the steps outside the main door of the church with a weak smile on his face. Rajan wondered if he thought it appeared beatific, one that imparted holy blessings upon his flock along with a saintly and knowing nod of the head as each of them passed by to enter the church.

Rajan looked at him with disdain. The Right Reverend Jackass, he thought.

Bee Bee opened her door but struggled to lift herself out of the seat. 'Yuh helpin' yuh granmother or what?'

Rajan sighed with irritation and walked round to help her out.

'Yuh should join me for de service,' she said.

He looked at her with his eyebrows raised in mock horror and said, 'Yuh know me better dan dat.'

'Yeah, I do,' she said. 'Wh'appen to yuh eye, boy?'

'I too busy. Wha' time yuh wan' me pick yuh up?'

'Half-eleven.' With that, she joined the throng of people walking up the path to the church entrance and the Right Reverend Kissoo's welcoming grace, all of them dressed in their best clothes, a kaleidoscope of colour, with hats for the women, smart shirts and trousers for the men, and the scrubbed children already bored, restless, and reluctant.

As he walked back to the driver's side, Rajan noticed a beat-up old Capri in which two men sat, observing the scene. Despite the tinted glass, he could see a white man in a strange-looking hat and a black man in a leather Rasta cap, both wearing shades, apparently observing the scene. 'Who de hell is dat?' he muttered. 'Dem lookin' like police.' He felt spooked and nervous.

Even though he knew he should drive away, he couldn't resist waiting and watching them. He lit a Broadway and wound down the glass, trying to appear nonchalant, looking straight ahead but stealing the odd glance towards the two men. It seemed as though the Rasta, in particular, was looking straight at him. 'It have to be police,' he thought, and his imagination ran chaotically in several directions at once, like chickens in the backyard when they knew one of them was ready for the chop and pot.

'If dey police, why dey lookin' at me?' he wondered. Had they followed him there? Was he under surveillance? The fact that one of them was a white man meant it had to be a serious investigation, maybe not just the T&T police but maybe the FBI or CIA, even.

'If it so serious, why dey checkin' *me*?' he wondered. Was it something to do with the Venezuelans? Had one of them been arrested and spilled the beans? Could he trust them? Did they have someone working for them who was police? Or was it to do with the girl? 'Damn dat girl,' he muttered as he exhaled two long plumes of smoke through his nostrils, 'she was nothin' but trouble from de start.'

He began to sweat and threw the cigarette out onto the road, trying to appear normal and calm. His hands were shaking, so he gripped the steering wheel to steady them. He felt sick. The hangover didn't help as the nervousness spread through his body all the way to his bowels. He shifted uneasily in his seat as though sitting on something sticky from which he couldn't extricate himself and then fired the ignition and drove off in the same direction his car was headed, so if they followed him, he could take some backroads, stop at a couple of bars on the way, try to lose them, and avoid them following him back home. He thought, with a shudder, how his father might react if he knew what was happening. He would beat me, he concluded.

For the next mile he drove the winding potholed roads through San Pedro towards La Brea, checking his rear-view mirror constantly, anxious and watchful like a wild animal who can smell a predator but has nowhere to hide. As far as he could tell, they hadn't followed him. Relieved, he cut up Dumfries Road to head back to Muga.

He parked next to the flamboyant tree and walked, trying to appear cool and casual, across the road into Neighbour's Bar. A few of the regulars were there, including Larry and Hero. Neighbour's husband, Kelvin, jerked his chin towards Rajan from the other side of the grille by way of saying hello, what do you want? or maybe both.

'Pilsner,' said Rajan.

'Raja! De prince a de village,' shouted an already drunken Hero by way of a greeting. Rajan ignored him and sat down on one of the bar stools, taking a few gulps of his beer.

'Wh'appen?' Hero continued as Larry pulled at his arm, telling him to leave it. 'Yuh cah seh hello to yuh friends no more? Yuh too big a man now, eh? Yuh cah even seh a muddacunt hello to yuh friends, big man?' He pointed to Rajan's black eye while turning to his audience. 'Look like some bigger muddacunt than you give yuh something sweet.'

Rajan turned to look at Hero. He had known him all of his life, and he remembered how, when he was young, Hero had tried to school him in the mysterious arts of spin bowling and had even taken him hunting and fishing. For all of which, Rajan had shown little interest or aptitude. For a brief moment, Rajan wished for that simpler life again, how it used to be when he'd helped out in his father's shop, didn't have much money, and lived the carefree Trini life, liming whenever he wanted, no commitments, no wife or child, and no untrustworthy Venezuelans, no damn pussyhole who'd black his eye and crack his ribs because he wanted to

show her some loving. His eyes narrowed. 'Leave me nah, man,'
he said. 'I busy.'

Hero re-joined Larry at their table and watched Rajan
down his beer, order another one, and pass a twenty-dollar bill
through the grille to Kelvin. 'Yuh okay, Rajan?' Kelvin asked.

Rajan looked at the barman, someone else he'd known all his
life and one of the few men in the village he was always careful
not to offend. Kelvin had borne a long scar down his left cheek
for many years now, and it never looked like it had truly healed,
still red and inflamed at times, serving as a constant reminder
to everybody of the rumour that he had killed his brother in
a knife fight. His brother's body had washed up on the beach
at Icacos Point, viciously damaged by the teeth of whatever
fish had fed on him; the official cause of death was drowning.
Despite the doubts and hushed insinuations, Kelvin had never
been investigated, nor had he been questioned, by the police, so
the villagers had made an unspoken but collective decision to let
the sleeping dog lie.

'I dey...jus' some tings on my mind,' he replied, and his
thoughts returned to the two men outside the church in the
beat-up old Capri. Who were those guys? He shook his head at
the mystery.

Birdy walked in, nodded at Rajan, who barely acknowledged
him, and took a glass and a bowl of ice from Kelvin before
joining Hero and Larry and their bottle of over-proof rum.
Rajan's thoughts quietened as he listened to the three friends'
foolish, inconsequential talk. Birdy had been hunting the night

before. He'd shot an agouti, so they were planning to make a cook whenever they'd finished at the bar but were unable to decide where. Then, Rajan's ears pricked up.

'I see he again today,' said Hero. 'He drive past in a Capri, an' a black man wi' a Rasta cap drivin' he.'

'Who yuh see?' asked Rajan a little too quickly, spinning his bar stool round to look at Hero.

'De white man. De one who sit under de tree dey.'

'Wha' white man?'

'De one wi' tattoo an' does wear a hat. I see he under de flamboyant tree, smokin' he cigarette.'

'Yuh talk to de man?'

'Nah, he disappear like a jumbie.'

'Who he is?'

'Me eh know, but he lookin' kinda strange wi' he tattoo an' he earring an' he federer hat like he voodoo, obeah, or maybe he some kinda cop like yuh see on de TV. Yuh know, like he bustin' drug gangs an' try to look like dem.' Larry laughed. 'Hero, yuh talkin' shit. He jus' some guy. A tourist or a friend a de painter man up de road.'

'When last yuh see a tourist in Muga?' mocked Hero. 'Now *you* de one talkin' shit. I tellin' yuh, he here for some reason.' Hero tapped the side of his nose as if to say it was something of which only those in the know would be aware.

His friends laughed gleefully at him as Rajan tried to look unconcerned, already aware he'd shown too much interest. He carried his beer to his car and drove off to collect his grandmother.

~ CHAPTER 20 ~

STILL BLACK AS pitch, and one of the cocks was crowing beneath their bedroom window. The night air was thick with heat, and Radhesh rolled onto his other side, trying to find a cooler spot on the sheets. The cock crowed again, lugubrious and haunting like some restless wraith condemned to wander between this world and the next. He lay on his back and stared into the void. Angel was making little puffing sounds as she slept, and what with the cock crowing and Angel's puff-puff-puffing, Radhesh got out of bed and went downstairs. He splashed his face in the washbasin under the house before going to pee in the adjacent toilet. As he switched on its light, an iridescent green bush cockroach of about four inches long and half as wide scuttled across the floor. He grabbed the toilet brush and tried to hit it but missed each time as it scurried away into the darkness.

He hadn't slept well, having been restless for much of the night, so he tried to analyse what was making him so. 'It's de damn boy,' he thought. 'He have me worried. He always was a jackass, but I thought he might be more responsible now he have a family a he own, and I growin' older, but he showin' no sign a dat. Out limin' all hour a de day an' night, Lord knows what he does do or who he does see. Then he reach home wi' a black eye, and he seh he crack a rib, seh he get rob in some bar in Fyzabad. Me eh even know me own son no more. Den dis business wi' de Spanish. I tell he it best to have no business wi' Venezuelans. Who dey workin' for? Dat boy suppin' wi' de devil, and like de jackass he is, he cah see dat. He cah see wha' really goin' on. We doh have to buy de flour from dem. Dis is damn stupidness. All we life we work so damn hard. No shortcut. I keep tellin' dis boy, but like he head hard, he feel he know best, and yuh cah tell he no damn ting. He cah destroy we business. Is we future. All a we future.'

The dawn sky was purple and grey, a crescent moon still shining, a few stars beginning to flicker and fade as he drove down the road, sounding his horn as he passed Hero with his planting hoe on his shoulder and who waved and shouted, 'Hoy!'

'Oh, for de simple times,' mused Radhesh as he pulled up in front of his shop and looked up at the faded sign above the wide, shuttered entrance: *Ramkissoon Mart & Licor Store – Quality Goods For All.* On one side of the sign was an advert for Stag beer: *A man's beer – quench your thirst with a cold stag today!* On the other, a sign in large, crudely hand-painted red letters, saying *BOODOOSINGH – PASSIONATE ABOUT PACKAGING!*

Rick Tucker

He sat down at the desk in the office at the back of the shop with a cup of sweet black coffee, switched on the computer, and waited for it to boot up. He rubbed his eyes, ran his fingers through his hair, and remembered he had booked a time with Taylor, the barber, later that morning. Meanwhile, his fringe kept falling over his eyes, so he went into the shop, switched on the fluorescent lights – which seemed to take an age to flicker into life – and looked for the shelf with the hair gel. He passed the fresh vegetable section, and above the cabbages was a sign, hand-written in red felt pen on a torn-off piece of cardboard box: *No Peeling off – of Cabbage leaf.* He looked at it, shook his head, and said out loud, 'What de hell?' He found what he was looking for – *Madam Glam Styling Gel* – took out a fingerful, applied it to his hair, and put the pot back on the shelf.

Back at his desk, he went online and logged in to the business account at the Republic Bank. Something didn't look right. The balance was much lower than usual for that time of the month, so he checked the credits and debits. Once a week, usually on a Monday, he or Rajan deposited cash at the bank in Point Fortin. What never happened was that the same amount was withdrawn the next day, which had happened twice in the last four weeks and a third time three weeks prior to that. Then, he noticed that no cash had been deposited all of the last week. He went to the safe situated in a cupboard next to the washroom, trepidation beginning to stir within him along with the pending realisation of something he had suspected but hadn't wanted to realise. Surely, the boy wouldn't be so damn stupid.

He opened the safe. There were two separate strongboxes in there, one for petty cash, the other for cash to be deposited at the bank. The petty cash box had about five thousand TT dollars in it; the other one was empty. Radhesh sat down and stared at the safe, its door still open, a sense of panic rising, and an unpleasant realisation coming into sharp focus, feeling like a thousand needles stabbing at his insides. He locked the safe, changing the combination as he did, and went back to the computer screen. His connection to the bank had timed out. Irritated, his hands shaking, he keyed in all the relevant information again and re-accessed the statements. Over the last three months there had been two weeks where the cash from the tills hadn't been deposited and eight occasions when large amounts of cash had been withdrawn. He changed the password and then the PIN number for the company debit card.

As shock gave way to anger, he got into the car and drove to Khalisha's house in the small trace opposite the mosque. The white dome of the mosque caught the morning sun, and the crescent moon above it was sparkling like gold. Khalisha and Ranesh were already up and sitting on the front porch drinking tea. 'Wh'appen Pappy?' said Khalisha. She must have sensed something bad as her father hardly ever visited them, especially at that time of day.

Rhadesh tried to calm himself before speaking. 'Precious, I need yuh to do someting for me.'

'Yes, Pappy.'

'When you open up de shop today, I wan' yuh to put de till money in de safe every couple a hours so we doh have too much in de tills at one time. Just leave enough for change. I go tell yuh de combination, and I need yuh to learn it an' not write it down.'

'Okay, but why?'

'I will tell yuh more later, but I done change de combination so only de two a we can use de safe.'

'How so? What about Rajan?'

Radhesh sucked his teeth. 'Doh say nothin' 'bout dis, Precious, but Rajan cah access de safe or de till or de bank no more. We losin' money, girl, and all dis ting wi' de Spanish is plenty problem for all a we now.' He looked at Ranesh, who was staring at him with his mouth wide open. 'Ranesh, yuh tell nobody. Allyuh understand? Nobody! I'll come by de shop later, but first, I have to go home and den to de bank.'

On arriving home, he picked up a thick bamboo cane from a bunch under the house, kept for gardening purposes but unused in years. He walked up the back steps into the kitchen, where Faith was drinking coffee. 'Baba, whey yuh been? Why yuh get up so early?' she asked, cocking her head like an inquisitorial pet.

'Angel, not now, eh. I need to see de boy.'

She looked at him and began to say something, but he pushed her aside and said, 'I say not now!'

He took the stairs two at a time and burst into Rajan's bedroom. Rajan was asleep with his bare back to Radhesh, who, without saying a word, brought the cane down across his son's shoulders with such force the bamboo split. He struck again and three times more as Rajan turned to face him, hands in the air as he yelped like a puppy. 'Yuh damn muddacunt!' yelled Radhesh, throwing the now useless bamboo cane onto the floor. 'Yuh damn stupid sour cunt. Yuh dotish, damn clown. Get up!'

'Pappy, please. Pappy, I – ' whimpered Rajan, shaking and getting unsteadily to his feet.

'Look at me, boy,' commanded his father.

Rajan looked up and had no time to avoid his father's fist connecting with his jaw. He fell back on his bed.

'Yuh wah a next black eye?'

Faith and Kajri appeared in the doorway. His wife grabbed Radhesh by the arms and shouted, 'Baba, stop!' and Radhesh, his fists still clenched, stepped away from his son. He shook free of his wife's grip and pushed past Kajri in the doorway. Then, he turned back round and said, this time so quietly he was barely audible, 'Dis business wi' de Spanish, it have to stop. Yuh hear me? Yuh eh no part a we business again.' He walked down the stairs.

Rajan was about to say something when his mother glared at him with a finger to her lips by way of warning him to not provoke his father anymore. Kajri smirked at him and walked back to her bedroom while his mother took his chin in her hand and pulled his face to each side to see if he was injured. His lip was bleeding a little. 'Get yuhself cleaned up,' she said before turning her back on him and walking away.

~ CHAPTER 21 ~

IT HAD BEEN a long day, and Radhesh leaned back in his chair in the office at the back of the shop and yawned. A bottle of rum and a glass were on the desk, and he poured maybe his fourth one for the evening, mixing it with a splash of coconut water from a small carton. After his confrontation with Rajan that morning, he had driven to the bank in Point Fortin, changed the business account signatories to him alone, and requested a new bank card to be issued in his name only. The process would take several days, so he arranged that any withdrawals from the account had to be made in person by him alone. Then, he went to see Taylor, the barber, for a haircut.

Taylor was an old friend, and they sat under his house, talking and drinking while Taylor went about his business with clippers, comb, and scissors. They talked about cricket – moaned, more accurately – a favourite topic of Taylor's almost to the point of obsession. 'Dem eh know how lucky dem is, boy, an' dey need tellin' that test cricket is de ultimate form a de game. De one yuh get real respect for, none a dis twenty-twenty malarkey go get dey name mark in de history books I tellin' yuh.'

Radhesh had heard it all before, but he patiently indulged his friend by nodding and agreeing out loud from time to time. When asked how the family were, he said nothing other than 'Everybody good.'

Haircut done and one for the road taken neat and quick, he drove back to the shop where Khalisha was working with two other members of the staff, Alexa and Grace, who had worked for the Ramkissoons for the past few years. However, events had now made Radhesh view anyone close to the business with suspicion. He called Khalisha into the office and told her to sit down and listen to him. On no account was Rajan to be allowed on the premises, and if he tried, she was to call him. If any Venezuelans came into the shop, she was to be careful, and if they – or anyone else for that matter – started asking questions as to his or Rajan's whereabouts, she was to say she didn't know. He was worried for her, but he tried not to convey it and said that he would try to be in the shop with her at all times until this business was sorted out, but in the meantime, she was to tell nobody of the new arrangements, including Alexa and Grace. He would tell them the business wasn't doing so well these days so that word would get around. It was a small gesture, but anything that made people think the business wasn't ripe for the picking might make anyone with dishonest intentions look elsewhere.

He decided to close the shop soon after dark and told them all to go home. He was still there at seven o'clock and thinking he should do the same when he heard someone banging on the shutter, making him instantly alert. It could be anybody, he mused. People wouldn't have expected the shop to close early, so it's possible it's someone needing milk maybe, or bread or beer. He walked through the shop toward the closed shutter. 'Who dey?' he called.

'We lookin' for Raj,' came the response.

'Raj not here. He eh workin' here again.' There was no reply, so Radhesh walked back to the office and picked up the cutlass he kept behind the cupboard.

Two men walked in through the side door and smiled at him. He could tell they were Venezuelans. 'Who de hell is *you*?' he asked.

'Is Ronaldo and Messi,' said a voice from the doorway as another man walked in: Indian, short, plump, sweating, a goatee beard, unshaven elsewhere, tinted glasses, and a walking stick. The accent was Trinidadian, and Radhesh felt his bowels loosen in fear. 'Sit down,' said the short, plump man.

'I go stand,' said Radhesh.

The short, plump man tapped Radhesh's desk with his walking stick. 'I prefer if yuh sit,' he said. 'An' put down de cutlass.'

Radhesh did as he was told. Ronaldo and Messi stood on either side of him.

'Yuh have pepper channa?' asked the plump man.

'Right dey on de shelf,' replied Radhesh, pointing.

One of the Venezuelans went to fetch a bottle and handed it to the short, plump man before taking up his place again at

Radhesh's side. The short, plump man opened the bottle and tipped a few into his palm. He crunched them, all the time looking at Radhesh. The only sound in the shop, in fact, the only sound in Radhesh's whole world at the time, was the short, plump man crunching his pepper channa.

'Who are yuh?' asked Radhesh after a while.

'Yuh really want to know?'

'Yeah.'

'Dey call me Dog. Yuh know why?'

'Nah.'

'When I was small, some fellahs tie me up an' call me fatty, an' dey make me swallow dog food till I get sick.' Radhesh turned his mouth downwards in distaste. 'Yeah, boy,' continued Dog, 'but me eh forget, yuh know? I jus' wait me time, an' when I did get dogs a me own – Doberman – dey get to know dem, an' now dey never forget me. One a dem blind in he eye, de other have no finger on he hand, so everybody know me as Dog.' He shrugged, smiled, and ate some more channa. A few more moments of crunching passed.

'I need to pee,' said Radhesh.

'Wait nah, man,' said Dog. 'Dis eh go take long.'

One of the Venezuelans put his hand firmly on Radhesh's shoulder and bent down to whisper in his ear, *'Cálmate, señor.'*

'So,' Dog continued, 'it have a problem, one I tink yuh can help me with.'

'How so? Me eh know nothin' a yuh business,' said Radhesh with sudden baseless bravery.

'Maybe, but I know all 'bout *your* business, so leh me tell yuh, an' doh yuh say a damn word and leh me speak. Dat boy a yours, he tell me plenty, yuh see, an' he very helpful. So helpful, in fact, dat we let him do a li'l business a he own wi' we. A li'l business whey he have to make a li'l...investment wi' we. Trouble is, it seem he cah finish wha' he start. He owin' me money is one ting, an' when he agree to a li'l arrangement which he cah keep to is another ting.'

'Is he business alone. I not involve,' said Radhesh.

'I see dat, but we bringin' in de sack a flour, an' yuh boy say he buyin' ten for heself, money up front, an' he need de ten sack so he could make enough to pay we back what he owe, an' den maybe have a li'l left for heself.'

So that was why Rajan had told him the cornflour was going to cost more – he was trying to raise cash. 'How much he owe?' asked Radhesh, toying with the idea that he should just pay the man off and let that be the end of it.

'Plenty. Twenty thousand US.' Dog pulled a phone from his pocket and tapped on the calculator icon. After a few seconds, he looked up and over his glasses towards Radhesh. 'Or one hundred and thirty-five thousand, four hundred and sixty-five TT dollar, sixty-four cent. I can forget de sixty-four cent.' He smiled before continuing, 'I real reasonable, yuh know? Yuh boy can work for we an' pay some off dat way. He can help wi' de distribution, but all a de sack an' dem have your shop address mark on dem.'

'What it have in de sack?' asked Radhesh.

Dog smiled again but said nothing. He threw a channa at Radhesh and then another, hitting him in the face both times.

'Man,' said Radhesh, 'how yuh know I won't go to de police?'

'Because that would be stupidness. Tell yuh boy to call me.'

One of the Venezuelans patted Radhesh on the head, and Dog got up from the table. All three of them left the way they had come in without saying another word.

Radhesh held his breath until he heard their car drive off. He hurried to the toilet and voided his bowels; then he poured a rum. He couldn't see a solution to this. It was beyond the realm of his experience, and so he had nothing to draw on. All he could do was talk to the boy. See if they could work a way out of this.

He looked up at a flyer pinned to the corkboard on the wall advertising the services of a Pandit Sanjay who described himself as an *astrologer & spiritual healer – world-famous Indian traditional – skilled in all astrology – if you having problems he has a solution!* – Radhesh thought he could maybe do with some help from the stars. He read the rest of the flyer: *INDIAN ASTROLOGY – HOROSCOPE – HAND READING – REMOVAL OF EVIL EYE – VASHIKIRAN EXPERT GET YOUR LOVE BACK - HELP SOLVING PROBLEMS IN: BUSINESS – SEXUAL – ENEMY – FAMILY ARGUMENT – HOUSE – MARRIAGE – LUCKY LOTTO – LOVE – PROPERTY – JEALOUSY – CHILDLESS COUPLE – SPIRITUAL PROBLEM – COURT – TRAVEL – BAD LUCK – HEALTH* and then in bold type: **we here to let you understand your strength and weakness base on the planetary configuration of your birth chart and we would also perform**

Rick Tucker

LAKSHIMI PUJA, VAASTU PUJA, DURGA PUJA, SHIVA RUDHRA HOOMA for HOUSE & SHOP & BUSINESS ESTABLISHMENT.

'What de hell,' said Radhesh out loud, 'is all damn stupidness. Damn stupidness.'

~ CHAPTER 22 ~

HERO HADN'T YET finished building his house, but at least it had a roof, electricity, running water, and stud walls between the two bedrooms, albeit with two-foot gaps between the tops of the walls and the roof space that was itself still in need of ceilings, so all the wiring remained exposed. The large living space, including the kitchen area, had a bare concrete floor, and there was a wooden trestle table where he would eventually build kitchen units and a worktop. The sink was full of unwashed dasheen, and next to it sat a bucket full of breadfruit. A solitary and threadbare two-seater sofa furnished the living area in which sat Hero and his uninvited houseguest.

'Why de house eh finish man?' said Rajan, looking around him.

'Why yuh tink?'

'Me eh know.'

'Dis take me three years already. I comfortable nah, man.'

'Yuh need money?'

'Everybody need money.'

'Doh tell nobody I here.'

Hero looked at Rajan and realised his life had just become more complicated than it used to be. He didn't like complications in his life. In fact, he put a significant proportion of his energy into making sure things never got *complicated* – no wife, no children, everybody's friend, never *maccoing* anybody – so he didn't like this situation now because it was already *complicated.* 'Wh'appen?' he asked.

'It have a problem. I need a little time to...deal wid it, yuh know?'

'Me eh know.'

'Jus' for a li'l while.'

'How long?'

'Until I deal wid it man.'

Hero nodded his head as though he understood, but he didn't. All he knew was that Rajan had arrived late last night and told Hero he wanted to stay there for a few days and he would make it worth his while. If Rajan Ramkissoon needed somewhere to stay, that meant he was in some kind of trouble. Enough trouble not to be staying with his family. Enough trouble to tell Hero not to tell anybody. Enough trouble that he looked scared, too.

Hero told him he could have the spare room, where there was a bare mattress on the floor, and now here he was, sharing his sofa with a man who wouldn't normally give him the time of day, a man who everybody knew was silver-tongued, mean, and brutish, someone who knew people Hero didn't want to know.

'Maybe here not de best place for yuh, man.'

'Doh let me down nah, man. I have money, yuh know? Plenty money.'

'Me know dat.'

'Yuh help me an' den I go help yuh. Help yuh build dis house good.'

'So, what yuh wan' me do?'

'I lookin' for a woman. I did meet she a few days ago, an' she maybe causing me a problem. I just need to check she out an' make sure she eh go make tings complicated for me.'

That word again: *complicated*. 'So, wha' yuh wan' me do? Me eh know where she dey.'

'She have family somewhere, in *La Brea*, ah tink. Yuh could ask around. Ent yuh have family right dey?'

'Me eh know dat side a de family no more, man. Dem eh people I see now.'

'She French, but she speak English wi' a strange accent, like French but Trini, yuh know wha'ah mean?'

'Nah,' said Hero, shaking his head in despair.

'Jus' ask around, man, an' it have another problem an' all.'

More and more *complicated*. Maybe Hero could run away, maybe go to Tobago to see his friend, Bullet, and hide out there.

Rajan continued, 'It have people lookin' for me, me family, me father.'

'Yuh father always good to me.'

'Just doh tell he I here, an' it have somebody else, too.'

Complications, man. 'Who?'

'Dog.'

'What de hell?' shouted Hero, 'Dog? *Dog?* Dat muddacunt would dig out me eye an' eat dem if I vex he. *Dog?* Yuh mad or what?'

'Is okay. Is okay. Doh worry. Jus' if he ask, yuh eh see me.'

'An' den he find out you livin' here? Yuh mad, boy. *Dog?* Yuh makin' joke, boy.'

'Dis eh no joke, nah, man. Gimme jus' a couple days an' I go organise meself. Go to work normal-normal. Whey yuh workin' today?'

'De village. Clearing some bush by de bar.'

'Good. I lyin' low till evenin'.' And with that, he went to shower.

A thousand thoughts whirled about Hero's brain but aside from running away and never coming back, he didn't know what to do. Should he talk to anybody about it? If so, who? If he told his friends, then they could also incur Rajan's wrath and maybe even Dog's as well. He could always go to Dog himself, but who knows what complications might ensue from doing that? The web could just get more and more tangled. He put on his work boots, shut the front door as normal, picked up his cutlass and planting hoe from outside the house, and walked down the road to work a troubled man.

After his shower, Rajan laid on the mattress, trying to work out a solution. He could go to his father, beg him for some of the cash, and explain to him how he would be able to clear the air with Dog and settle the whole affair. Then he could meet up with Dog and give him the cash, promising to do anything for him to clear the rest of the debt. Or he could just go straight to Dog and ask him what he needed to do, tell him that he was completely under his command and that so long as Dog left his family alone, he would do anything for him. Anyway, he already knew so much about Dog's import business that Dog was bound to want him on the inside of his organisation rather than risk making an enemy out of him. He could take over the distribution, drive up north for him, go to Tobago or even to Venezuela, anywhere Dog wanted him to go. He would pledge his allegiance and become one of Dog's soldiers. Or he could go straight to the police.

This was another idea that needed thinking through. Hero kept once-wild birds – finches – in small cages attached to the joists outside the house, and Rajan could hear one of them singing. He stood up and looked out his window. The tiny bird was hopping along a perch, cocking its head from side to side and chirping loudly. 'Wha yuh tink, li'l birdie?' he asked out loud. 'We much de same. Somebody capture yuh an' put yuh in a cage an' now all yuh can do is sing but eh nobody listenin' to yuh. Yuh tink if yuh sing some more, somebody gonna let yuh go? Let yuh go free? Me eh tink so li'l birdie. Ah sorry.'

If he went to the police, it would mean telling them everything he knew about Dog and his enterprise. The police would want proof, and he would have to be protected, as would his whole family. There would be violence and a court case. Everyone would know it was he who had given Dog away, and he might never be safe again. He would have to ask the police for immunity from prosecution and a new identity, maybe. Or he could just give them the information anonymously and wait for them to act, set Dog up but make it look as though it had nothing to do with him.

The bird stopped singing. He looked out the window and saw a chicken hawk circling the garden at the back where Hero's neighbours had planted packchoy and Irish potatoes. A pair of blue and yellow macaws flew towards him, screeching their harsh call with a flash of turquoise and green as the sun caught their foreheads. He had to find a way out of this. He called his father from a new cell phone.

'Who dis?'

'Papa, is me.' He was met with silence. 'Papa? Is me.'

'I know is *you*, yuh jackass. Whey yuh?'

'I cah say. Papa, I in trouble.'

'*You* in trouble? Boy, all ah we in trouble 'cos of yuh damn stupidness. Whey you, I say?'

'Papa, I in trouble wi' Dog.'

'I know dat. He tell me to tell yuh to contact he. I tell he I eh know nothin about whey yuh dey. He act like he doh believe a damn word I sayin'.'

'Papa, if I could give he a li'l something, a few thousand maybe, maybe he let me work off de rest. I...I – '

'A few thousand, eh? A few *thousand*? Boy, yuh owe he more dan a hundred thousand. He say one hundred an' thirty-something.'

'If I could jus' give he *half* ah it, den maybe he go ease me up for de while.'

'Sixty or seventy thousand dollars? From *my* business? Yuh talkin' shit, boy, 'cos even if he agree to dat, it mean we in hock to him every day a we life until.'

'Papa, it have enough dey in de bank. I go make it up to yuh, I promise yuh. Please, Papa.'

'Yuh scared, boy?'

'Yes, Papa.'

'So yuh damn well should be.' Radhesh hung up.

~ CHAPTER 23 ~

I T WAS WAY too hot in the house. Tanty Jo had switched on one of the two fans she possessed, a dusty black metal relic with three speed settings, all of which were mostly sluggish and inconsistent and served little purpose. Sometimes, its blades would speed up and emit a frenzied high-pitched screech, not unlike the call of a macaw except that it would continue unabated until someone switched it off and on again a few times and it reverted to its original state of fatigued unarousal.

The other fan was a white circular tower – the one Tanty Jo called *de new fan* – which she had bought in San Fernando in April 1983, memorable because it was the day Gus Logie, a local cricketer from Sobo Village, right there next to La Brea, had scored his maiden test century at the Kensington Oval in Barbados against India.

Logie's achievement had caused wild celebration all over Trinidad, especially in the rum shops around La Brea and Sobo, and she remembered borrowing a wheelbarrow from Barnie

Jacobs, the owner of Barnie's Bar by the crossroads where the maxi taxis stopped and from where, strong as she was, she couldn't face carrying her new acquisition all the way home. Normally, someone would have given her a ride, but such were the celebrations and rapt attention directed towards Barnie's television set by the cricket-mad crowd, no one had paid her any mind, so she'd just helped herself to the wheelbarrow propped up against the wall outside.

One day, a week or so later, she'd wheeled it back and Barnie – who would normally have cussed anyone who had taken anything of his without asking him first, maybe even threatened them with physical violence – decided that, due to her reputation as an obeah woman, discretion was the better part of valour. He smiled sweetly at her, said, 'Tanks, Jo,' and waited until he thought she was out of earshot before sucking his teeth and calling her *dat ugly fuckin' witch*, which he then had great cause to regret when she'd emerged from the ladies washroom and said, 'I hear yuh, Barnie Jacobs, I hear yuh.'

The following week, his car had come off the road on one of the bends in Aripero, writing it off and causing Barnie to suffer whiplash and a couple of broken ribs. The fact that he had been drinking Puncheon rum all afternoon at a friend's house in Dow Village where a few of his cronies had gathered to make a cook of curry manicou, and that he had evidently not been fit to drive, was something ignored by most people in La Brea, who found it suited their natural tendencies towards the dramatic and mysterious rather than the mundane truth. They attributed the cause of the accident to Tanty Jo having put a curse on Barnie for calling her an ugly fuckin' witch.

She had never thought it necessary to buy another fan. If the days were intolerably hot, then she would sit on her back gallery with a damp flannel on her forehead and take a little breeze. Also, she wasn't used to having anyone stay with her and so wasn't accustomed to having to consider whether or not they were comfortable. They could adapt, after all. But on that particular day, it was hot, even for locals, with hardly a breeze and a rumbling cloud cover that threatened without ever delivering the storm that would freshen them all up and cool them down. She still only switched on the one fan.

Accompanied by Lola in her skin-tight t-shirt and shorts and a small but persistent swarm of bush flies that would not let her alone, Camille walked down the steep pathway to the beach, waving her one free hand frantically in front of her face. Lola had seen her leaning on Tanty Jo's back gallery, looking hot and sad and had wandered over to suggest they take a walk. More nervous than she had been a few days before, Camille took some persuading, but eventually, instinctively drawn to the kind, pretty, Spanish-speaking woman and trusting her as a result, agreed to go with the proviso that if there was anyone they didn't like the look of down there, they would quickly head back up the path.

Lola carried a cutlass in one hand and slipped the other into Camille's as she led the way. This action, childlike *and* lover-like, innocent and knowing, aroused in Camille both sadness and desire, both of which she rationalised as being born of both her sense of displacement and insecurity and her innate need to be held and protected. The physical security of her life in Paris seemed far out of reach, and she promised herself she would never take it for granted again if she ever went back there.

They sat on a blanched dead tree trunk and looked out at the calm, barely rippling sea. A frigate bird, with its long prehistoric-looking wings, soared black against the billowing grey and white clouds as a small group of corbeau hopped and hassled on the water's edge. 'I'd like to go in the water,' said Camille.

'So go,' said Lola, pointing towards the sea with an upwards nod of her head.

Camille indicated her clothes – shorts and shirt – as a way of saying she didn't have a swimming costume. Lola mimed pulling down her shorts and pointed along the beach. 'No people,' she said, standing up.

Camille watched Lola pull down her shorts, revealing the triangle of a bright red thong edged with a white border that went around her lower belly to join the thin strip behind. Lola turned her back to Camille as she bent over to fold her shorts on the trunk, showing, deliberately, thought Camille, her perfectly rounded and muscular backside. Lola turned back to face Camille and opened her palms while raising her eyes expectantly, gestures that asked if Camille was going to join her.

Camille stood and dropped her shorts, revealing her underwear, and she couldn't help but notice how Lola immediately directed her eyes towards her thighs and what lay between them. With a flash of her brilliant white teeth, Lola grinned and again took Camille's hand and led her to the water. They continued to hold hands as the first gentle waves hit their bodies, making them gasp and laugh.

Lola released Camille's hand and stood waist-high in the water before pulling down her thong and washing herself. 'The water good for here,' she said, pointing down below her waist and laughing.

Camille beheld the beauty of her companion, once more feeling the arousal of longing. It was something more than sexual desire, but she was undeniably physically aroused. How easy it would be to love a woman, she thought. Here, simply and naturally, instinctively, safely...how easy it would be. All of that falling in love with men and then trying to sustain a relationship with them, how exhausting it all had been. She thought of Philippe, Liam, and Fingal and sighed at the effort each of those relationships had needed. There was nothing more attention-seeking than an urgent man.

They swam and floated for a while before, upon seeing a group of three young men arrive on the beach a hundred yards or so away, Camille decided it was time to go. Lola followed her back onto the sand and once more bent over in front of Camille to pick up her shorts before turning round to pull them up slowly over her wet thighs. Camille cocked her head and looked Lola straight in the eyes, the two of them locking gazes with looks of serious intent before a wry smile from Camille and a mischievous laugh from Lola broke the tension. They walked hand in hand back up the path, Lola leading and carrying the cutlass as before.

It was a hot climb, the path steeper than Camille had realised on the way down, and when they reached the top, they were both breathless and beaded with perspiration. 'Bathe by me,' suggested Lola, and Camille silently assented, allowing herself to be led through the door of the shipping container.

The interior was surprisingly roomy. The long, rectangular space of the container was empty of furniture but for an array of floor cushions and a couple of rugs. There were three further rooms built with wooden boards leading off the basic structure, one containing only a mattress on the floor and clothes piled up against the walls, the other a wet room with two buckets full of water and a plastic cup. A kitchen area led out onto a small gallery at the back.

Lola bathed first while Camille wrung out her shirt and underwear and left them on a window ledge to dry. Then, Camille bathed with the cup and water, relishing the sensation of the cool water on her hot skin. She remembered her mother telling her how she used to bathe like that as a young girl when there had been no mains water and how she had learned to use the standpipe on the main road that had run through the village, where she would fill buckets to take back to her mother's house. Camille got dressed in only her shorts and a t-shirt Lola had given her.

Lola was lying on the floor of the main room, and she gestured for Camille to join her, which she did. She lay on her back with her head on a cushion, a foot or so away from Lola who, after a few minutes, leaned towards her and with the back of her hand, gently stroked Camille's face. Camille sighed, too tired to decide whether she should succumb or not. When the back of Lola's hand brushed her breast, Camille turned to look at her, and without smiling, gently pushed Lola onto her back and rested her head on her belly. 'I'm tired. I need to rest,' she said. Lola stroked her hair for a while before the two of them fell into a light sleep.

From her kitchen window, Tanty Jo had watched the two women return from the beach and go to Lola's house. She thought about this for a few minutes, scanning the trees in her garden for snakes or any other signs that the spirits might be trying to tell her something. The candle beneath her incense burner flickered. But it's a day without a breeze, she thought. Maybe there was love in the air. Or maybe not. She couldn't tell. But there *was* something in the air, she knew that. It was time to take precautions.

~ CHAPTER 24 ~

FINGAL WAS FINDING it difficult to be alone. The strange events he'd witnessed at the beach on Sunday had unnerved him, made him feel vulnerable. Israel had left early that morning, soon after they had got up, and had made it clear that whatever he was going to do was best done alone. So Fingal spent the morning languidly, the heat so dry and oppressive it was easy to do nothing. After a few hours, the sense of alienation and aloneness began to unnerve him, and by early afternoon, he had had enough, so he decided to walk into the village and drink a beer or two.

He took a bottle of water from the fridge and put on his hat. The sun was now high, and his face, already more burned than he had ever experienced, needed some protection. He then walked down *Trace Off Point Carlos Trace* to its dead-end and onto the path through the dasheen that led at a slight incline up to the village. He had considered bringing the cutlass and thought better of it as a white-looking stranger carrying a cutlass might arouse too much curiosity among the locals, but the dasheen was head-high and so thick in parts where it had overgrown the path he wished he had brought it. Several times, he had to part the thick stems like curtains in order to progress but managed to keep going in the right direction, the thought of an ice-cold beer in a cool bar encouraging him in his efforts.

The village was quiet. No one was walking its main street, and just a few cars passed as Hero swung his cutlass from side to side like a scythe, cutting the dasheen and accompanying bush behind the flamboyant tree. It was hot work – nothing he wasn't used to – and he stopped to slake his thirst from a pouch of water he carried on his belt.

'Muddacunt a job dis,' he whispered to himself. 'Me take a five soon.' He worked robotically, one-paced and efficient, systematically cutting away the foliage until he had cleared about twenty square metres down to a hard, unyielding stubble. He stood straight, wiped his brow, and poured some water onto the nape of his neck, letting it run down his back. His shirt was so wet with sweat it didn't matter, and anyway, it would soon dry off in the heat. From where he stood, he could see all the way to the forest at Point Carlos and a glimpse of the sea beyond. He noticed something black moving above the tops of dasheen. 'What de hell?' he said. 'What de hell is dat? It lookin' like somebody hat. Who de hell walkin' through dey in dis heat? Wheyyy, boy, it lookin' like...a...federer, an only one man wearin dat round here. De white man comin'. Lord, I *sure* he some kinda jumbie. Whey he come out from? He comin' out de forest, I sure ah dat. Or he could be from de sea. He headin' straight here. Me eh like dis *at all* at all.'

Hero re-sheathed his cutlass and walked over the road to the bar. Neighbour was leaning on the counter behind the grille, asleep on her folded arms. Larry was sitting on one of the bar stools with a bottle of water and a shot of rum in his hand. 'He comin', boy,' said Hero, unable to hide his excitement.

'Who comin'?' said Larry laughing with a wide, gap-toothed mouth. 'De lord mayor a London? De queen?'

'Doh make joke nah, man,' said Hero. 'De white man who sit under de tree – I see him in de dasheen bush!'

'Why de hell a white man walkin' through de bush – he pickin' to make callaloo? Yuh mad, boy.'

'I tellin' yuh! He comin'. I see him. He federer. Dey. Through dey. Look nah, man.'

Larry leaned over a bit and looked out towards the road. 'Me eh see nothin'.'

Hero sucked his teeth and rapped on the counter, stirring Neighbour to raise her head. She looked at him with one eye closed. 'Puncheon,' said Hero, and with a sigh, Neighbour got up from her stool and reached for a miniature bottle from a stack on the shelves behind her. She passed it through the grille along with a glass tumbler, and Hero unscrewed its top, downing it in one before reaching for Larry's water with which he chased it.

'Next one,' he said, looking at Neighbour who had just sat down again. With effort, she got up once more and passed him another miniature before sitting back down with an even heavier sigh.

'Sorry to disturb yuh,' said Hero sarcastically. 'Hush nah, man,' she said, lowering her head back onto her folded arms.

Fingal sat down under the flamboyant tree and took a few gulps of water before lighting a cigarette. He felt suddenly hesitant about going into the bar. An unsettling self-consciousness pervaded his being, sapping his confidence, and so, despite his longing for a cold beer, he decided to wait a while and see how the land lay. Also, he wasn't sure if Israel would think it a good idea, but if he kept to the plan and gave little away about who he was or why he was there, then it should be all right. He might even learn something. He noticed one of the locals peering round the pillar in the middle of the bar's entrance, casting a glance in his direction before darting back behind the pillar like a rabbit scared to leave its burrow in case it was attacked. Now and again, another rabbit looked out and darted back in again.

'Doh stare at de man,' hissed Hero.

'He kinda lookin' strange wi' he white skin an' all ah de tattoo,' said Larry, 'but he eh nothin'.'

'He bound to be someting. Someting, I tellin yuh. Why it have a white man in de village? It doh have nothin' here for he.'

'Go ask de man.'

'You go ask de man.'

'You de one who frighten.'

'Me eh frighten.'

'You is de big man. You go speak wi' he and find out who is he, if he jus' somebody passin' through...or you frighten?'

'Me eh frighten!'

'Watch nah. He comin'!'

'Wheeeyyy!' said Hero, stumbling off his stool in fearful agitation. 'He comin', he comin', Lordie, he comin'. Oh, Lord.'

Hero turned around and leaned on the bar with his back to the road, glancing nervously over his shoulder to see how close the white man was. Larry tipped his pork-pie hat backwards and laughed.

~ CHAPTER 25 ~

THIRST AND CURIOSITY having got the better of him, Fingal walked into the bar and removed his hat as he crossed the threshold. A small man with filthy sweat-stained clothes and laceless muddy boots stood at the bar with his back to him. Another man with a pork-pie hat wearing slacks and a short-sleeved shirt was sitting on a barstool. He looked at Fingal briefly before turning his gaze to the floor. 'Good afternoon,' said Fingal.

The man in the pork-pie hat nodded back at him before averting his eyes, and the small man didn't turn around at all. A woman behind the grille appeared to be asleep on her arms as Fingal stood there awkwardly. A few seconds passed before Fingal said, 'Excuse me?'

She didn't respond.

The man in the pork-pie hat turned towards the woman and said, 'Neighbour, look, a customer,' before walking to the edge of the doorway and lighting a cigarette.

Fingal asked for a beer. She looked at him, blinking rapidly, making it difficult for him to hold her gaze, but he persisted in doing so, nevertheless. 'It have Carib...Stag...Pilsner...Miller lite...an' Guinness,' she said after what felt like an unnatural amount of time.

'Pilsner, please.'

She passed a bottle through the grille and didn't ask for any money.

He asked, 'Do you sell cigarettes?'

'Twenty-pack...ten-pack...or single.'

'What do you have?'

'Eh?' she said, frowning and turning an ear towards him.

'What cigarettes do you sell?'

'It have Broadway or Du Maurier.'

'I don't know.' He looked at Larry, who had moved to the open door and was standing there, smoking, 'What do you smoke?'

'Broadway.'

'A pack of Broadway, please.'

'Ten or twenty?'

'Twenty.'

'Wait nah, man,' said Larry, holding his pack out in front of him.

Hero turned round, his eyes wide as though in horror at what was about to happen. 'Try it first. Yuh might find it too strong.'

'Thanks,' said Fingal, taking a cigarette, thinking it an opportunity for a friendly exchange, but as he lit it, Larry flicked his cigarette stub into the road and returned to the bar, leaving Fingal standing there. Fingal had left his beer on the bar with his hat, wanting to drink and smoke at the same time, but he didn't know whether he should walk back inside with the lit cigarette or rest it somewhere while he retrieved his drink. There wasn't an ashtray anywhere. The noise of the fan suspended on the wall above a sign that read *No Obscene Language* was the only sound.

The man in the pork-pie hat and the man in the dirty clothes both stared at him for a few seconds before the former picked up the beer and took it to Fingal. 'Thanks.'

'No problem.'

Fingal stood smoking and drinking his beer quickly and feeling frozen to his spot by the door as though any move he made would amplify his presence further and increase his feeling of self-consciousness. No one else in the bar was engaged in any conversation. A red hatchback car with numerous dents and scratches and minus a passenger's seat stuttered into the parking bay outside the bar. A man with a James Brown haircut in an oil-stained blue boiler suit and shiny smart black shoes walked in, and the woman handed him a beer and a pack of Du Maurier without any exchange of words between them before he walked back out again. He had glanced up at Fingal on his way in but ignored him on the way out.

'Could I have another, please?' asked Fingal, passing his empty bottle through the grille. 'And a pack of Broadway, too, please.'

'Eh?' said the woman looking at him, her eyes blinking with even more fervour than before.

'A next Pilsner for de man,' said the man with the pork-pie hat, 'an' a pack a Broadway.' She passed them through the grille in silence. 'Can I pay?' asked Fingal.

'Eh?' she said, adding a frown to accompany her blinking.

'De man want to pay he tab,' said the man in the pork-pie hat.

'Fifty-four dollar,' she said.

He handed her three twenties, and she pushed the change under the grille without another word. That was about five pounds in the UK, thought Fingal. Two beers and a pack of fags for a fiver seemed ridiculously cheap. He reflected again upon life in the first world, its obscene consumerism, and the wasteful, expensive way its citizens had to live.

Fingal turned to the man in the pork-pie hat and offered him a cigarette. 'Nah...tanks,' he replied.

Fingal took his beer to the doorway and stood there smoking a while before the man in the pork-pie hat came alongside him. 'Whey yuh from?' he asked.

'London.'

'Inglan?'

'Yes.'

'How much beer an' cigarette costin' across dey?'

'Two beers in a bar in London and a packet of cigarettes? Maybe two hundred TT dollars.'

'What? So much?'

'Yeah.'

'Whey, boy. Inglan expensive, man. Like yuh hadda be real rich dey jus' to smoke an' drink.'

200

Fingal felt awkward. Being from the first world, regardless of how liberal and informed he felt himself to be when confronted by the comparative poverty of the third world, he just felt out of place, an impostor almost. 'I guess so,' he said, 'but it's relative. People earn more money but have to pay more for everything – cars and petrol, houses, clothes – there's plenty of poverty in England, too. In many ways, you've got it right here.'

'Larry,' said the man in the pork-pie hat, offering his fist for a bump.

'Fingal,' said Fingal, offering his fist.

'Fingal?' asked Larry. 'Me never hear dat name before.'

'It's Scottish...and a place in Ireland.'

'Scotch, eh? Yuh like whisky?'

'Yes.'

'I cah drink dat at *all*. Even if I chase it wi' de coconut water it too hot.'

'Yeah, it's for a cold climate.'

'How cold it is in Scotland?'

'Right now it's probably less than twenty degrees but can be warmer. Much less in winter. Minus degrees at night. Sometimes minus in the day.'

Larry nodded as though he had heard of this phenomenon before. 'I have a brother livin' up New York...Queens. He seh it does make real cold in winter, but he stay dey. He workin' an' married an' ting. Yuh ever went to New York?'

'Yes, a few times. You ever go?'

'Nah.' There were a few moments of silence before Larry, this time accepting an offered cigarette, asked, 'So why yuh here in de village? Yuh have friends?'

'No, I'm just passing through. I'm a writer. Just researching, you know.'

'Which part yuh stay?'

Fingal hesitated. 'Not far. Won't be staying long, I don't think.'

'Yuh know it have a white fellah livin' here. Jus down de road. He a artist. He married a girl from de village. Nice fellah. He from Inglan, too.'

'Oh?' Fingal was interested. Maybe this artist could be someone he could talk to, and maybe he could help with the search for Camille.

It had taken him by surprise how different Trinidad was to where he knew, how the spoken language wasn't English as he knew it, how the culture was so different – he laughed at his own naïvety – as though he was in a foreign country. There was a tendency among those in the UK who had never been anywhere in the Caribbean other than its resorts, for the most part in the other islands, or who had never been there at all, to imagine the former colonies to be tropical versions of Britain, where everything bar the weather would be familiar and where the obvious legacies of empire would still be apparent, thus making it somewhere Brits would feel at home and made to feel welcome. There were some obvious signs of that, but the imperialist legacy was far more complex and multi-layered than just a few leftovers from old British culture. Spanish, French, Dutch, and British influences converged in Trinidad with the forcibly imported cultures of Africa, the ways of old India courtesy of indentured and exploited East Indians, as well as Arabic, Chinese, and North American incursions in various guises, not the least in harvesting oil, sugar, and other natural resources or setting up businesses, buying land, and political influence.

Then, there was Trinidad's link with the international drug smuggling chain. Perfectly positioned as a staging post between the coca fields of South America and Western markets with their insatiable appetite for its effects and profit potential, Trinidad's culture had become deeply influenced by this dynamic. As the supermarkets and clothes shops and fast food outlets all increased in number, so did the murder rate, one of the highest per capita in the world. Alongside some people getting very rich by fair means, foul, or both, many others struggled with extreme poverty and a consequential limiting of their horizons. Others still – the majority, no doubt – worked hard and managed to make ends meet. Physically stunning and culturally chaotic, Trinidad was not what Fingal had expected at all. He was in a strange land, and he wondered how Camille would have found it on her naïvely romantic quest – which he had naïvely encouraged – to discover her roots. What the hell are roots, anyway? Just a tangled mass beneath the land with which there's no need to make sense of or come to terms.

Larry had rejoined his friends at their table, and, not wanting to intrude, Fingal ordered another beer and sat alone at the end of the bar, underneath a stuttering fan.

~ CHAPTER 26 ~

VICTORIA PERSAD SAT on the front gallery, eating phoulourie, which she held on her lap in a single sheet of kitchen towel. She had cut an incision in each one and filled them with coconut chutney after finding them covered loosely with a tea towel in a bowl on the kitchen worktop as she made her morning sweet black coffee. She didn't know who had made them or how they had got there – maybe a neighbour's birthday had been celebrated the previous day, and someone had brought them over – but she couldn't resist them. 'Pepper hot,' she said to herself after biting into the first one. 'Nice.'

She preferred to sit at the front of the house so she could see the comings and goings of people in the village. She missed the old house, which used to be right on the road, where she could wave to passers-by, some of whom would stop for a chat or even come through the gate to sit down with her and keep her company for a while as they took a sweet drink or a coffee and caught up with the local news and gossip.

She appreciated the new house with all its space and its three bathrooms, all with running hot and cold water – one of which was for her sole use – and she could still, at least, see the road, even though the house was set back too far from it for anyone to drop by on the spur of the moment. Then again, she did enjoy the status the new house afforded her in the village, and she relished being seen as belonging to a family who was obviously doing well.

People in Trinidad admired those who got on. Social status was important, even if it did lead to some people becoming spiteful and jealous, and no one could say Victoria Persad – known as Bee Bee to all – hadn't done well in life, albeit vicariously, and not because of her own efforts. However, she did miss some of the old ways of life when the whole village had lived in wooden board houses, and life seemed so much simpler, but living in a large concrete house with all its modern conveniences was evidence she had come up in the world. There was no more bathing with a cup and bucket, no more having to fetch and carry water from the standpipe up the road, no more having to do her laundry with a barrel of water and a washboard, and best of all, no more having to relieve herself in a foul-smelling, insect-infested latrine.

The family's enhanced status in the village, it had to be said, was down to the hard work of her son-in-law, Radhesh, but this was not something easy for her to acknowledge or give credit for. The man had always been a hard worker, no doubt about that, and he had never raised a hand to her Angel, but in all the years she had known him, she had never really liked him. He was a *grocer* – a shopkeeper, after all. It was just a small business. He might have worked hard and provided for her Angel and the family – including herself, she had to admit – but he wasn't a bright man, really; he was dotish, in truth. She had always thought her daughter would marry someone with *real* status, a *professional* like a doctor or lawyer or accountant. Radhesh had no education to speak of, and he had grown up in a family who grew their own vegetables and sold them at the market. Nothing wrong with that – everybody had to get by, after all – and they were an honest family, but he wasn't the type of man she had wanted her Angel to marry. She used to tell her, 'Now Faith, Angel, my sweet, doh settle for less when yuh could have more. Yuh go grow up to be one a dem tings bright and beautiful, an' some clever rich man go sweep yuh off a yuh feet, and yuh go live de good good life.' Instead, she hook up wi' he, she thought, though it doh matter he a Hindu, really – plenty people we know are so – jus' he eh who I did expect she to marry. He come from a *low* family, an' we probably originally come from a higher caste than he.

'Mummy, whey yuh dey?' called Faith.

'In de front, Angel.'

Faith brushed aside the doorway curtains. 'Yuh find de phoulourie, I see.'

'Pepper hot, but it nice.'

'It have kurma an' sugar cake, too.'

'Somebody married?'

'Shianne dey.'

'Who she?'

'Yuh know she: Kaneesha daughter.'

'Kaneesha?'

'Mouthy...Brandon and Anya daughter. She youngest.'

'Brandon granchil'?'

'Yes.'

'She have enough years to married?'

'Plenty. Nineteen.'

'Lord. I remember she from small. Nice chil',' then adding after a few seconds' thought, 'But she get fat now.'

'Anyway, Mouthy pass by in de evenin'.'

'I eh see she.'

'Yuh was sleepin'. I goin' town jus' so, den to see Shantel. Yuh wah anyting?'

'Shantel?'

'Gloria cousin.'

'Long time I eh see Gloria.'

'She dead, Mummy. Las' June.'

'For true. I forget. Which part she livin'?'

'Who?'

'De cousin.'

'Debe.'

'Yuh goin' Debe?'

'Yes, Mummy.'

'Bring some saheena for me nah. Roll up saheena, not de chip up kind.'

Faith left her mother to ponder the passing of time and the people and places inhabiting her memories. It had been a long time since Victoria had been to Debe. She'd like to go again and walk along the main road there, sampling the different snacks from the street vendors. She had always enjoyed that, and saheena was her favourite of those snacks. It had always been a treat for her, ever since she could remember. She used to make it, of course, not the chip up version people seemed to favour these days, that was just lazy cooking in her opinion. No, she made the *rolled* kind in the traditional way, where you make up the paste of split peas, haldi, and green seasoning and wipe it between layers of whole fresh dasheen leaves, then roll them up tight before boiling them in a sealed bag for a few minutes and coating them in more of the paste and frying them until crisp. 'Make sure is de roll up one, eh! Not de chip up,' she said out loud as though Faith could still hear her.

The house was empty now. All she could hear was a kiskadee calling and the breeze rustling the leaves. She watched a pair of blue macaws preening themselves on the chataigne tree for a few moments before her eyes began to droop, and she was just about to nod off when she heard a noise coming from the kitchen, the fridge door opening and closing and some cupboards being banged shut. Frightened, she got up from her chair and peered through the doorway curtains into the shade of the sitting-room and the kitchen beyond, where she saw a figure moving around, searching for something. 'Who dey?' she shouted.

'Is Rajan.'

'What de hell yuh tryin' to do, boy? Yuh frighten me.'

'Sorry, Nani.' She liked it when her grandchildren referred to her as *Nani* in the old Hindustani way. 'Boy, come nah. Spend some time wi' yuh Nani.'

Rajan thought quickly. She evidently didn't know he had been banished from the house, and this gave him a bit more time and maybe opened up an opportunity. He didn't want to be seen on the gallery, however, so he called out to his grandmother, 'Sure, Nani, but come inside de house nah. I lookin' for some ting.' She wandered into the kitchen. 'Wha' yuh lookin' for, boy?'

'I have a surprise for Papa.'

'How so?'

'I have a chance to make de business some real, real money. Plenty profit. Yuh see, Nani, I make a good deal wi' some fellahs, real good. Dey top businessmen from town.'

'Oh, dat nice.'

'Yeah, Nani. Real, real nice, but it have a problem.'

'Wha' dat?'

'I get rob. Some fellah teef me wallet in de market dis mornin'.'

'Wheyyy...yuh get it back?'

'Nah.'

'Yuh tell police?'

'Yeah, I tell dem, but wha' dem go do? An' I need to get to de bank to get de cash to pay de fellahs for de deal. Dey gonna supply we wi' all de sweet drinks and snacks at a real low price. Yuh ever hear about Sunrise Food?'

'Nah, boy.'

'Oh, dey real big, Nani. Real businessmen. Trouble is, if I doh seal de deal dis mornin' we gonna lose out.'

'Seal de deal, eh?'

'Yes, Nani. An' me eh find de bank card, de spare company one, so me eh get no cash.'

'Oh, dat's a shame.'

'Nani, yuh could help me out? Yuh have cash? As soon as de deal seal, I can tell Papa, an' den we give it back to yuh. Den, we can celebrate. I wah buy a li'l something fuh Ma...an someting fuh yuh, too, Nani.'

'How much yuh wan'?'

'Only twenty thousand, Nani.'

'Wheyyy, boy – dat plenty money.'

'I know, Nani, but is jus' for a li'l while. Please, Nani.' He kissed her on the forehead.

'Doh follow me,' she said before shuffling through the curtains that separated her bedroom and bathroom from the rest of the house. After a few moments, she returned with a wad of cash and handed it to Rajan.

'Nani,' he said, smiling at her, 'yuh is de best. I go see yuh later, when I give it all back to yuh...an' more. Papa go be real happy. Ma, too.'

'Wha yuh buyin' fuh she?' she asked.

Rajan tapped his nose and said in an excited voice, 'Surprise!' and then hurried out the back door and climbed over the back wall into the uncultivated land behind the house, hoping his grandmother didn't see him.

The old lady sat down again on the front gallery and closed her eyes. I know he was always kinda wild, she thought, but now he grow, he a good, good boy. He generous and nice, and maybe he a better businessman dan he father.

~ CHAPTER 27 ~

AS THE EVENING sky grew dark, Neighbour's Bar began to get busy. Fingal stood outside and smoked a cigarette, watching the strips of yellow, purple, and pink clouds signal the day's end. He was beginning to relax. The locals seemed friendly enough if naturally a little wary of him, and the beers were ice-cold and easy to drink. Two women – he guessed Venezuelans – sat down on the bench outside the bar without going inside. One was older than the other, and they chatted to each other in Spanish, the younger one glancing over at Fingal a few times. He couldn't help but notice how attractive she was, her dark hair tied back in a long ponytail and wearing a tight red dress that had him fighting his natural inclination to look at her body. He smiled at her, and she smiled back.

'*Un cigarillo, por favor,*' she said. Fingal walked over to her and proffered the open pack from which she took one, smiling a gap-toothed smile at him. He offered the older woman one as well, and she declined with a wave of her hand. After lighting her cigarette, Fingal stood there awkwardly for a few moments before speaking. *'Hablas inglés?'*

'No mucho.' He tried to summon up a few of the Spanish words he knew in order to start a conversation, asking her if she had work.

'Yes,' she said, pointing with her chin up the road. *'En el otro*...bar.'

'Es bueno?'

'Es duro. Muy duro.'

'Donde vives?'

She gestured again with her chin in the same direction.

'Ingleesh?' she asked. *'Americano?'*

'English.'

'I want *aprender* Ingleesh.' She smiled again. 'Maybe jou...' He noticed the accent, finding the way she said *jou* instead of *you* alluring.

'You want a drink? *Un bebido?'*

'Una bebida? Sí, cerveza.'

'Comó te llamas?'

'Rosa...jou?'

'Fingal.'

'Feengal.'

She sat at the table where Larry and Hero were sitting, leaving her companion outside while Fingal fetched two beers. They clinked bottles. The beaten-up red hatchback he'd seen before pulled up outside, its front bumper so close to the building it overlapped the step up into the bar, and the man with the James Brown haircut got out of the driver's side. A white man got out of the passenger door, a big man wearing a loose Hawaiian-style shirt. He strode into the bar confidently, looked around him, and said hi to Larry and Hero, his gaze resting momentarily on Fingal and Rosa. He nodded in their direction. He probably thinks I'm Venezuelan, thought Fingal, which may be no bad thing.

There wasn't a lot of conversation at their table. Hero was quiet and wary, Rosa didn't understand much, and Larry and Fingal were still awkward with each other, though they managed to speak of a few things, mostly sports and London life, which Larry wanted to know all about.

The bar began to fill with locals. All of a sudden, Larry nudged Hero and jerked his head in the direction of the flamboyant tree on the other side of the road where a black Hummer four-door pick-up with tinted glass had pulled up in the space alongside it. Most of the people in the bar were also looking.

'Wheyyy, boy,' said Hero.

'De dogmobile,' said Larry.

'Why he here so?'

'Me eh know, but best we watch out. De dog is in town.'

'What's that?' asked Fingal.

'Is a fellah name Dog. He eh no man yuh want to know. He eh too friendly. Best keep away from he.'

Rosa looked nervous and put her hand on Fingal's thigh, which he didn't move away. He looked at her and said, 'It's okay.'

She then took his hand and interlaced her fingers with his.

Everyone in the bar carried on as normally as possible, but Fingal could tell the atmosphere had undoubtedly changed since the arrival of the dogmobile. People were tense, often glancing over to the road where it was parked but not holding their gaze lest they be seen to witness whatever business Dog was up to. One of the Hummer's rear doors opened. A figure was pushed out and nearly fell over onto the ground. The bar fell silent, and everybody watched.

'Is Rajan,' whispered Hero.

Rajan brushed himself down and looked back at the dogmobile with his hands held together as though in prayer as the rear door closed. He glanced over to the bar, held his head up in an attempt to show he was fine, perhaps hoping the witnesses in the bar would think he was working with Dog, but likely knowing, deep down, that most people would see it for what it was and would understand that Dog had chosen the location on purpose and for maximum effect. Rajan turned on his heels and walked away. The dogmobile stayed put. Everyone in the bar turned their gaze away from the road and tried to continue as though nothing had happened.

Fingal sat down again with Rosa. Larry and Hero had joined two other men at another table and were playing a card game – one unfamiliar to Fingal – and he watched the way each player made strange gestures across the table to their partners, twitching their noses, scratching their heads, or tapping their shoulders in what appeared to be like a surreal and frenzied game of bridge that only made sense to the players themselves. Every now and again, one of them would whoop as he slammed a card down on the table. Another would write a score down on the table-top with a piece of chalk.

A car pulled up alongside the dogmobile, and it slowly dawned on Fingal as he peered through the half-light that it was Israel's old Capri. He's come to give me a lift back to the house, he thought, and he started to get up and walk over when he saw Israel get out of the driver's seat and get into the back of the dogmobile through the same door from which Rajan had been thrown out. The customers in the bar had noticed this, too, but carried on doing whatever they were doing regardless. If Dog had wanted any business with them, he would have come over by then. Fingal kept his eyes on the Hummer.

'*Qué pasa?*' asked Rosa, looking afraid again.

'*Nada,*' said Fingal, 'it's okay.'

Only about three or four minutes had passed when Israel emerged from the car. He said something indecipherable, addressing it to whoever was in the back seat and then laughed. So, Israel knew the bad man, observed Fingal, and maybe that wasn't so much of a surprise.

Israel walked confidently over to the bar, and with a big toothy grin, high-fived Fingal and rested his hand gently on Rosa's shoulder. '*Qué tal, hermana?*' he said, looking away from her before she could reply.

Fingal couldn't determine whether he knew her or not.

'Beers?' asked Israel, and without waiting for a reply, went to the grille and bought three Pilsners. They stayed a while longer before Israel indicated they should get going.

'Yuh wah a drop?' he asked Rosa.

She looked puzzled. '*Tu casa,*' he said. '*Quieres?*' and he simulated driving a car.

Rosa and Fingal sat in the back, and when Israel pulled up outside Uncle's Bar about a half-mile down the road, she leaned over to kiss Fingal, slipping her tongue between his lips. They kissed for a few seconds while Israel lit a spliff and exhaled out of his window.

'Jou teach Ingleesh?' she said.

'I will look for you,' said Fingal, fighting the urge to get out of the car and go with her, finding the likely and imminent prospect of sex with Rosa hard to resist. She stood outside the car and took his hand, pulling him towards her while he remained seated.

'Come,' she said, looking earnestly at him.

'Tomorrow,' he answered.

She let go of his hand, and he watched her backside as she walked towards Uncle's Bar. Before reaching there, she stopped to bend over and pick something up, lingering momentarily, fully aware he was watching her. She was framed in the doorway as the dull lights of the bar and the gaudy yellow walls beyond made for a composition so compelling and spell-binding it made Fingal think how easy it would be to stay there in that country with its lack of hang-ups, its easy-going ways, and beautiful women. He could just get drunk and stoned and have sex with Rosa and forget all the stresses and strains of his life in London. Not for the first time, he wondered what he was doing there, realising that the mission to find Camille was unexpectedly peeling away his defensive layers, leaving any efforts to keep them in place redundant and pointless. This was as good a time as any for him to surrender.

~ CHAPTER 28 ~

SPARKS FLEW UP into the night as Israel stood over the barbecue, turning chicken thighs. A bottle of rum sat half-empty beside the two friends as they sat outside on a hot night under the stars. They hadn't said much to each other, and Fingal was deep in thought. The last couple of days had been the most challenging so far, from the scene on the beach to his time in the bar and then seeing Israel speaking with the man they called Dog and then, at the end of it all, Rosa, sweet and unguarded, overtly sexual, and wanting. All of it led him to reach shifting conclusions, like milestones on the meandering pathways of his thoughts and feelings that didn't yet lead to an actual endpoint. Moreover, the whole journey now seemed infinite and unpredictable. He realised he had travelled so far out of his comfort zone that he might actually be lost. Nothing was familiar, and if he didn't make a conscious effort to stay aware of where he was going and what was around him, who knows where he would end up? It had dawned on him that, however his journey progressed, it was looking increasingly possible that in the end, it would involve violence, either by his own hand or that of another – most likely Israel – and he supposed, there was bound to be a brutal quality to some or all of the proceedings.

He was entering into something he had little or no control over, a realm of unknown forces vying for supremacy – visceral, raw, and without rules, but always real. And being there, where rules were easily broken, where life was cheaper, where people had to bend and sway to the forces of nature much more than in the first world, where the potency and power of ancient impulses still influenced decision-making and behaviour, was as real as anything he had experienced in his life. Until going to Trinidad this time, he had believed there wasn't much more the world could show him, and maybe there wasn't in the world he normally inhabited, but there, he was learning something new, not least about himself. That call to oblivion he was bound to answer, the easiness of surrender, not only to nature and its gifts that were so on hand and accessible there, but also to drink and drugs, to easily-attained physical gratification and comfort. He had gone there to find Camille, who he believed to be the love of his life, but even that force might not be enough to divert him from the nihilistic path to which he was so drawn. He thought of Rosa, a siren's voice he could barely resist.

He picked up his harmonica and began to blow. Israel beat out a rhythm on the step he was sitting on, and Fingal began to sing as though his life depended on it:

'I'm heading for the border, gonna leave this town behind
Heading for the border, got to ease my troubled mind
I'm heading for the border, gonna leave this town behind

I'm heading for the border where the air is pure and clean
I'm heading for the border where the air is pure and clean
And look out on the ocean, beauty like you've never seen

Moonshine on the water, red sun setting in the west
Moonshine on the water, red sun setting in the west
Now I've crossed the border I can lay me down to rest.'

He finished with a forty-eight bar harmonica solo that filled the night air. Israel nodded his approval and complimented his singing.

'Yuh write dat tune?' he asked.

'Yeah.'

'De blues, eh?'

'Yep. The blues.'

'An' a white man singin' it.'

'I'm not white.'

'Eh? Yuh lookin' white to me.'

'No, man. I'm not white. I'm mixed. My mother was mixed. Dual heritage, they call it. Black African and white.'

'An' yuh father?'

'White.'

'Then yuh mostly a white man.'

Fingal took a while to speak. 'I don't feel I am. I don't identify with being white. I don't describe myself as a white man.'

'How yuh describe yuhsel, den?'

Fingal paused. 'Non-white, I guess.'

'Wheyyyy, boy. Dat kinda strange. Kinda mix up. Yuh lookin' to me like yuh is a white man.'

'When I was at school, the fact my mother was not white was a source of...interest, shall we say, to the white bully boys. I was called all the names – half-caste...choc-ice...son of a nigger – so I could never identify with *them*, and the black kids and the Asian kids, well, they just ignored it, I guess, but I never really fitted into their cultures either. Maybe it had nothing to do with colour or race in the end anyway. My mother was drunk for most of my growing up. I didn't fit, man. Maybe that's why I sing the blues. But as time went on, I found I felt more comfortable if I wasn't just with white people. I felt I couldn't totally relate to them. I kinda gravitated towards black culture, I guess. It's where I felt safer, more able to be myself, not judged because of my skin colour or heritage. People think I'm Greek or Spanish.'

Israel nodded like a sage. 'It real mix up, boy, but, boy, yuh sing nice.'

They ate the chicken and drank the rum. The sky was cloudless, and Fingal looked up in awe at the myriad constellations on view. He could make out the Plough and maybe Orion's belt, but he didn't know any of the others.

'Look at the sky, man.'

On hearing his words, Israel walked over to the car and beckoned Fingal to join him. They both leaned back on the side of the car, Israel's locks spreading over its roof, and looked skyward. As Fingal's eyes adjusted, more and more of the night sky became visible until he was looking upon an incomprehensible expanse full of time-bending wonder and brilliance. 'Yuh know what yuh seeing dey?' asked Israel.

'Not really. I can make out Orion's belt. I don't really know the constellations.'

'De Spanish call de belt *Las Tres Marías*, yuh know. Can yuh see all a he?'

'I don't know where to look.'

'Look...yuh see whey he shoulders are an' he head above...like a triangle above he belt, de left-hand shoulder? Above dey yuh see a line to a next star, and den a next line that reach a shape like a square with one side missin'. Da'is he club. He raisin' de club above he head. Den look to he other shoulder whey a line stretchin' from dey to a curve line a six stars. Da'is he shield.'

'Amazing.'

'Yuh can see Canis Major an' Minor. He huntin' dogs just dey behind he. An' den, Lepus de hare or rabbit – me eh know which – below he feet.'

'So much more to Orion than I realised.'

'He straddlin' de celestial equator. Artemis send he dey because he get too big for he boots.' He laughed.

'What else can you see?'

Israel pointed. 'Da'is de North Star.'

'Where?'

'Yuh see what yuh call de Plough? Well, de North Star in a straight line from the right edge of de Plough's square...yuh see?'

223

'Yes...wow, that's wonderful.'

'It all part of de Great Bear, Ursa Major.' He proceeded to direct Fingal's gaze along the lines of the constellation. 'Now, lookin' to de north...da'is Cassiopoeia right dey. Five stars shape like a drunk W...yuh see? She another one who get too big for she boots.'

'How come?'

'She vex Poseidon, man. She say she more beautiful dan all a he nymphs, an' de nymphs didn't like dat, so dey tell de boss so, an' he punish her. She was Queen a Ethiopia, man...Rasta Far I. She doh wah nothin', but she get too big for she station in life – keep wantin' more than she merit, is a message for us all to learn from. She not only stuck way up dey, she have to circle de pole, de celestial pole, an' she have to hold on tight, man, or she gonna fall from de sky. Imagine...until eternity she have to cling on.'

The two were silent for a few minutes, Fingal reflecting on the fate of those forever banished to the skies in unending punishment, having to look back down at the life they could have had instead. It made him wonder if there wasn't a lesson for him to learn from that, but he couldn't organise the thought enough for it to become clear.

Israel turned and looked in the opposite direction.

'Look dey,' he said, 'something yuh wouldn't see whey you live...de Southern Cross...or Crux, to give it de proper name.' He pointed, and Fingal found it easily.

'I thought you could only see that from the southern hemisphere?' he said.

Israel looked at him with an amused expression as though he was humouring a child. 'We close to de equator, man. De Earth curve in both direction, an' we can see far both ways, man. Yuh lookin' at both de southern and de northern sky...beautiful, eh?'

'Yes, but...hard to understand.'

'For real, but it just a li'l bit a science, physics, an' astronomy, a li'l bit a history a how dey discover all a dis, Galileo, Newton, all a dem. An' den what about de Islamic scholar an' dem, or de Egyptian? Plenty a dem knew even more dan dat. Look at all a dem mosaic dey have in de ancient world – dey knew about the infinite, man.'

'Did you study all this?'

'Yeah. Long time I did start study a degree in physics an' ting, den me leave all a dat.'

'Why?'

'Tings happen, yuh know? I decide to go to sea. I go all over. I work tankers, mostly, all over de world, so I learn to navigate de old way, yuh know? Usin' de stars.'

'You didn't want to finish your studies?'

'Man, I learn enough a de world. All I need to know.'

'But you could – ' Fingal was interrupted by the sound of a car coming down the trace, its headlights shining on them. He looked nervously towards Israel, who calmly told him to go back to the house while he remained where he was.

It was a police car. It pulled up alongside Israel's Capri. Two uniformed officers sat inside, and one of them wound down the passenger's window. Israel leaned into it, and Fingal could hear them talking but couldn't make out the words. Occasionally, Israel gestured back towards the house without turning round.

Eventually, Fingal heard them all laughing, and then the police car backed into their driveway, turned around, and headed off down the trace the way it had come. Israel, chuckling, loped back to where Fingal sat on the steps of the house. He looked up expectantly, and Israel smiled. 'Is okay. I know dem.'

'What did they want?'

'Dey jus' checkin' we out. Once dey see me, dey know we okay.'

Fingal fetched two beers from the fridge, and the two sat on the step together and continued looking up at the stars. After a period of silence, Fingal asked, 'Did something happen to you to make you leave and go to sea?'

'Plenty.'

'You want to tell me?'

'Not really.' Israel stood up, finished his beer in a couple of swift gulps, then patted Fingal's shoulder before saying goodnight.

~ CHAPTER 29 ~

RAJAN WAS IN a panic. Before dawn, he had heard Hero get up, and then he couldn't get back to sleep as he listened to his reluctant host going about his morning routine, making coffee, heating roti to carry with him for his lunch, and then taking a shower. Rajan cursed him but knew he couldn't afford to express his irritation out loud as he needed to keep Hero in his confidence for the time being. No one knew where he was hiding, as far as he knew, and that was how he needed it to stay. As he lay on the mattress watching the day come slowly to life through the curtainless window of the bare room – such a comfortless sanctuary – he felt the panic rising. Even a kiskadee calling from somewhere nearby was getting under his skin, its carefree, innocent song a stark contrast to his deteriorating state of mind.

He had choices, the most obvious being to make a run for it and get away, go to Port of Spain and either stay there or take the ferry to Tobago, hoping Dog or the police wouldn't follow and be able to find him, but he would need money, and plenty of it if he was going to do that.

He could go back to his family like the prodigal son and repent, confess to all the mistakes he had made and all the subsequent misdemeanours, beg for their mercy, ask his father to repay Dog, and then he would promise to work all hours to repay the debt. It would be humiliating, for sure, but worth it just to make life simple again. But what if his father refused to help? Or what if Dog didn't accept that as the end of their arrangement and still required the family business to be a front for his smuggling and money laundering?

The last option, and the one he least wanted to contemplate but was now reluctantly accepting, was that he had to get hold of some real money so he could pay off Dog once and for all. And that meant robbery and all the risks it entailed. He could see no alternative other than going to the police and asking for their protection in return for telling them all he knew about Dog's enterprise. He quickly discounted that option because he knew Dog was bound to have police officers on his payroll, and he didn't know how high up Dog's influence reached into the force as a whole.

Apart from anything else, there was still the French woman to consider. What if the police were looking for him in connection with her? Dog had been so angry when Rajan had tried to elicit his help, he'd slapped him twice across the face and terrified him with a chokehold on his Adam's apple, so hard and with such murderous intent that it had made him fear for his life. 'No soldier a mine does do dis kinda ting,' Dog had said. 'It can only bring trouble to *all* a we, yuh stupid boy...damn stupid.'

How many times had he been called that in recent weeks? Not the least by himself. Dog had been furious, as though he paradoxically lived by a strict moral code when it came to behaviour towards women. Rajan wondered whether Dog wouldn't have cared so much if the French woman had been a local, but because she was a foreign national, a visitor to the country, it meant she couldn't be made to disappear without drawing some considerable heat. Dog had said he would look into it, but he made his deep disapproval of Rajan more than apparent. Rajan feared him, experiencing a dread he had never felt before in his life. There had to be a solution.

His body began to shake. He hurried out of bed and ran to the latrine at the back of the house, where he voided and fought back the tears, biting his lip until it bled.

The name Plum Valle came to mind, a small village not far from Manzanilla. A few weeks ago, he had heard Larry and Clock talking in the bar about *sou sou* and how the local scheme was paying around forty thousand TT dollars a hand when once it had paid much more. It seemed fewer people wanted to save money the old way, preferring banks to earn them interest on a regular basis rather than waiting for their hand to come around. There had been talk of the government trying to regulate and tax the savings, but it was so widespread and such an intrinsic aspect of village life in Trinidad that locals had dismissed the idea out of hand.

'How dey go do dat?' Larry had laughed, 'It everywhere, man, every little village, every neighbourhood, in every town.'

'An' some a dem payin' big hands still, yuh know,' said Clock.

'Doh make joke,' Larry continued. 'It have a sou sou in Plum Valle. Me cousin, Royston, de treasurer, an' he tell me dey payin' seventy-five thousand a hand; a li'l li'l place like dat an' dey still takin' so much.'

'Which part dat is?'

'Manzanilla side.'

'Dese days, I wouldn't want to mind all dat cash.'

'He doh keep it in he house. He run de community centre, an' it have a safe dey.'

'Seventy-five thousand – dat worth it, eh?'

Rajan took a back road out of the village, and even though the potholes slowed him down – some of them deep enough for a vehicle to get stuck in – he knew it was unlikely that anyone would see him there. The cocaine he'd snorted after his shower was still bitter at the back of his throat, but it had given him the impetus he needed to take action instead of staying confined in Hero's house. He had decided to take the long drive to Manzanilla, somewhere he wasn't known, to see what he could find.

He headed through Debe and Princes Town and then onto Rio Claro, where he pulled up outside a restaurant called Ali's BBQ and Smokehouse. He felt like eating some chicken wings or fried pork, so he walked up to the double glass doors at the front of the building, but they were locked. He peered through the glass and saw an obese Indian man in a vest and shorts sweeping the floor. He knocked. The man looked up and shook his head, shouting, 'We close,' before returning to his chores.

Rajan knocked again. The fat man put down his broom, walked ponderously to the doors, and opened up one side of them. Rajan looked at him. The man was sweating, his vest stained and wet. 'We close,' he said.

'I jus' wan' some wings. Yuh have?' persisted Rajan.

'Nah, man. We close. We eh open till six dis evenin'.'

Rajan acted quickly, pushing the door and the man back into the restaurant, pulling the gun from the back of his jeans as he did so, and levelling it at the man's temple while grabbing the man's throat with his other hand. 'Whey de cash?' he whispered, trying to sound as menacing as possible.

The fat man's eyes were wide with fear. 'Dey eh no cash,' he said.

Rajan hit the fat man across the face with the butt of his pistol, drawing blood and a squealed yelp. 'Whey de damn cash, yuh muddacunt?' said Rajan. For an enhanced effect, he added, 'Tell me or I kill yuh.'

The man was breathing heavily, and he extended his hands in a submissive gesture before saying, 'Okay. I show yuh. Just now.' He led Rajan behind the counter and into the kitchen, off of which was a small office. With the gun pressed against his head, he opened a drawer, pulled out a cashbox and a set of keys, and managed to unlock it despite his trembling hands.

He handed a thick wad of notes to Rajan, who asked him, 'How much it is?'

'Maybe ten thousand...maybe twelve.'

'Dat all yuh have?'

The man nodded.

Rajan stuffed the wad into his pocket and told the man he was going to leave, and that if the man promised to do nothing, then he wouldn't kill him. The man nodded again. Rajan demanded, 'Gimme yuh cell phone...an' yuh keys.' The man handed them over. Rajan backed out of the office into the kitchen and ran to the glass doors, locking them behind him and walking slowly back to his car.

He drove towards Mafeking and stopped by the crematorium to throw the phone and door key over its wall before hitting the coast road en route to Manzanilla, where he would turn off to find Plum Valle.

The sea at Cocos Bay was sparkling under the midday sun, frigate birds soared effortlessly above, and the long stretch of road hugged its expanse of sand, bringing back memories for Rajan of family days out there when he was a boy. The boot of the car would be filled with food and drink, pilau, pilhourri, roti, and fried fish with beers and sweet drinks in the cooler, his father at the wheel, his mother fanning herself in the front passenger's seat as he and his two sisters irritated each other in the back, provoking admonishments from his father who threatened them with all kinds of horrors if they didn't shut up. 'Allyuh wan licks? Den licks is what allyuh go get, so shut de hell up!'

Rajan couldn't help but smile at the memories. How simple life had been then. How simple he would like it to be again. If he could just pay off Dog then he could settle down once more and resume the peaceful life he'd had before it had all gone crazy. He would stop drinking, stop using cocaine, and eventually get rid of his gun. He felt it digging into the small of his back as he drove and wondered how it had ever come to this.

I go give it all up, God, he promised, *let me just pay off de Dog once and for all and free meself to lead a normal life again.*

Past the beach, the road headed inland, ceasing to be the Manzanilla-Mayaro Road and becoming the Eastern Main Road from where he had to look out for Plum Road. It wasn't hard to find – it was the first major turn on the left after about five miles – and soon, he was in Plum Valle, a place he had never been before.

It was a village like countless others in Trinidad. Mostly board houses and a few concrete ones lined its main road. The jhandi flags outside many of them told Rajan it was a mainly Indian area. Agricultural. Poor farmers, mostly, he reckoned. He recalled something he had seen on the news about how the area had been badly flooded following the rains of the year before, during which a fifteen-foot anaconda had swum down a residential street. Perhaps it was there, he wondered.

It was quiet on the road, with a few people walking slowly in the heat, carrying baskets of vegetables or fruit. Children ran about and shouted in the playground of the Presbyterian school, next to which some small football goals had been erected on a rough piece of ground. And there was the community centre, a cream-coloured, concrete building with bright white fencing at its front, in the middle of which was a tall gate. Rajan parked fifty yards away and waited, trying to determine his strategy. It didn't take long.

After about twenty minutes, an elderly man wearing a pork-pie hat walked through the centre's gate, which, to Rajan's surprise, was open. That must mean there's at least one other person inside, he thought, maybe more, so he would have to act quickly and decisively. He drove up to the building and parked outside the gate, then took a petrol canister and a length of coiled rope from the boot. Upon walking in, he saw two men – the one with the pork-pie hat and another even older man – sitting at a table. They looked up in surprise.

'I lookin' for a fellah name Royston,' said Rajan confidently.

'I is Royston,' said the older man, looking quizzically at the stranger and the rope and canister.

'I have news from yuh family,' said Rajan with a smile.

'Oh...wha' news?'

'Dey say yuh must hand over all de sou sou to me...right now.' Rajan pulled his gun from the waistband behind his back and pointed it at Royston.

The old man looked at him with an expression of grim determination. 'Yuh cah do dat,' he said.

Rajan pressed the gun against the back of Royston's companion's head. 'Yuh wah me to kill he?' hissed Rajan at which point Royston seemed to summarise in his head all the available options and quickly reached the conclusion that he had little choice.

He nodded his surrender to Rajan and spoke to his friend in calm, reassuring tones. 'Doh worry, Patrick. Is okay. We go be okay.'

Rajan then tied Patrick's hands to the chair behind his back and proceeded to douse him in petrol. Patrick's face crumpled, and he wet himself. 'Yuh muddacunt,' said Royston. 'Dey eh no need for dat.'

There was so much cash in every kind of denomination, Rajan couldn't believe his luck; there were enough blue notes there to tell him there were tens of thousands. He ordered Royston to find carrier bags to put the cash in, which he did after emptying out packets of paper plates and plastic cutlery onto the floor.

Rajan now had a dilemma. In his planning, he hadn't made a contingency for if there was more than one person in need of tying up. 'I wah yuh to be a good boy, Royston, an' take off yuh clothes, nah. All a dem.'

'Muddacunt,' said Royston.

The old man slowly removed his clothes, the last item being his boxer shorts, which he hesitated to take off before Rajan waved the gun at him. Rajan then ordered him to sit down, and using the discarded shirt and trousers, he tied Royston's hands to the back of the chair and poured petrol over him as well. He then trailed petrol back to the front door and waved a cigarette lighter at them. Patrick let out a sob.

Rajan put a finger to his lips to tell them to be quiet, then walked calmly out the door and back to his car. He was possibly four hundred thousand TT dollars richer than he had been ten minutes previously.

Under the Flamboyant Tree

The drive home was unremarkable, taking longer than it needed because he took some back roads and stopped off in a couple of bars along the way to quench his thirst with some cold beers. Pleased with himself and his day's work, he drew up outside of Hero's house and got out of the car to open the gates, moving quickly so nobody would spot him. He saw a beaten-up old Capri parked under the poui tree fifty yards or so down the road, but didn't pay it any mind.

236

~ CHAPTER 30 ~

THE STONES PLAYING at an overly loud volume provided an appropriate soundtrack to the scene of decay Mireille encountered when Philippe finally answered the door and let her into the apartment. The place was wrecked. Clothes and cushions were strewn across the floor, dirty glasses, cups, and plates were on virtually every surface, including bookshelves and windowsills, ashtrays were full, there was some broken crockery on the floor in the hallway, and the smell of foul drains and cannabis smoke combined to create a heady, suffocating effect. Philippe himself was unshaven in a stained t-shirt and unbuttoned jeans, his belt loose, the skin inflamed and flaking on his forehead and cheeks, his eyes red like open wounds.

He didn't say anything to her, just walked back into the living room, leaving the door open so she could follow. He sat down on the sofa, head in his hands, and stared at the floor.

She stood speechless in her smart beige coat, patterned scarf, and hat. Sylvie had let her into the block as there had been no answer to Mireille's frantic ringing of Philippe's doorbell. Seeing the distress on Mireille's face, Sylvie had asked what was wrong, and Mireille had told her of her concerns about Camille's possible disappearance and how she was worried something terrible had happened to her friend. She thought she had better check on Philippe to see if he had heard anything.

Sylvie had grimaced at the news while giving a cursory jerk of her head in the direction of apartments upstairs, adding, 'He's an idiot, that boy. Doesn't know how lucky he is to have her for a wife.'

Mireille had noted Sylvie had used the word *boy* to describe Philippe and thought it perfectly apt. He was so immature. It was as though he had reverted to childishness when things got difficult for him, blaming everyone but himself, waiting to be rescued and spoiled by some non-existent adult figure whom he hoped might be Camille. She had tried to fulfil that role for him, eventually running out of patience and tiring of the relentless burden he had foisted upon her.

Mireille had climbed the spiral marble stairs with reluctance and foreboding, her flat shoes sweeping the surfaces the only sound in the building, until she neared his front door when she heard the music. Philippe eventually opened the door.

'Have you heard from Camille?' she demanded, looking down at him, trying to suppress her disgust at what she was bearing witness to.

'That bitch.'

'Do you know where she is?'

'How would I know? Some man, maybe? Whore. Are you going to tell me?'

'She's in Trinidad.' Philippe looked up at her, confused, his eyebrows tensing so much that a vertical crease appeared between them and bisected his forehead. His eyes narrowed as if trying to make sense of what Mireille had just said.

She turned the volume down. 'Yes...Trinidad.'

'How?'

'She had enough of you, you pig.'

'Trinidad? Why would she go there, do that?'

'If you ever bothered to care for her, maybe you would understand why, you idiot.'

'Don't lecture me, woman. Who the hell are you to tell me that? I love Camille, more than you could ever know. I sacrificed –'

'You sacrificed nothing, Philippe! You gave up. You...you... took her so much for granted, you did nothing for her these last years. You – '

'Fuck off, Mireille. Leave me, please. Go...now!'

'So, she hasn't been in touch?'

'No.'

'Look, Philippe, I'm worried about her. I think she is in some kind of trouble.' She proceeded to tell him of Camille's promise to make contact with her every day and that she was no longer responding to her calls or messages. She had no idea where in Trinidad Camille had been when making the call, but she hadn't heard from her since. Her phone was obviously out of action, and she'd disappeared.

'Have you told the police?'

'I reported it, yes, but they said they couldn't do anything yet. They didn't really take it seriously. It was all so...I was so... vague, I guess. They wanted to wait to see if she got in touch. I called the embassy and the police there.'

'And?'

'They said it's not always easy to contact people if they are travelling in Trinidad...phone signals...Internet inconsistent in places, that if I heard nothing from her in a week, they would inform the local police.'

'She's probably okay...who knows?' He said this defiantly as though his pride was more important than Camille's disappearance, but Mireille could see fear in his eyes. She didn't know if he knew about Fingal, but she doubted Camille would have told him.

'I know someone, a friend of mine...from London. He was going to Trinidad. He said he knew someone there who might be able to help. He's a good guy.'

'I need to tell the boys...and Yves.'

'Yes, the boys need to know, but maybe not yet. You will worry them, and Yves...he's not well. He's old. Maybe leave it for now, but I can tell him. I know you and him...you don't really –'

'Yes.'

'Tidy up this fucking mess, will you? You need to be a grown-up, Philippe, now, especially.'

'I could go out there, maybe.'

'Maybe it's better if you stay put for now.'

He looked at her as if trying to summon up his defiant spirit, but his lips began to quiver, and within seconds, his face crumpled like a collapsing wall, and he started to cry. All she could bring herself to do was to place her hand lightly on his shoulder by way of offering him some comfort and reassurance, but she was too contemptuous of him to offer anything more. She surmised he wanted to be held, the pathetic, self-centred man-child, and she wasn't about to do that for him. She left him standing there, the sound of his primal sobbing cushioned when she closed the door behind her.

She knocked at Sylvie's. The old woman ushered her inside and gestured towards a sofa for Mireille to sit upon, telling her she had a pot of coffee on the go. She went into the kitchen, and Mireille heard her preparing crockery. The apartment smelled like a mixture of incontinence, lavender, and cologne. It was airless, too, and Mireille's instinct was to open up all the windows to let the fresher air of the streets into the tiny, dimly-lit apartment. She resisted doing so and waited for her coffee. It arrived served in delicate china cups, which rattled on their saucers as Sylvie's bony, blue-veined hands carried them into the living room. The coffee was bitter and thick, and there had been no offer of milk or sugar.

Sylvie sat down on a battered, green leather armchair that made a sound like breaking wind upon first bearing her diminutive weight. 'Well,' she said, 'now, tell me.'

~ CHAPTER 31 ~

AS GIGS GO, it was an awkward one. Small stage – actually, not so much a stage as a space cleared of tables and chairs adjacent to the swing doors of the gents' toilets – and a seemingly precarious arrangement on which to mount the PA speakers. There were no monitors or mixing desk, so they weren't able to do a sound-check, and there was bound to be a noisy, fluid crowd, many of whom would be more likely to engage in their drinking and personal conversations than listen to the band. Even so, the four of them were looking forward to playing as they sat at a high table upon high stools, drinking beer, chatting, and joking. It was their first-ever gig without Fingal, their reluctant leader and songwriter, their arranger and nuanced, creative driver.

It was also their first-ever gig in the Man O' War, a Soho pub with an august musical heritage, not so much because of the gigs which had taken place there, but more for the musicians who used to frequent it. When you sat at its tables and looked upon its aged décor of etched glass, mahogany, and dim Art Deco lights, you were sitting where the likes of Jimi Hendrix, The Who, The Pretty Things, and David Bowie among others had all sat and soaked up its sleazy but vibrant atmosphere. And with Ronnie Scott's jazz club only a five-minute walk away, many a jazz legend had also soaked up the vibe and alcohol of that Soho institution over the years. A large painting of an anatomically correct man o' war sailing ship turning broadside in rough seas hung above the bar, faded and cracked, a blue admiral's pennant on top of the mainmast being buffeted in the wind while the sails on the fore and mizzen masts billowed like sheets on a washing line, smoke puffed from the gun decks, and the Union flag flew on its bowsprit above the figurehead of a big-bosomed mermaid; the incongruity of the faded empire among the bohemians, artists, copywriters, and tourists of old London.

Thabo told his companions how he often bumped into fellow jazz musicians there, and how London was as vibrant a jazz scene as anywhere in the world with its young artists brought up on reggae, hip-hop, R&B, garage, jungle, and grime, all relishing the freedom jazz gave them to create and express the universal themes of love, happiness, and the blues, as well as those of being young, poor, and marginalised in an austerity-ravaged urban and disunited part of the country. Thabo could talk, eloquently, rapidly, and with passion about the heritage of jazz and blues, and the three band members listened intently, not a little in awe of their new friend. Perhaps only Goose wondered about Fingal, how he would feel about it, whether they were being disloyal to him by agreeing to a gig in his absence, riding on Thabo's billowing coat tails into a whole new experience, one Fingal might not have wanted to share. Kieran and Bobby seemed cool about it all, and it was apparent they hung onto Thabo's every word.

As they sat there loosely discussing the setlist and arrangements, they watched a scene unfold that was typical of London life. A tall, athletic-looking white man in an expensive blue suit, white open-neck shirt, and smart black raincoat was arguing with the barman, a man much shorter and stockier than him, who looked like he was from another time and class, dressed like a 1960s mod with a black-and-white checked button-down collared shirt, maroon waistcoat, and close-cropped hair with long sideburns. He was leaning over the bar, jabbing his index finger towards the taller man's chest. 'I told you: finish your drink and then fuck off out of here. I'm not serving you anything more. Go on and fuck off,' he said.

'Why the fuck should I?' slurred the other. 'I've done nothing wrong.'

'You know why...now, get out.'

The tall man looked over to where the band were sitting and stretched his arms out like Christ the Redeemer, as though appealing to a referee who had just awarded a free kick against him. 'What have I done?' he beseeched them.

All four returned his look with impassive stares, the neutral but confident look men often adopted when violence was in the air, not wanting to get involved but letting any potential antagonists know they were hard enough to defend themselves.

The barman came round from behind the bar, took the man forcibly by the arm, and pulled him towards the door.

'All right...all right, I'm going,' he said, shaking himself free from the barman's grip.

The barman opened the door for him like a bellboy at a hotel. The tall man gave him a sarcastic grin and then punched him, dealing only a glancing blow. The barman instinctively rode the punch, which connected, nevertheless, with enough force to knock him off balance.

'Cunt!' shouted his protagonist, before running off down the street.

As if nothing had happened, the barman walked over to the band's table and cleared the empty glasses. 'Sorry about that, lads,' he said.

They played two forty-five-minute sets before finishing off about ten-thirty. The sound had inevitably been dominated by Thabo's virtuoso alto sax and improvised vocals, which, in the absence of Fingal's harp playing, was the only soloing that took place to any great degree. Goose had struggled to keep pace at times, unsure of where to play lead or rhythm, unwilling to solo within a framework much looser than that to which he was accustomed, while Bobby performed only one drum solo and kept it short, only twenty-four bars, and Kieran didn't solo at all.

Thabo was full of enthusiasm afterwards, telling them that for a first gig, it had gone really well and that he had heard something special in the way they seemed to transcend the basic structures of the songs on the set list. However, Goose felt Thabo had directed most of his comments towards Bobby and

Kieran, and he took this as confirmation that his own playing had been uncertain. 'We need to see what Fingal thinks when he gets back,' he said.

'Fingal will be cool,' said Thabo.

'If he comes back,' said Kieran. 'He's the one leaving it all a bit tight in terms of us having enough time to prepare for the tour. He shouldn't have gone away, man.'

'It isn't the best timing,' added Bobby.

Goose looked at them all and shook his head. 'He'll be back in time, man. He's a man of his word. When has he ever let us down?'

'True,' said Bobby, 'but it was him who kept going on about us having to be more professional than ever, to get really tight before we went on the tour, then he fucks off to the Caribbean.'

'He didn't fuck off,' said Goose getting angry. 'Someone he cares about is in trouble. He's doing what he thinks is the right thing to do. We'd be fucking nowhere without him for, fuck's sake.'

'Goose, man, you're right, ' said Thabo, 'but y'all need a contingency plan. This was nothing, man, just a little gig, just keeping your hands in. It's good to do that so y'all don't get slack. I love Fingal, man, and I don't doubt he'll be back...I'm just getting to know how to play with y'all.' He looked to Bobby and Kieran with a smile, and they both nodded in agreement.

Goose got up from the table and went to the bar. John Coltrane's version of *My Favourite Things* was playing as a barmaid with a ring through her septum, and Celtic knot tattoos on her earlobes, washed glasses while asking him what he wanted.

~ CHAPTER 32 ~

'IF DEY EH nah rest fuh de wicked,' thought Radhesh Ramkissoon as he climbed the back steps to the house and went through the kitchen door, clutching a pair of *chataigne* in one hand and a cutlass in the other, 'I mus' be do plenty wrong in me life to be sufferin' so.' His vest was stained with sweat, his shorts and ankles muddy, but he could at least comfort himself with the thought of curry chataigne and roti that night. Even if it always made him fart, he loved it, especially the way his Angel prepared it. The second one had been difficult to get down from the top branch, and he'd nearly fallen off the ladder – he wasn't as sure of foot as he once had been – but he had managed to cut its stalk in the end, and it had dropped to the ground with a satisfying thud. He put the chataigne in the kitchen sink and walked into the sitting room, where he could hear the television.

Angel, Khalisha, and Kajri were all sitting on the settee, and that old she-goat, Bee Bee, was sitting in the armchair with her mouth wide open, a startled expression in her eyes. She lookin' like she poop she pants, he thought.

Alicia was also there, sitting on the wooden chair, holding her baby daughter. The news was on, and he heard the female announcer talking about a series of robberies that had happened around Mayaro way within a short time of each other and how the police believed they were the work of one man they were seeking, warning the public not to approach him. A sou sou pot had been robbed, and two elderly men had been stripped, then tied up and had petrol doused all over them.

Radhesh stood listening and then spoke: 'Wha' kinda man go do a ting like dat – robbin' poor people hard earn savings so, and den frightenin' de old man an' dem so? Wickedness. Stupidness, too, because de police go hold he.'

An artist's impression of the supposed perpetrator was on the screen, the thin, bony face of a young Indian man that could have been anybody. 'Fat lot a good dat go do,' he added.

Faith turned off the television with a jab of the remote. As Radhesh made to leave the room, she said, 'Baba...wait nah.'

'Wh'appen?'

'We worryin'.'

'About?'

'Rajan.'

'Who is dat?'

'Baba, please. Dis situation eh right.'

'How so?'

'Da'is we son, we blood. If he in trouble den we bound to help he.'

'He make he bed, so he bound to lie in it.'

'Papa, please,' said Kajri.

He looked at his daughter as if he were weighing up what to say, an exaggerated a look of incredulity aimed at her. 'You, too, eh? Well, Precious, yuh doh know *what* you talkin' about.'

Then his mother-in-law spoke: 'He take money from me, too, yuh know.'Everyone looked at her.

'When?' asked Radhesh.

'Two days now. He say he need some to go make a deal...for de shop...de business.'

'He lie.' Radhesh looked to Khalisha for some kind of support or confirmation. 'He a damn crook, an' he rob he own family. He make he bed.'

Victoria continued, 'But he still we family, an' if he in trouble, den it have to be family to help he.'

'What de hell is dis?' shouted Radhesh, his face reddening with anger. 'De boy rob we. De boy mix up in all kinda ting wi' some bad people, de Dog an' he crew.' He paused for effect. 'An' he bring dat wickedness into de family...we home...we livelihood. Khalisha, wha' yuh seh?'

'Is true, Papa...de shop – Raja take plenty, put we in trouble an' we have all kinda men watchin' de store...Venezuelans.'

'Venezuelans?' asked Victoria as though Khalisha had actually meant Martians.

'Yuh see wha I tellin yuh?' said Radhesh. 'De boy bring badness to all a we. He rob we, he rob he own grandmother, an' if we doh distance we self from he, den all ah dem – Dog an' dem, de police, everybody – go tink we a part a all dis.'

Faith started to cry. 'But if he in trouble, we eh know whey he is. He could be in a ditch. He could be in prison – '

'He make he bed an' he – '

'Stop saying dat!' shouted Faith. 'Da'is yuh son, yuh blood – yuh cah jus wash yuh hands. Please, Baba, help de boy.'

'Well, even if I wah help he, me eh know whey he dey. If he fix he problem an' he willin' to work off he debt to he family, den maybe he can come home, but he *have* to fix he problem. He owe de gangsta an' dem money, real plenty money.'

Faith sobbed some more, and Kajri put her arm around her mother. Throughout all of this, Alicia had stayed quiet, looking down at the innocence of her sleeping baby. Radhesh stood there, clenching his jaw and staring out of the window.

After several minutes, he addressed Alicia. 'Yuh doh have nothin' to say, girl?'

She shook her head and replied, 'No...nothing, Baba. I jus' wan' to feel safe...for de baby.'

'Yuh see? De damn jackass doh even look after he wife an' child. Doh worry, girl. Yuh always welcome by we. You an' yuh child always have a home.' They all remained silent for several minutes. 'It have two chataigne in de kitchen,' he said.

No one acknowledged him other than Khalisha, who offered a weak smile. He nodded back at her, grateful for some kind of affirmation and watched his mother-in-law struggle to get out of her chair. He didn't offer to help, thinking she looked like one of those seals he had seen on a wildlife programme, undulating laboriously towards the sea. 'I go pray for allyuh,' she said. 'Who go carry me to church?'

~ CHAPTER 33 ~

THE ROAD HOME always felt longer than the road out. Ten hours' toil takes its toll, and the homeward-bound stride is always less purposeful and more laboured than the way it had been at dawn. Still, that evening, thought Hero, there is a cool breeze and a pretty sunset, so it isn't so bad. It doesn't matter how many times you see a sunset, it's always different, and the one lighting his way home that night was particularly worthy of his acknowledgement.

There was a band of thick, blue-grey clouds motionless above the world and underneath them, stripes of an orange, pink, and purple sky glowing above the rooftops with the coconut palms and telegraph poles like ghostly silhouettes punctuating the landscape at random. If only Rajan wasn't home. When would he sort things out and move on? He thought about stopping off at Neighbour's Bar to slake his thirst with a cold beer, but he was sticky and dirty from his labours and needed to bathe. He was hungry, too. The older he got, the harder the clearing and cutting and planting became as his body stiffened up much more readily than when he was a young man. He noticed how it would sometimes ache in the morning, especially when the weather was cool. Maybe he would come out again later for a drink if he didn't fall asleep in the chair. As he walked past the bar, he didn't see any of his partners, so he just waved to Neighbour and shouted, *'Hoy,'* to her as he walked past without stopping.

'Man, me foot tired,' he muttered to himself, knowing he had another twenty-minute walk ahead of him. Maybe someone would give him a drop. The crapaud were singing loudly, and the kiskadee making their last calls before settling down for the night. A few cars went by, but none stopped for him. Until, as he turned the last bend in the road before his house, he heard someone slowing down.

A car pulled up alongside him, but he couldn't see the driver through the tinted glass of the windscreen and windows, so he was immediately on his guard. The passenger's door opened, and he peered inside. The Rastaman was in the driver's seat, looking straight ahead. 'Hop in,' said Israel.

'Thanks, but I almost reach,' replied Hero, feeling a rising sense of dread, as though he were getting caught up in quicksand. It didn't matter how calm he stayed or how hard he tried to avoid it, it was swallowing him.

'Get in de damn car nah, man,' said Israel, still not looking at him.

'Me hoe. It have no space for me hoe.'

'Jus' leave it right dey so...we eh goin' nowhere. I jus' have some ting to tell yuh.'

'Den tell me. If I standin' here or sittin' dey it doh make no difference.'

Israel sucked his teeth in irritation. 'Boy, I eh go hurt yuh or nothing. I have a message for yuh...lodger, an' I need yuh to take it all in, yuh understan'?'

Hero lay his hoe down at the side of the road and climbed into the car, unbuttoning the scabbard for his cutlass as his did so.

Israel laughed. 'Boy, yuh safe,' he said in an attempt to reassure. 'Shut de door.'

Hero closed the car door and looked with fearful expectation towards Israel, who manoeuvred the car off the road onto the grass verge. He spoke slowly as though imparting some vital information that needed to be easily received and understood. 'Yuh doh have to understan' all a dis, just relay de message to de little prince stayin' by yuh. Tell he we know whey de woman is, whey she go be, an' when. She stayin' in La Brea wi' she tanty, a obeah woman, name Josephine. Everybody know she by Tanty Jo.' At the mention of obeah, Hero let out a whimper and said, 'Oh Lord, dis too much.'

'Yuh doh have to worry – yuh eh goin' dey – but if Rajan wah find she, it have to be tomorrow...in de night. She go be there late, about nine an' ting.'

'Me eh know nothin' about she. Who she is?'

'The less yuh know, de better tings go be for yuh. She somebody, an' he wah find she...me eh know he business. Anyway, dis Josephine livin' on de cliff dey, above de beach. Tell he dat he bound to find de French woman dey...tomorrow in de night. Yuh have all a dat?'

Hero nodded. 'Me hear yuh,' he said, 'but I doh wah nobody to know I involve in all a dis.'

'Yuh not *involve*...every ting sweet as far as yuh concern. Jus doh tell no*body* but Rajan.'

'Okay.'

Hero opened the door, but before he could step out of the car, Israel placed a firm hand on his forearm. 'One more ting,' he said. 'Tell he dat de Dog is cool. De Dog helpin' he here to show he doh have no hard feelin'...okay?'

'Dog?' said Hero, sounding alarmed again. 'De Dogman an obeah...an'... an'...dis too much a...'

Israel tightened his grip on Hero's arm. 'Jus' give he de message. Tell nobody again an' nothin' go happen to yuh.' He jerked his head towards the passenger's door by way of telling Hero their conversation was over.

Hero got out and picked up his hoe as Israel drove away, the exhaust sounding like a racing car as he changed gear and accelerated over the hill and out of sight. Hero was shaking. All his life, he had made a point never to get involved with criminals or obeah, but there he was, acting as a go-between for the gangsters and potentially incurring the wrath of an obeah priestess if he didn't get it right. He walked on down the road to his house.

When he walked through his front door, he saw Rajan sitting at the table with a glass of rum in his hand, looking red-eyed and drunk. The bottle was half-empty. He looked up at Hero but said nothing. Hero took a glass from the sideboard, sat down at the table opposite Rajan, and poured himself three fingers of rum. 'I jus' see de Rastaman.'

'Wha' Rastaman?'

'De tall fellah. De one we all see recently.'

'Me eh know.'

'He have a message for yuh.'

'Eh?'

'De Rastaman have a message for yuh...two message, really.'

'Why he have a message for me...an' why he tell *you*?

'From de Dogman.' Rajan now looked at Hero. 'From Dog? How so? Wha' goin' on?' he said, trying to stem the fear rising inside him, so much that he struggled to speak.

Hero looked at him with contempt, pausing to take a slug of his rum. 'He tell me to tell yuh two tings. One, he know whey yuh can find some woman yuh lookin' for.' He paused to watch Rajan, whose speechless reaction was wide-eyed with surprise. 'She go be in La Brea tomorrow in de night, after nine. She by some obeah lady name Josephine...Tanty Jo. One a dem house up on de cliff dey. An' he tell me to tell yuh dat Dog doh have no problem wid you again. He jus' wah help yuh.'

Rajan took a while to take this in and his thoughts raced as he tried to make sense of it all. Dog had found the French woman? How so? Well, Dog did know *everybody*. So this could be good news. The Rasta was working for Dog? Or was he just a messenger boy? Who would have guessed *that*? But then again it made sense. So, Dog had listened to him and had somehow located the woman for him. This *was* good news. A sense of calm and equilibrium returned. It meant the nightmare was over, that Dog had realised he was a good man, one that could be trusted, and it meant he could give Dog some of the money he'd stolen as a gesture of goodwill and good intent, and maybe keep some back to give to his father. Then, he would be able to go home again.

He looked up at Hero with a big grin and slapped his hands on the table. 'Wheyyyyy, boy,' he shouted, 'good news!' He poured another rum.

'Yuh stayin' long?' asked Hero.

'Why de hell would I wah stay wi' *you*?'

'Yuh was happy enough to take advantage de last few – '

'Hero, nah stupidness nah.'

'Who de hell yuh tink yuh is, Rajan? Yuh could see I doh have much an' you stay here by me, usin' current, usin' food, drinkin' *my* rum, yuh muddacunt.' Rajan stood up suddenly, knocking over his chair. He strode to his bedroom, returning seconds later, holding a carrier bag.

He put his hands into it, pulled out a handful of notes, and threw them at Hero.

'Here, yuh muddacunt yuhself. See...see...I have money, boy, more money dan a damn gardener like you go make in a year... two years...three years...in all yuh damn life. Yuh a damn loser, boy, too stupid to make some *ting* a yuh life. Yuh live *here*, dis board shack, dis *hovel*, an yuh sweat so in de garden every day, an' everybody give yuh right as yuh walk by dey house...dey laughin' at yuh? Dey pityin' yuh? Wha' yuh tink? Damn loser... take de damn money. Tomorrow, I go be gone, an' yuh go get back to yuh little life.'

Tears of rage and of humiliation welled in Hero's eyes. If he had a gun, he would have shot Rajan there and then. If he'd had his cutlass, he would have lashed him. 'Go to hell,' he said and walked out of the back door to the space behind the house where he lay down in the hammock tied between two pillars. It was made of an old canvas sack and was grey with the grease and dirt of decades. The very same hammock used to hang under his father's house, the house in which he was born, and his father used to lie in it with him when he was a child. His father used to call him Boo Boo after Yogi Bear's companion, and Hero used to call his father Yogi.

'Dis damn life,' Hero said out loud to himself. 'Dis damn life.'

~ CHAPTER 34 ~

MAYBE IT WAS the pepper. Or the rum. Or the beer. Or their combined efforts to disrupt his digestive system during his fitful sleep that found Fingal sitting in the latrine, not daring to call his morning evacuation complete. The pain in his lower intestine felt like someone was twisting his bowel with an intent so vicious it felt persecutory, it felt like hell, and as the heat rose and the stench intensified, the jack spaniard wasps moved creepily around their nest in the corner of the wooden ceiling, no doubt eyeing him up for a sting or two. Bent double, Fingal stared at the floor as a lizard, its body about the length of his hand, its tail twice that size, fluorescent green with bulbous blue surrounds to its eyes, scuttled through a gap in one of the wooden boards, stood stationary inches from his feet, and swivelled its head, eyeing him impassively before darting off behind the plinth upon which he sat.

The food had been good – curry conch, same and peas, and sada roti – and Israel had prepared it all with a practised hand that made it look easy. They had sat back in the folding chairs afterwards, drinking beer and rum, looking at the night sky, and not saying much. Now it seemed Fingal was paying the price for something that hadn't agreed with him, or his body was telling him enough was enough, and it was time for scrambled eggs, mince and tatties, or a bacon roll and a cup of tea.

When he finally emerged, he saw his friend cutting off the top of a coconut with his cutlass. Israel looked up and smiled at Fingal, passing him the fruit and telling him to drink its water. With gratitude, Fingal raised the coconut to his mouth and poured, letting some of its juice trickle down his chin and onto his bare torso. Then, he went to take a shower. Beautiful as he found the country, he was beginning to tire of the heat, the mosquitoes, and the basic features of the house. Oh, to be in a hotel. Three or four stars would do – two, even. As he stood under the cold water, he began to sing:

Sometimes I feel like a motherless child,
Sometimes I feel like a motherless child,
Sometimes I feel like a motherless child,
Such a long way from home.

Sometimes I wish I could fly like a bird up in the sky,
Sometimes I wish I could fly like a bird up in the sky,
Sometimes I wish I could fly like a bird up in the sky,
Closer to my home.

He dried himself and put on shorts and a vest.

Sometimes I feel like freedom is near,
Sometimes I feel like freedom is near,
Sometimes I feel like freedom is near,
But we're so far…

He paused before speaking the last phrase, *so far from home.* Israel applauded. 'Sweet song, man.'

'You know it?'

'Yuh know.'

Fingal told him about a text message exchange with Goose first thing that morning. He had awoken, his head full of memories – the cottage in Scotland, its surrounding terrain, and of course, Phoebe and the grief he still felt when he remembered her – as if the past had been calling to him, reminding him it was always there and would never let him go. It made him feel dispirited and sad. Then, he read Goose's text message telling him the band had played the Man O' War in Soho, an unplanned gig arranged by Thabo, which they had all gone along with even though Goose had felt uncomfortable about it, and how the gig had gone well, how they were all wondering when he was coming back and whether he would return in time to rehearse before the tour.

His reply had been short and to the point: *It's cool I will be back soon,* but he actually felt a sense of insecurity for which he didn't know the source. The thought occurred to him that maybe the band didn't need him anymore. Then, of course, they did if they were going to continue playing blues, and they needed a singer to sing the blues. Maybe his insistence on keeping

263

traditional blues as an integral component to their music, the foundation upon which their sound had been built, was holding them back. Thabo's influence had shown him and the band they could play very well – and with an original sound – within a less rigid structure to their songs.

'How yuh feel 'bout dat?' asked Israel.

'Don't know.'

'It's *your* band, man.'

'Well...maybe. I've been the leader, I guess, but we're more of a kind of...a...a...collective, I guess...you know?'

'Sure, but it wha' yuh do, man? It's your ting.'

'Yeah, but you know, sometimes, being here, I don't really give a shit. Something about being here makes me just want to give it all up, just free myself of all of the...hassle, the stress of it all. All that performance, standing up there trying to pour my heart out to people I don't know, wanting them to like me, to love me...all that bullshit. We're good, but we ain't so good it matters if I'm there or not.'

'Yuh wah live *here*? Live like we?'

'Maybe, you know. Maybe I could just give it all up, live a natural life, get high, drink myself to oblivion.'

'Dat is stupidness. Life here eh easy, brother.'

'I know, I just...I don't know. I don't know why I'm here sometimes, but it's having a surprising effect on me.'

Israel jerked his head in the direction of the latrine. 'Sure is,' he said, and they both laughed.

The sun was getting high in the sky, casting a light so dazzling and clean it turned the trees in the forest to a lucid shining green, the spiked leaves of the coconut palms swaying and glittering like fingers sprinkling particles of white gold into the air. What wasn't there to like?

Fingal looked over at his friend, washing in the oil barrel, wringing out his locks and then swinging them behind his head before securing them in a ponytail. Israel walked towards him, drying his back as he approached. 'Yuh can get home real soon if yuh want.' Fingal looked at him quizzically, encouraging him to continue with the slightest jerk of his chin. 'We make progress, an' we have some information. Yuh go find she...tonight. I know whey she be.'

Fingal leapt up excitedly, smiling at his friend. 'Wow – that's amazing! Where is she? How do you know? Man, so many questions but...'

Israel gave him a crooked grin and gestured for him to calm down, telling him he would explain. 'She stayin' by a woman up by La Brea,' he said, 'an' we can go find her tonight.'

'Why do we have to wait?'

'It's complicated.'

'How?'

'Me eh know exactly, but it seem she maybe in some kinda trouble.'

Fingal felt a surge of adrenalin. 'What kind of trouble?'

'It have a next fellah who wah go find she, too – me eh know why, exactly – but he some kinda muddacunt, an' so it's necessary we careful.'

'Who is he, and why is he after Camille?'

'Me eh know.'

'Is she in danger?'

'Possibly.'

'Then why can't we go now?'

'Trust me...I have a plan, an' it jus' need we go follow it, den tings will be okay. Trust me nah, man.'

'I do trust you, but if she's in danger, then – '

'Den we go see she is okay. Doh worry nah, man. We go fix dis.'

Israel told Fingal as much of the plan as he decided he needed to know. He would collect Fingal from under the flamboyant tree opposite Neighbour's Bar around eight o'clock that evening, so he should go into the bar a little earlier and hang out as though everything was normal, but he should be mindful of who else was there. They would then drive to the house where he believed Camille to be staying. If all looked quiet, then they would just go and knock on the door and find her. 'If tings...complicated, den we will...we will deal wi' dat dey and den, okay?'

Fingal nodded without feeling that things were particularly okay, but he had no choice but to follow Israel's instructions. All of a sudden, things were coming to a head, and he couldn't help but feel nervous.

Israel went into the house and emerged a few minutes later, carrying two guns, one slightly smaller than the other, which he laid down on the table outside the house where Fingal was standing. 'Yuh ever use one a dem?' asked Israel. Fingal shook his head. 'Dis one here is a Beretta ninety-two, nine millimetre, semi-automatic. It loaded. It have fifteen rounds. Dis here is de safety catch. Yuh jus' turn it so...point, and pull de trigger.' He studied the look of horror on Fingal's face and made to reassure him. 'Look nah, man, dis just a precaution, yuh unnerstan' me? I have one, too, as yuh know, an' I eh expecting yuh to be involved if it come to me having to defend we...or de woman, but I wah yuh go carry dis when we reach de house she in, jus' in case. Is a last resort.'

Fingal nodded his assent, feeling he was making a pact with the devil.

~ CHAPTER 35 ~

WHILE ISRAEL DRESSED, Fingal sat at the table and pondered the situation he was now in, one that had accelerated to a point where, if he had felt outside of his comfort zone before, he now felt a million miles away from it. He watched the hummingbird all but disappear inside the hibiscus flower. Again, he asked himself what he was doing there. His love for Camille had never gone away no matter how hard he had tried to bury it, no matter that he had long accepted they were to lead separate lives and most likely never see each other again. So, why had he been so reckless in coming out here? To have made that fateful decision. At its most complicated, he had only ever anticipated speaking to the police, maybe the French embassy, perhaps having to check some of the hospitals. The worst-case scenario he had imagined was that she had been in some kind of accident and was injured, perhaps in hospital, waiting to recover before going home. He had often rationalised her disappearance as her being typically

Camille, suddenly cutting off contact as she dealt with whatever issues were troubling her at the time and not considering that others might be hurt by her behaviour or even concerned for her wellbeing. She was probably having a great time connecting with family, travelling round the island, and seeing the sights. Maybe she'd lost her phone or wasn't in signal range. Whatever the reason, he was probably a fool for thinking she would appreciate him turning up out of the blue at a time when she was discovering her roots and making a connection with her mother's homeland. But then, who was this other guy? Probably someone she'd had a fling with and then spurned, some other poor bastard who'd fallen under her spell only to have her walk away from him. Ha! They could compare notes if they ever met.

Then he considered the implications of Israel asking him to carry a gun. There had to be a good reason for it. So, there must be a real possibility of violence and of Camille – and them – being in a dangerous, possibly life-threatening situation. This was madness, he decided, but he knew he'd have to see it through. There was no escaping the nervousness he felt or the impulse to take flight.

'Doesn't the prospect of violence concern you?' he asked as Israel stepped out of the house wearing a smart shirt, jeans, and desert boots, his locks bundled into his leather Rasta cap. He smiled at Fingal.

'I prefer if it eh happen, but if it go happen, it go happen, an' I eh lookin' to be taken by surprise.'

'Couldn't we just tell the police...ask them to help?'

'Nah.'

It was a simple answer and said with enough conviction to convince Fingal to accept his friend's judgement and not ask about the police again. Things were different there, he knew that. Sometimes lines were blurred between those who were on the side of law and order, those who definitely were not, and those who straddled the two. He knew Israel was someone who lived on the edge of what was legal, who was prepared to do what had to be done, legal or not. The reassuring thing about him, though, was that he was moral, someone who clearly understood the difference between right and wrong and who appeared to have a deep, if unforgiving, sense of justice.

'Are you scared?' asked Fingal.

'Nah...nah so much scared as...preparing for de unknown. It make me be cautious.'

'But you're prepared to use violent means to...to...?'

'If somebody wah use violence on me, den yes, I prepare. Look, nah, man, I is a Rasta, me nah wah to do any *body*...any *ting* on dis earth...anyting bad, but yuh know too damn well it have wickedness an' evil in de world, an' if Babylon come to me, den me have to meet fire wi' fire, yuh unnerstan? Yuh get one damn life, an' boy, I go make sure I go look after it.'

'I get it. It just doesn't sit easily with me. I'm not as...I don't know – not as...confident...strong...I don't know.'

'Look...yuh needed me help to help yuh. Me eh know how tings turn out de way dey do, but now we in fuh de penny an' de pound. Yuh girl maybe in a li'l trouble so we go save she...simple. Anyways, maybe she cool nah, man, happy an' ting...nah worry... soon come.'

Israel went back into the house, returning a few moments later with two beers. He sat down. They chinked bottles in a gesture of friendship, Israel intending to make Fingal feel more confident. He studied his white friend, whom he had grown fonder of over the last few days. He knew he wasn't a gangster, knew he wasn't a natural fighter, but he liked the strength of character Fingal showed in other ways. His upbringing had been tough, sure, but it was more than that. He had refused to be conventional. He had stuck by his music despite it not making him that much money. He had led the band, written songs, and led the life of an artist when the world tended to frown upon those who chose such a path. He had the courage of his convictions and didn't mind being an outsider if it meant being true to his beliefs and his calling. That's where they were similar and why they got on. If he had been the kind of white man who thought he owned the place, the arrogant, condescending type of rich white people who buy property in the Caribbean or who just came as tourists and never tried to understand what real life was like there, then he would never have been his friend, would never have agreed to help him out on his mad adventure. Fingal was different. He was humble and intelligent, and he was colour-blind. Maybe blinded by love, though.

'Yuh ever read de Greek myths?' asked Israel.

'Some. A bit. I never really remember them, though. They're kind of complicated.'

'Yuh should. Dey teach me plenty.'

'How?'

'Dey show me how de world be...de nature a people...help me unnerstan why tings de way it is.'

'Go on...I'm listening.'

Israel took a gulp of beer then leaned back, putting his hands behind his head. He spoke with confidence, obviously enthused by the subject matter: 'If Pandora never open she jar den de human race would a live in harmony an' peace for all eternity, but de point is she did open it, an' den it mean we go deal with all de tings she release: lies, war, sickness, misery, an' more, like jealousy an' covetousness – '

'But then what about beauty, love, art, nature, the good things...what about them?'

'For sure, but she...Pandora, nah...she leave one ting behind in de jar, meant to be seal up forever.'

'What was it?'

'De very *las'* ting mankind need.' He chuckled. 'Hope. Hope, man. We can enjoy all a de good ting yuh talk about, but we also subject to de bad ting, an' dem too, an' if it have no hope, it mean de human race eh ever go change, an' we jus live with it, get on wi' tings. Trouble is dat hope make we wah for tings to be different when we could jus' accept tings de way it is, all de bad in de world all have a common factor an' dat is violence an' greed. It doh mean yuh have to be violent or a greedy man, but yuh have to know it dey an' know yuh cah eradicate it from de world. Rastafarians is men an' women a peace, yuh know, but all de persecution an' violence Babylon bring down on dem mean we have to defend we self, stand up for we rights, good over evil. Dem Greek gods an' dem...dey let we see we selves in de mirror, de intensity a we existence, so much of it beautiful an' so much a cruelty an' violence. To enjoy de beauty, yuh have to unnerstan de ugly. It doh mean I wah live a ugly life...a bad life. I doh wah shoot my gun, but if some fellah wah hurt me or me bredren and sistren, den I ready for he. Me always ready.' He paused for a few moments. 'But hope, man, de desire for tings to be different... dat is what fuck we up.'

Israel stood up, and confirmed the arrangements for later one more time. Then they shook hands brother-style. 'Doh worry, man,' he said again with a little chuckle.

After he left, Fingal showered before walking down to the beach. The tide was in, making it look as though the coconut palms that dotted the sand were growing out of the sea. They all leaned towards the horizon, the west, and reminded him of Anthony Gormley's sculptures at Crosby looking out in the same direction. *Another Place*, they were called, and the reason for their name suddenly became clear to him. He sat on a rock, smoked a few cigarettes, and looked towards Venezuela, its coastal hills blue on the horizon, the rigs in between like ghost ships, all of them flying flags of eternal flames that flickered into the air like the angry orange tongues of serpents.

He realised that all he had known so far had mostly been safe. Sure, there had been hard times, sometimes frightening, sometimes hurtful, sometimes confusing and unpredictable, but he had always felt the hard times would eventually end, that there was always the likelihood of better, calmer times. He had never really felt mortal before. Until now. Suddenly stripped of the comforts and privilege his life had afforded him, he was facing an unpredictable future in this, his immediate world, possibly one that held a threat graver than he had ever encountered before. And there was nothing to stop him from packing his bag, finding a ride to the airport, and checking in at a five-star hotel from where he could arrange a flight home. He could be there in a day or two, back in his London flat, back with his bandmates, back in his local pub with all its familiar faces and voices.

Weirdly, being there in the wilds of Trinidad, he had also been stripped of the persona so carefully constructed over the years by both his conscious and unconscious decision-making and his reactions to events – the guise that persona wore as he went about his life, the image he projected and the shield it provided. Where was the real person behind it all? If he were to peel off all the layers, what would he find? Would he find his true self?

He thought of the drunken man pawing at his mother's breast, saw her glazed eyes looking towards him, and then saw the long, meandering journey he had since embarked upon to reach the point he was at now. And all for what? To be sitting alone on a beach in a strange land, a gun in his pocket, and the prospect of the most *uncertain* contingency he had ever known. The past was pointless, the future more *unknown* than he had ever imagined. There he was, watching a vulture picking at a bloated dead fish washed up on the shore as the tide began to turn.

~ CHAPTER 36 ~

YVES SAUVETERRE LOOKED out from his third-floor apartment on Rue du Boccador in the 8th Arrondissement, and with a detached air, watched the lack of any significant rush-hour activity. There were few pedestrians because the road offered little advantage to them if they were trying to access *Avenue George V, Avenue Montaigne*, or the metro station at *Alma Marceau*. Likewise, car drivers would gain nothing from using the street as a shortcut, so all in all, it was a quiet district at all times of day and night, and this particular quality had appealed to him and Elma when they'd moved there in the mid-eighties.

They had lived in the 11th before that, an area they'd enjoyed and where they'd made a few friends among the locals, but Yves' career had progressed to the point where they could afford an apartment that offered considerably more space and comfort. He remembered how Camille had resisted the idea and sulked accordingly until she'd seen her bedroom-to-be, which was three times the size of her previous one and acquiesced, much to her parents' amusement.

How he wished Elma was with him now. He knew it was selfish of him to wish to share the burden, one that she was free from, but because he could not help but imagine the worst outcome to Camille's possible plight, not having the reassuring presence of Elma meant that his anxiety was a free-flowing current, gradually increasing in force and turbulence with endless swirls and whorls and eddies and undercurrents, each one threatening to carry him away and drown him.

He played *Canteloube's Chants D'Auvergne*, a go-to piece of music whenever he needed calm, the *Bailèro* having been one of Elma's favourites, even though she didn't understand the words, sung in the original Occitan. He had managed a rough translation, and the last verse made him weep as it often had done in the past:

Shepherd, the water divides us
And I can't cross it,
Sing bailèro lèro
Then I'll come down to find you.

And now, with Camille seemingly out of reach, he feared life itself and the state of complete aloneness that it could suddenly impose upon you when every reference point became either too insubstantial to offer any stability or, in the case of human relationships, all but disappeared. The fear it struck was that of being alive but without those you love, not being able to help them if they needed you, to have them suffer when you couldn't stop that suffering, to have them fearful and threatened when you couldn't protect them. But you couldn't protect someone from a brain aneurysm, one that lay hidden only to suddenly weaken and burst at random while she was taking a shower, but the thought he could never eradicate was how she'd felt in that instant, that microsecond – had she known what was happening? Had she felt any pain? Or fear? The thought of her suffering was unbearable. His impotence, his *failure* to protect her and comfort her, was the most human aspect of it all. We cannot hold hands forever. When he realised that aloneness, it made all the past seem futile and the future non-existent.

If Mireille hadn't called him, he might not even have realised Camille wasn't in the country, let alone missing, such was the nature of their relationship these days. No lack of love – an abundance of it, even – and underneath it all an unbreakable unspoken bond, but since his wife had died, the remoteness of his relationship with his daughter had become more apparent to him. As they stood at the graveside watching Elma's casket being lowered, Camille had slipped her arm through his and thus taken him with her to drop the yellow roses and handfuls of earth onto the coffin's lid. They had stood bound together, sharing a few moments of grievous reflection, and Yves, ever since then, had imagined that had been what the future held for them: father and daughter in an inseparable inosculation whose synthesis would become a barrier too formidable for anyone who might dare intrude. Including Philippe.

Bereft and suddenly cast into the empty space that for so many years Elma had filled with such love, energy and good-naturedness, Yves took comfort that his relationship with the daughter he adored remained intact and strong and was one he could look forward to experiencing at a level of fullness he hadn't enjoyed since she had been a young girl. It hadn't turned out that way, though, and it became apparent Camille had intended to just carry on living her life, watching out for her children, and sharing domestic space with her husband.

Yves admitted to himself that he had become jealous. As the first stages of grief had passed, they inevitably saw less of each other, and Camille had retreated gradually back to the way things had been before her mother's death. Yves wanted her back, and he had become possessive, angry, petulant, even, and he realised with self-admonishing clarity that his behaviour had driven her away.

He angrily blamed Philippe most of all, yet he also blamed Camille for choosing not to see the blind and desolate alley into which Philippe had led her. He also blamed the fates for taking Elma away from him so suddenly, leaving him unreconciled, which meant that much of life was now led in a state of dissonance with the forces surrounding him. He had tried in vain to reach out to Camille, to draw her back to him, but her marriage had stood resolutely in the way of that, whether in Yves' imagination, Camille's misguided loyalty, or Philippe's deliberate obstruction. When they did spend time together, he loved it so much he over-compensated, pressuring her to stay longer, visit more often, and inevitably, to be shot of her useless husband. In response,

Camille had displayed the kind of wilfulness and determination to do what she felt was right that he often displayed himself, and he both admired and castigated her for it. When Mireille had told him that Camille had left Philippe, it was the only silver lining to what was a disquieting and threatening cloud.

Thinking of his child and her current status of being incommunicado, possibly lost, possibly in trouble, and in Trinidad, of all places – not the laid-back safe zone of the colonial past but now, in his jaundiced view, a lawless, corrupt, and dangerous place – it had triggered his anxiety. It rippled violently through his body as though a boulder had been hurled into the calm waters of a mountain lake, inducing tears to well once again in his eyes. Eight years had passed since Elma's unexpected death had pulled life's rug from under his feet, leaving him feeling vulnerable, his hold on life tenuous and seemingly under threat from powerful forces he had never encountered before. How he missed them both now. It was a restless, gnawing feeling in the pit of his gut that could not be calmed.

He still had contacts in the diplomatic corps and was itching to use them, but Mireille had counselled against that for the time being and had told him of this unknown-to-him friend who was helping to find Camille. Who the hell was he? And why wasn't Philippe, the useless bastard, flying out there to help find her? And why did Camille go in the first place? Foolish, wilful, hot-headed girl. He smiled at the thought of her doing something that everyone would have advised against. Typical Camille. He spoke out loud to himself, *'Rentre bientôt, cherie.'* Come home soon, darling, please come home.

The doorbell rang, and he looked into the screen above the security panel by the entrance door to see Mireille. He buzzed her in without speaking, and a couple of minutes later, she was knocking on the door.

Mireille felt tiny as she sank into one of the opulent armchairs in the living room and watched Yves as he poured two cognacs without asking if she wanted one. He sat down opposite her, leaning forward, stroking his brandy glass and looking her in the eyes. He told her to tell him all she knew and to not hold back on any details. She didn't believe he meant to be intimidating, but then again, perhaps he knew exactly what he was doing and wanted to convey the fact he was likely to take control if whatever she told him wasn't enough to satisfy his need for accurate information and his understandable sense of foreboding. In telling him what she knew – which, on the face of it, was very little – she actually began to wonder if she had overreacted.

The only evidence she had was that Camille hadn't contacted her for several days, having promised that she would do so every day, nor had she responded to any other form of communication, of which Mireille had tried the lot: phone calls, emails, text messages, Twitter messages, Messenger messages, and WhatsApp calls and messages. The simple explanation could be that she had lost her phone, and being where she was, was having trouble replacing it or getting it repaired.

'She could have called from a hotel,' suggested Yves.

'She might be staying somewhere else. She mentioned an aunt.'

'There's only one aunt out there, and she was...mad. Jo... Tanty Jo. No one knows if she's even alive let alone where she lives. I can't believe Camille would have been able to find her. So, tell me about this Fingal...who the hell is he?'

'He's a musician, and – '

'A *musician*, for fuck's sake. How does she know him?'

'She met him when he was playing a gig in Paris – '

'A *gig*, for fuck's sake. What kind of musician?'

'Yves, it doesn't matter. He's a good guy. She trusted him. They...they...' She hesitated to tell Camille's father a secret only she knew. What would Camille think of her if she did?

'They had an affair,' asserted Yves.

Mireille nodded. 'It was a loving relationship,' she said. 'He is an honourable man. I thought...I hoped she might leave Philippe for him, but she broke it off. Broke his heart, I think.'

'So why *him*? What can *he* do to find her?'

'He's been there before and knows the place,' she exaggerated, 'knows people there who can help.'

'We should call the police. I can phone the French Embassy.'

'I called the police, and they've opened a file but said there was little they could do. They would check the hospitals and get back to me if they found out anything. Let's give him a couple more days. He told me he was making progress.'

'I mean the French police. Mireille, I am going out of my mind with worry, and I can't...' He stood up and turned away from her so she wouldn't see his tears, but he released a guttural sob, betraying his feelings of grief and desperation.

Mireille stood and went to him, placing her hand on his lower back, patting him in sympathy and reassurance. 'She is strong. She will be okay, Yves. We will find her.'

'And I want to kill Philippe.'

'I went to see him. He's so useless – don't waste your energy on him.'

'That bastard should be out there looking for her.'

'Believe me, Fingal is a better option for that. Camille walked out on Philippe, and he's probably the last person she wants to meet over there.'

Yves swallowed his cognac in one. 'Keep me up to date with what this Fingal is doing. If we hear nothing by tomorrow, we have to take some more serious action, and I will use my contacts to put pressure on the police there.'

Mireille looked at her text messages as though to demonstrate her capacity to stay in touch with Fingal, a man she barely knew herself. She re-read the last exchange with him that had taken place a few hours previously:

– there's been a breakthrough maybe, I'll know more tonight/tomorrow

– is she ok???

– as far as I know yes but no details

– what about the police?

– shouldn't be necessary, theyre not to be trusted apparently, my friend here reliable

– let me know as soon as you know something, her father is very worried, so am I

– I know, I'll let you know as soon as I do

– take care

– x

Now, she faced the dilemma of whether or not to tell Yves of this particular, albeit vague, development. She decided not to.

~ CHAPTER 37 ~

HOW CAN YOU smell in dreams? And it was such a sweet smell, one she loved – wet leaves on a forest floor in late autumn or winter with all their musty decay and earthiness – the headiness of which fuelled Camille's perception as she dreamed of *Le Forêt de Retz* and walking there with her parents when she was a child. That smell of the leaves, thick and damp upon the paths, as she picked chestnuts and acorns from the forest floor and filled her pockets. Sitting on a fallen tree trunk with her mother, who looked so pretty and kind as she gazed down at her and held her hand. *'Maman...veux-tu me tenir la main pour toujours?'* she'd asked.

'Yes, child, I will always hold your hand...forever. Even when you grow up, I will still do that.'

She'd run ahead of them along one of the trails in her pink puffa jacket, woolly tights, and walking boots, her curly hair blown behind her by the strengthening wind. *'Papa...Maman... vous ne pouvez pas m'attraper!'* she'd cried as she'd ran.

'Coming to get you!' shouted her mother.

Camille had hidden behind a large oak and waited, panting, her breath billowy and damp and rising towards the branches. She couldn't hear their footsteps – where had they gone? They *must* be coming soon – and as she'd waited, the smell of the wet leaves and rotting chestnuts had overpowered her senses, making her feel sleepy. She had to stay awake so she could jump out from behind the tree and surprise them, but she'd felt so very tired, she'd closed her eyes and felt the irresistible force of sleep entrench her, pulling her down into unconsciousness and away from her beloved Papa and Maman. Where *were* they? She'd forced herself awake as though struggling out of a morass, feeling the alertness of fear.

Camille opened her eyes to look upon the gentle, perfect curve of a mons pubis with its tuft of untamed hair inches from her face as she breathed in an unmistakable aroma. She eased herself up into a sitting position and looked down at the now naked Lola, who, as she slept, emitted delicate puffs of air from her mouth as though she were blowing kisses. Camille wondered at what she might have slept through. She was still clothed, and although puzzled, she smiled indulgently at her sleeping companion, amused at her boldness and stark disregard for convention. It was all so intriguing, undoubtedly alluring, and thrilling, too, if she could only allow herself to think so.

Leaving Lola asleep on the floor, Camille went to stand on the overhanging gallery and looked out over the sea. More pelicans flew past, heading south. She recalled her dream and felt the

sadness it had induced. I must call Papa, she told herself. He will
be worried if I haven't returned his calls. Maybe he thinks I'm
missing. I will call him first and then Mireille as soon as possible.
The boys, too. I must ask Tanty Jo where I can go to make the
call. Maybe I should go back to the hotel to collect my luggage,
my phone, and my passport. So many maybes. What on earth
has happened to me? Why am I here? What am I supposed to do?

She walked back over to Tanty Jo's house.

Tanty Jo was in her garden, picking petals from a yellow
hibiscus bush, placing them in a wicker basket she had hooked
over her arm. The petals looked like soft-hued shavings of gold,
thought Camille.

Tanty Jo turned at her approach. 'Yuh dream?' she asked.

'How do you know?'

'I see it in yuh eyes. Dream good or dream bad?'

'Started good...finished bad. Papa and Maman, they – '

'Yuh dream yuh mother an' father?'

'Yes, but they – '

'Couldn't find yuh. Yuh lost.'

'How do you know?'

'Me see it.'

'Do you know what it means?'

'Chil', it can mean many ting. Yuh mus' wait before yuh can
tell exactly wha' it try go tell yuh, but it...*dey*...dey tryin' to tell
yuh some ting.'

'I was scared. It felt like something wanted to take me away
from them. I made myself wake up.'

'Difficult?'

'What?'

'To wake up from de dream?'

'Yes. It was like being possessed or something,' said Camille, looking like she couldn't quite believe she was having such a conversation.

'Yuh wondrin' how me know all a dem tings?'

'Yes, it's so strange.'

'Yuh doh need to worry, chil'. Dey plenty good spirits lookin' over we.'

They were standing at the front door, and before entering, Tanty Jo put down her basket and took hold of both of Camille's hands, and looking her sternly in the eyes, spoke in the most serious tone Camille had heard her use. 'Girl, I need yuh go do someting for me.'

Camille felt scared but answered, 'Okay.'

'Me need yuh to go and wake Lola and tell she to come by we as soon as she can. Tell she me wah she to stay by we for de whole evenin' and de night...maybe even de next day...so she need to lock she door an' window an' pack clothes an' ting – not that it seem she like to wear dem – and she cutlass.'

'Is everything okay? You're scaring me.'

'Everyting go be good, girl. Yuh may tink dis all of a stupidness...and maybe it so...but I feel I need the two of yuh here. Me feel we jus' need to be together for a li'l while. Go nah. Tell she.'

Tanty Jo went back into the house and collected a bottle of Puncheon rum and a bowl of uncooked rice, which she scattered around the outside of the house, dousing it with the rum and repeating the phrase, 'Feed good ones and do my work,' as she did. Then, she took a stick of chalk from her pocket and drew a circle on the wooden floor of the gallery in front of the door. In the middle of the circle, she drew three stick people around a cross. Then, she went back inside to fetch three pairs of kitchen scissors she kept in her bedroom. She hung them, open and pointing downwards, from hooks attached to a piece of wood screwed to the wall above the interior doorframe.

As the day hurriedly descended towards dusk, Lola and Camille walked back together, carrying a couple of carrier bags holding some of Lola's clothes and toiletries, and they saw Tanty Jo encircling the house with the hibiscus petals she had gathered earlier, leaving a gap at the front gallery through which she ushered them. Once all three of them were inside the house, Tanty Jo completed the circle with the remainder of the petals and closed the front door.

Looking at the scissors, Camille asked, 'Tanty...why are you doing these things?'

Tanty Jo smiled and said, 'I go tell yuh jus' now,' as she went to the cupboard beneath the shrine to the Black Madonna. She brought out the skull of a small animal and placed it on a table so that it faced the front door. 'De cat have a watchful spirit,' she said before addressing her dead dog. 'An' Rocky boy, let we know if anybody come.'

Lola and Camille sat down next to each other at the dining table, and Lola, evidently scared, took Camille's hand. 'Wh'appen?' she asked.

Tanty Jo sat down opposite them and held their hands so that the three of them were linked together. She smiled a reassuring and benevolent smile and spoke softly and calmly, 'Every ting is okay, an' yuh have no need to worry. Tings though maybe a li'l strange. Camille, since yuh reach, chil'...that yuh reach by me *at all* is strange, in truth...it tell me some *ting* happenin' to yuh, maybe to all a we, an jus' like Lola, yuh reach here for a reason, an' de signs are dis hadda be de right ting to happen, so everyting go be good, but maybe...an' only maybe...dey be some kinda ting we have to go through before every ting is real okay. Dey been signs – '

'What signs?' asked Camille, her eyes wide and fearful.

'Me eh know for sure, but first de sea duck – so many a dem flying so.' She swept her arm across an imaginary sky. 'Den, de bush fly swarmin' around yuh face.' She nodded towards Camille. 'Den, de two fowl peckin' dey beaks. Maybe dat was to let me know yuh reach, but maybe dey tryin' to tell me more... me eh know. De candle flicker when it eh have no breeze, den yuh dream a yuh mother an' father an' someting tryin' to take hold a yuh. Den de black cock, he lookin' me in de eye jus' so.' She cocked her head and gave a wide-eyed stare. 'Me eh know, but if anyting bound to happen, it bound to happen soon, so I tink it better to be safer dan sorry, so me ask de spirits to protect we – '

'The petals and the scissors?'

'Me eh know if dey go do anyting, but if we have visitor an' dey know anyting about obeah, den dey maybe scared a dem, an' if dey mean no harm den it not a problem to we or to dem, but me serious, children, me eh know.' Then she chuckled and sang:

'Since me born
Me nebber de know
Crapaud is wear shirt and pants.
Since me born
Me nebber de know
Crapaud is going to dance.'

She lifted all their hands into the air and said, 'De Lord is we shepherd, an' it have salt fish an' tomato an' hard food to eat, so let we eat.'

'Hard food?' queried Lola.

'Ground provision,' answered Camille.

'Ground provision?'

Tanty Jo cackled. 'Cassava, eddoes, dasheen, an' green fig.'

'Fig?'

'Banana!' said Camille and Tanty Jo in unison, making them all laugh.

~ CHAPTER 38 ~

AS SOON AS the sun set, mosquitoes in their hundreds, until now happy buzzing the surface of an adjacent pond, swarmed into the space at the back of the house with a blind and ravenous frenzy. Rajan slapped his neck and arms as some settled on his skin to feed, and he eyed Hero, lying in his hammock, with contempt. 'It like yuh live in a swamp,' he said.

'Eh?'

'Damn mosquitoes.'

'Dey eh botherin' me.'

'I never unnerstan why, in all a nature, it have mosquitoes.'

Hero turned to face his houseguest, and propping his head on one hand, addressed him: 'Is because dey serve a purpose.'

'Wha' purpose? Wha *you* know about de purpose dey serve? Dey come like a vermin. Dey serve no purpose at all at all.'

'Oh, yuh be surprise. Dey does pollinate. De birds an' de bats eat dem an' crapaud eat dey larva an' fish, too, does eat dey larva an' – '

'Yuh talkin' shit. Wha' yuh know about dem tings?'

'De mosquito – it name so because it be de Spanish word for little fly. It have three an' a half thousand species, an' dey be more danger to humanity dan de shark or de snake. Maybe one million people die every year from mosquito disease. Each female lay maybe one thousand eggs, an' de *aedes aegypti*, it have plenty a dem here, carry de dengue and yellow fever. An' another ting –'

'Enough a yuh stupidness. Dirty people live in dirty house, an' mosquito like to live in dirty house.'

'Dem eh botherin' me.'

'Well, dey bother me.'

'Dey like yuh sweat, an' boy, yuh sweatin' now.'

Rajan looked at Hero and tried to convey both threat and superiority, but Hero just smirked back at him. Rajan cut a long line of cocaine on the back of a magazine. He snorted half into one nostril and took a deep breath before snorting the rest into the other. Sniffing exaggeratedly, he again observed his host, and with all the disdain he could muster, said, 'Hammock is a lazy man ting.' He rose from the table as though he had just delivered a final blow, a brilliant concluding riposte that would stun his opponent into silence and demonstrate his higher intellect and social status.

'An' cocaine is a loser man ting,' said Hero.

Enraged, aroused, and red in the face, looking as though he was chewing a stale crust of bread flavoured with lemon peel as his mouth twisted and gurned, Rajan stood over the hammock and shouted, his spittle a shower of rancour and indignation that made Hero protect his face with his hands, giving an impression of a fear he actually didn't feel at all.

'Me a loser, man?' shouted Rajan. '*Me?* Yuh joke. Look at yuh. *You* de loser, man. *You* de nobody, yuh hear me? Watch yuh damn mouth, yuh stink li'l muddacunt. After tonight is me back at de top an' *you?* Yuh still go be here in yuh shit house an' shit clothes an' yuh damn mosquitoes, an'...an'...yuh best remember me an' de people I know. Yuh best show me some respect, yuh damn muddacunt, like a lot a people go have to show me nah. Yuh nobody...nobody! An' I is de very opposite of yuh. I have friends...contacts. I have money like yuh never go see, so who de loser, eh? Who de damn loser now, muddafucker? Yuh go see. After tonight, Rajan Ramkissoon, de prince back on he throne.'

With that, he went inside to bathe. As he poured water from a bucket over his body with a plastic cup and washed himself with an exaggerated vigour and thoroughness, he started to plan the evening ahead. He would shave with precision and leave just a goatee and pencil-thin moustache. It was a shame he didn't have his expensive aftershave with him, but he did have his Lynx deodorant, and he would dress well and look smart and eye-catching, so when he saw that bitch again, she would know what she was missing, know he was a man of class, someone to be taken seriously, and then he would show her who was the boss. He would have his way with her and scare her so much she would never do anything to betray him. How dare she try to humiliate him? He would leave her in no doubt that if she messed with him again, she would suffer the consequences. Bitch, take that! He imagined striking her across the face, punching her in the mouth, and the thought aroused him so much that an erection started to grow. He looked down at it and smiled. And then, once he was finished with her, he would call round to see Dog and give him the money, shake hands, and discuss future arrangements, maybe even a partnership.

After dressing and preening in front of the mirror, Rajan took another line of cocaine. It was still too early to go to La Brea, so he decided to head to Neighbour's Bar. He put the money, still in plastic carrier bags, into the boot of his car and thought about his next move. If he parked down the track opposite the bar, no one would notice, but on second thoughts, he didn't care anymore if he bumped into anyone from his family because he could now tell them that everything with Dog was okay again, and they didn't have to worry anymore because he had sorted things out and demonstrated how he could be relied upon and trusted to do right by the business and the family. In fact, that night was a night to celebrate. By the next day, everything was going to be so sweet. So, he would park right outside the bar and show the whole village he was back.

The bar was busy, and there were no spaces to park in front, so he pulled up over the road. He saw someone sitting under the flamboyant tree, smoking a cigarette. It was the white man, the one with the tattoos and earrings, the one he had seen with the Rasta outside the church. Who de hell he? he wondered. But he eh lookin' like a fed, so who cares? Me eh no worries about he.

Neighbour wasn't there, but her husband, Kelvin, nodded a silent and cursory greeting from behind the grille as Rajan walked into the bar. He looked around him at the familiar faces, most of whom he had known all his life, all of them drinking, talking, shouting, and laughing. Losers, every damn one a yuh, he thought.

Kelvin jerked his head at Rajan by way of asking what he wanted to drink. 'Vodka,' he said. Kelvin passed a bottle of Swedish vodka, a jug of water, and a glass through the grille. Rajan poured a couple of fingers, downed it in one, and chased it with some water. 'Who he?' he asked, jerking his head over the road and pouring himself another drink.

'Who who?'

'De white man dey...under de tree.'

'Wha' tree?'

'De tree dey. Over de road.'

'Me eh know. Some fella.'

'Which part he does stay?'

'Me eh know.'

Larry walked into the bar with his loping gait and swinging arms and a smile for everyone. He bought two Pilsners, and with the air of someone who was party to some important information, said, 'He a writer. He doin' some kinda research. Nice fella.'

Rajan ignored Larry but took in what he had said. Eh nothing for me to worry about there, then, he thought, as Larry walked across the road with the two beers.

~ CHAPTER 39 ~

THERE HAD BEEN simpler times. On that very site where he now stood next to the julie mango tree – the very same tree from which he had picked mangos as a boy – Radhesh Ramkissoon could still bring to mind, like ancient snapshots of a life gone by, the first board house his father had built. Supported by timber stilts of no more than three feet in length, the three-roomed structure – one bedroom, a sitting area, and a kitchen – made entirely of wooden boards save for the roof, which had originally been of carat leaf but had been replaced after a few years by galvanised iron – was the not so proud family home where his parents and he, the eldest of nine children – the first four of which all lived there – had existed in relative comfort and peace for the first six years of his life.

Progress came sometime around independence in 1962, when Britain had allowed Trinidad and Tobago to manage their own affairs and finally break free from centuries of colonial occupation. Optimism and excitement pervaded the up-until-then acquiescent culture of its people as they – like teenagers on the cusp of adulthood getting the keys to their front doors or their first cars, or bringing home their first wages – took their first baby steps towards what they believed was true independence, shaking off their colonial shackles while remaining grateful and reverent towards their former masters. It was an over-egged gratitude and reverence that remained to that day and hampered cultural and economic progress even though those masters had, in effect, long ago washed their political and judicial hands of their former slaves and indentured labourers, even though they still, through economic and corporate imperialism, maintained control over what remained vastly profitable natural resources: sugar, to a degree, and oil to a much greater degree.

The building of a new house on the site where the old board house had stood seemed fittingly symbolic of a hard-working, god-fearing, honest family looking to make their way in the brave new world of the 1960s. It was a much larger building, one now connected to an electricity supply, still constructed from wooden boards and galvanised iron, three bedrooms, a large kitchen, and an even larger sitting area, now supported by ten-foot-high concrete pillars, thus creating a wide space beneath the house for life to manifest itself in all its noise and hullabaloo. It was where hammocks swung, dogs barked, cockerels crowed, and children played, where dhal was ground, coconut grated, and paratha was buss up shot, where the extended family gathered to play cards, play cricket with a tennis ball and a coconut branch for a bat, celebrate births, christenings, and other Christian festivals, Hindu celebrations for the lights of Diwali, the powdered paint throwing of Phagwa, all sorts of pujas for which another jhandi flag would be placed in the ground, birthdays and weddings, and to mourn the dead in wakes that lasted days and nights, and in forty-day prayers and one-year prayers, where, throughout it all, they ate their fill and drank even more.

The village was a place where mutuality meant survival, where cooperation and neighbourliness meant no one starved. Yes, there were rivalries and jealousies, feuds and fights, affairs and curses, but like some independent living organism – each family constituting a vital (some more vital than others) organ that worked for the good of the whole, that couldn't, or so it seemed at the time, have survived without its counterparts up and down Moncoeur Road, the lively stretch of potholed pitch they all called home – the village in its own way thrived.

When the standpipes were replaced by large water tanks filled by the water company on a regular basis, it was a cause for wonder, gratitude and reverence. When mains water arrived, and showers were taken for pleasure rather than necessity, the village finally felt it was a part of the modern world, even if the electric current maddeningly cut out without warning sometimes, suddenly plunging them into darkness or defrosting their freezers without anyone knowing when or if it would return.

When the first telephone had been installed at the home of Steven 'Semi-Colon' (so nicknamed following an operation to remove a part of his intestine) Seepersad and his wife, Avril, aka Bouncy (because she never liked to wear a bra), it caused some amusement, as they were one of the poorest families in the village. Nevertheless, some friends and neighbours had popped round under the pretext of wanting to borrow something just to see the contraption, maybe be invited to hold it to their ears just to hear its dial tone, while others actually wanted to make calls, handing over the few dollars Semi-Colon had estimated the call to cost, clutching numbers scrawled on scraps of paper and shouting down the receiver when connected to some distant relative in Toronto, New York or London – 'Yuh hearin' me? It's me. Yuh hear me? Hello? Hello? Yuh hearin' me?' When the phone had been disconnected by the operators due to the Seepersads not having paid their bill, and not actually realising they had to pay it, no one seemed to mind that Semi-Colon and Bouncy had kept their friends' money for themselves rather than put it towards the payment. For a while, again, there were no phones in the village, but gradually, those, too, became commonplace.

In time, his brothers had left to build their own homes, where they would raise their families or, in the case of his three sisters, to marry local men and have children of their own, leaving Radhesh to run the house and the now substantial plot of land it sat within, allowing him the space to marry Faith – who, over the next few years, would bear four children, one of whom had died in childbirth – and move in her ageing and bossy mother.

When the day had come to break down the house once more in order to build the Pink Palace sometime around the turn of the century, Radhesh, although proud of the way he had built up the family business from one that sold home-grown vegetables at the market to one that was now a thriving local supermarket, an elevated social status achieved by wealth alone had never been one of his aspirations. In fact, it had been something that had made him uneasy – to be the subject of gossip, envy, and ridicule from those who coveted their neighbour's wealth, most of whom he'd known all his life and most of whom he'd considered to be friends – and so, he'd resisted, for all of a day, the idea that the house should be painted pink on the outside. Faced with the unified fervour of his wife, mother-in-law, and youngest daughter who were all *pro* pink and the indifference of his lazy son and heir and his sensible daughter (who had married and moved out) he'd given in. Give dem what dey want, he thought, if it go make dem happy. But all those ghosts, all that ghostly noise and bacchanal of the past had gone, never to return.

Like de macaws, he thought, looking at the dead and hollow coconut tree that stood in the middle of what had once been bush and was now a part of their garden. It had housed mating macaws for decades until, in trying to rob the nest of its chicks for what would have been a short-lived monetary gain, two hapless thieves had broken the two unhatched eggs on the ground as they'd missed catching them from the nest they had tipped over with a piece of scaffolding pole. For the next two days, the parent macaws sat in the adjacent chataigne tree, squawking in grief and incomprehension at man's vulgarity and arrogance. The macaws, symbolic of the old ways, never returned.

Radhesh trudged up the back steps and into the kitchen where he poured himself a Puncheon rum, squeezed the juice of half a lime into it, and knocked it back in one. Then, he had another one and soon felt its heat course through him. 'Who de hell have de idea to make a rum so strong?' he wondered, looking at the label on the bottle. 'Seventy-five per cent proof an' de cause a so much argument an' fightin' an' wife-beatin'... me eh know, but it hit de spot okay. Me jus' eh sure which damn spot it hit.'

He had one more, telling himself it would be his last one that night before joining Faith and Kajri on the sofa in the sitting room where they were watching television. It was a hot night. Sweat beaded across his forehead and dripped from his armpits.

Faith turned to look at him. 'Yuh drinkin' rum,' she said, not as a query but a statement of a fact, one laced with disapproval.

They were watching reruns of *The Honest Honestest Truth*, and Radhesh couldn't be bothered to follow it – some story of a policewoman who is mad and can't stop herself from stealing while she tries to solve crimes – but he stayed quiet, trying to find some comfort in the bosom of his family, though a bosom, he couldn't help but think, that was not as welcoming and comfortable as it once had been. Everyone seemed to be separate from one another, even he and Faith. Everyone was just going about their own business. The spirit of a collective, one body with all its connected parts working towards the common aim of prosperity, security, and wellbeing, was dissipating like the smoke from a fire drifting on the breeze away out of reach.

He knew why, as leader of the pack, he had to bear some responsibility. 'Why had de boy turned out so?' was a question he had asked himself many times over recent years, and all his cajoling, encouraging, arguing, berating, and beating had made no difference. In fact, he admitted with an emerging and unfamiliar reluctance, like that of a miscreant who suddenly sees the error of his ways that maybe he had it wrong where

306

the boy was concerned, treating him too harshly, expecting too much of him. Maybe he should have been more nurturing.

He remembered the boy when he'd been a boy, a skinny, shy thing who was more interested in feeding the fowl than playing cricket, who, when the family had gone on a beach lime, would sit in the shade by himself, playing with sticks and stones rather than joining in the small-goals football games his father had dominated with his loud voice berating the players around him. It was the same boy who'd seemed scared of the world, who had been called *Raja* by his mother, as if he was a little prince – she'd even called him Prince as a nickname. The same child who hadn't seemed to have a brain for schoolwork, who hadn't seemed to make friends easily, and who'd witnessed the one and only occasion his father, drunk at the time, had struck his mother across the face in order to conclude an argument in the most brutal of ways, demonstrating that even the most stable structures sometimes crack.

All these excuses aside, the teenage version of Rajan had been a problem; his behaviour and language – aggressive and foul-mouthed all too often – had an unsettling effect on the whole family. Surly and withdrawn in the early part, mouthy and defiant as he'd grown physically stronger, he had clashed so often with his father and taken so many beatings from him that their relationship never matured into something even vaguely functional. And yet, because he'd been a boy, the only boy, Radhesh believed Rajan had to be the one who would take over the business, and so he'd set about grooming his son for the role. The first mistake had been to show him the books, show him how much profit could be made, how much money had to be banked each week, and how much had to be hidden away. He'd recalled the astonished look on Rajan's face when he'd realised his family's wealth in terms of dollar signs and bank balances.

The second mistake had been to encourage the cutting of costs wherever possible and by whatever means when purchasing wholesale goods. 'Look for de bargain,' he'd told him. 'Go be on de good side of the importers, but never trust dem... an' look for deals that make we a quick profit, preferably so dey eh bound to go into de books. Doh leave a trail, an' move easy an' confident so people take yuh serious and tink dey can rely on yuh. Doh get in no debt, an' doh offer credit to nobody.'

It had become apparent early on that Rajan had neither the brains nor the patience for the financial minutiae of running an expanding business, but he did seem to show a flair for finding cheap stock, striking deals, and building up a network of new contacts. At first, it had been impressive and reassuring. Maybe he had found his niche, something he was finally good at. The books and the staff could be managed without him because Khalisha had been showing an aptitude for that side of the business, and Radhesh himself still had a few years to go before retirement and so could exercise the necessary control as and when the need arose. But that confidence all too quickly weakened, turning into doubt and disquiet, a nagging anxiety-provoking suspicion that something wasn't right. Now, all hell had broken loose. Radhesh admonished himself for not handling the boy better and for not stepping in to manage the situation when he suspected it might be getting out of control. Where was the solution?

If the boy came home and demonstrated he had got the gangsters off their backs, if he started to be responsible, if he stopped the late nights and the drinking, the cussing of his wife and sisters, if he would just damn well settle down and work hard and accept there are no short cuts in life and that if you're prepared to graft, then you'll reap the rewards. Radhesh felt the world was now his burden sitting squat upon his shoulders and weighing him down. He glanced at Faith and Kajri, the former trying to keep her eyes open and the latter filing her nails, and for the first time in his life, he felt a despair so deep and affecting that he questioned both his ability to carry on and whether or not the whole bacchanal was worth it.

I'll give de boy a few days more, he told himself. Den, if he eh come home, I will go find him, talk to him man to man, an' see if we cah find de solution to all a dis. He couldn't stand the soap opera anymore, so he returned to the kitchen, saw the Puncheon bottle on the worktop, contemplated it for a while, and muttered out loud to himself, 'Ah, what de hell.'

~ CHAPTER 40 ~

FINGAL RESTED THE fedora on his knees as he smoked a cigarette. He liked sitting there under the flamboyant tree, watching a small part of that small part of the world go by. He felt a little nervous, but at the same time, he rationalised away his fears by telling himself how unlikely it was that anything would go wrong, that Israel was not a man who took risks or acted impulsively. Israel was a careful – even calculating – man whose friendship was genuine, as was his regard for their safety, but over the last few days, Fingal had realised that the fundamental differences between them were stark. Israel was the weary, battle-hardened warrior who gave shit to nobody but never took it from anybody either, and Fingal, himself the life-weary artist, who could – until now, he noted – always take the easy option to avoid risk and hardship. One of them hard as steel, the other more pliable, one sure of himself, the other less so. Some men were fighters; some men described the fight. Both, though, were self-reliant and principled, detested bullshit

311

and insincerity, and had rejected many of society's norms and expectations. And they both loved to feel carefree, to laugh, drink, and smoke weed under a starry sky.

Then there was the land, the country, which had taken him by surprise with its untamed beauty, its extraordinarily rich cultural mix and history, its tough, honest, un-neurotic people who called it as it was and took you for who you were, all of which was in contrast to its harshness of climate, its apparent lawlessness, incomplete infrastructure, sometimes corrupt administration, propensity for casual violence, drunkenness, argument, and a weird combination of both reverence and bitterness towards the white man. None of that multiplicity was in the holiday brochures that showed tanned white couples clutching cocktails and showing off their perfect bodies as they strolled on some white-sanded beach along the edge of a turquoise sea, grinning inanely as they attempted to show us just how *fab* life could be.

Luxuriant in flora and fauna, complex, chaotic, languorous, and excitable in the way it went about its business, Trinidad was far from being a simple place. If he wasn't on his madcap mission to rescue a woman who might not need rescuing and rekindle the unquestionably deep relationship he'd had once had with her – that neither of them now might actually want or be suited to – he would have liked to travel the island to get to understand it more. Was he on a righteous path? He had no doubt of that as he remembered his instinctive reaction to Mireille's initial message – he had to act, he had felt compelled to put everything aside in order to respond, as though his unconscious mind had, at last, found a rationale his conscious mind could accept and once more be in pursuit of love. It even felt as though it could be his last chance to establish that particular force in his life; she meant that much to him.

The severing of contact had taken such an effort on his part to sustain. The denial that had followed – and with it the emotional turmoil and self-loathing – had once more threatened to cause him irreparable damage as if a desperate old friend had turned up at his door, giving him no choice but to let them in and then allowing them to drain away his life force as they emptied his cupboards and overstayed their welcome. Suppressing what is natural – be it hunger, talent, or emotion – can only result in a troubled spirit, he knew that. Its persistent noise had to be drowned out by numbing his senses, and its nagging presence had to be elbowed aside with an ever-increasing effort. Their connection had been so strong, undeniably so, but when it had come to the crunch, she had denied it, negated it, and reduced it to something base and inconsequential, when he *knew* she had experienced the same as him but wouldn't allow herself to believe it was real. *Or* he had completely misread her, and she was more shallow than he believed. She had seduced him, knowing that she would discard him at a later date, a new accessory worn until its novelty had lost its shine with familiarity, a trinket she no longer favoured. *Or* she just wanted to be unencumbered and unhindered by yet another relationship with a man when she knew, maybe unconsciously, that she was about to change her life irrevocably and make one of those decisions from which there would be no going back.

He remembered Israel had told him to hang out at the bar for a while, but he couldn't summon up the energy it took to face down the self-consciousness he felt as a stranger surrounded by curious and watchful locals, not always able to understand what they were saying to him, and just wanting to be anonymous and unnoticed. Maybe if Rosa had been there, it would have been easier, but he hadn't seen her, so he lit another cigarette and sat there, watching the liveliness over the road, happier to be an observer than a participant.

A car pulled up opposite the bar. A thin, young Indian man in smart clothes emerged and glanced at him before walking over to join the throng. Fingal had seen him somewhere before. The church – he had been parked there after dropping off an old lady.

Flicking his cigarette butt into the road, he noticed Larry approaching the tree. Larry cocked his pork-pie hat, gave Fingal a gap-toothed grin, and handed him one of the beers. 'Thanks. Good to see you,' said Fingal.

'No problem.'

'You okay?'

'I good. Yuh eh comin' to de bar? Yuh lookin' like yuh waitin'.'

'Yeah, I'll come over in a little while, but yes, I'm waiting on a friend. We're going...erm we're going out. San Fernando,' he improvised.

'De Rasta fellah?'

'Yes.' Everyone knows everything, he thought.

'I could join yuh.'

'In San Fernando?'

'Nah.' Larry cackled. 'Here. Under de tree.'

'Of course.'

When they'd finished their beer, Fingal suggested they go over the road so he could return the favour and buy Larry one. While walking in a few heads turned, but it seemed as though people were getting accustomed to seeing him. Conscious of the gun in his waistband, Fingal stood with his back to the bar a few feet away from the thin, smartly dressed man, who sat staring into a void, drinking neat vodka and sniffing, wiping his nose on the back of his forearm.

Larry had rejoined Clock and the man who looked like James Brown in dirty overalls, so Fingal was left with no one to talk to, and his self-consciousness returned. The smartly dressed, sniffing man glanced at him, so Fingal smiled and was about to say something when the man turned away again; his brief look in Fingal's direction had been empty of any warmth or interest.

Larry beckoned him over to their table and introduced him to Clock, who bumped fists with him, and, by way of greeting, said, 'Nice.'

'How come you're called Clock?' asked Fingal.

'Wha' he say?' Clock asked Larry.

'Yuh name – why dey call yuh Clock?'

'Ah!' He stretched his arms out in front of him, the left at least six inches shorter than the right. 'Because me like a clock.' He laughed.

By the time Israel called to tell him it was time to go, the bar was full, and Fingal was a few beers down, enjoying the company of Larry, Clock, and James Brown, whose name he hadn't yet determined. Israel was parked by the flamboyant tree, and when Fingal sat down in the passenger's seat, Israel pointed to the car parked a little further up. 'De driver a dat vehicle in de bar?'

'Yeah. Drinking vodka and sniffing coke by the looks of it.'

Israel smiled a thin smile that conveyed no amusement. 'He have company?'

'No. He's alone at the bar and not talking to anybody.'

'Cool. We go wait a li'l while an' see wha' go happen to he.'

'He was at the church. I remember him.'

'I know.' Israel was deep in thought, looking as though he was trying to solve a difficult equation. After a few minutes, he said, 'I go park over dey.' He jerked his head in the direction of the unmade track behind them on the other side of the road.

'Aren't we going to find Camille?'

'Doh worry nah, man. Soon come. I jus' wah go check dis fellah first.'

'Why? What's he got to do with it?'

'Me eh know. Some ting, maybe. Doh worry nah, man. Everyting cool. More cool than me tink it go be a li'l while ago. Relax nah, man. We go wait to see when he move...and whey he go.'

Relax? thought Fingal, how the hell can I relax with a fucking gun digging into my back? 'Shit. I left my hat in the bar,' he said and made to open the car door, but Israel put a gentle restraining hand on his arm.

'Leave it.'

'But it won't take me – '

'Leave it nah, man,' said Israel in a voice that left no doubt. 'We doh wah nobody to know you eh leave.'

'I said we were going to San Fernando.' Israel nodded without looking at Fingal, keeping his gaze fixed on the entrance to the bar.

'Cool,' he said.

~ CHAPTER 41 ~

THE WAIT WASN'T long, but Fingal would have extended it if he could. Even at that point, from which there was seemingly no turning back, he would have welcomed a postponement, a change of strategy, or to have been excused his duties, but he knew that wasn't going to be an option. In the silence of waiting, he tried to work out a way of telling Israel that he couldn't go through with it, that he didn't have what it took; whatever *it took* was, he didn't feel anywhere near having it.

Then, Rajan walked out of the bar and crossed the road a little unsteadily as he glanced around him without seeing the front of Israel's car peeking out from the shadows like a predator watching an oblivious prey. He took what seemed like an age to start his car and then suddenly and violently reversed across the road with a crunching screech, turned, and drove straight past them, heading for the Southern Main Road. Israel waited several seconds before pulling out and driving in the same direction. 'Are you following him?' asked Fingal.

'Yeah, boy.'

'Has he got something to do with all of this?'

'Yeah, boy. I tink so. I *know* so.'

'So, where are we going?'

'I tink La Brea, but let we go follow he and see.'

'Where is La Brea from here?'

'Jus' so.'

'How far?'

'Jus' so.'

'Israel...can you explain what's happening?'

'Me eh know exactly, but I know dis: de Indian boy we following? He lookin' for de girl like we, an' me tink he goin' where she go be, so we followin'.'

'How do you know this?'

'I ask questions, I find some answers. Doh worry nah, man. Dis workin' better for we than me expect.'

'How so?'

'De boy bein' in de bar...I worry he go leave from where he stay an' we maybe lose he, but nah, man, dis good for we.' Israel turned up the volume on the car radio, which until then had just been an irritating background hum. Dub reggae drowned out any other sound. Fingal took this to mean he shouldn't ask any more questions.

Israel turned the volume down again. 'He drunk, though – look how he does drive.'

Rajan's car occasionally veered into the opposite lane, and then, as he approached the village of Vance River, he took one left-hand bend too quickly, brushing the bushes on the right-hand side of the road. Israel sucked his teeth. 'Slow down nah, man. Me wah yuh dey in one piece.'

They passed the locked blue gates of the Vessigny Beach Facility, and Fingal soon saw a weather-beaten sign on his left – *Welcome to the Pitch Lake La Brea – The 8th Wonder of the World! Visitors welcome!* – as Israel slowed down to a point where the car was barely moving. He peered over his steering wheel, scanning the road left and right as though looking for a turning. 'Lost him?' asked Fingal, now also peering.

'Me eh know,' replied Israel. 'Me see him mash he brake, maybe he stop or he turn some whey.'

As they drove around a slight bend where the road undulated at random, tipping the car to almost forty-five degrees, they saw Rajan's car parked a little further up the road, where a man was leaning into the passenger's window and pointing straight up in the air. Israel killed his lights, stopped the car, and lowered their windows. 'Jus' so...jus' so,' the man was saying, 'by de football ground, take a left so,' and he pointed exaggeratedly behind him by way of indicating the direction Rajan should take.

'Foolish boy,' said Israel, 'he must be hopin' de fellah as tight as he an' cah remember he askin' de way.'

'Why?' asked Fingal.

'Case anybody ask, none a we wah witness.' It wasn't a reply to calm Fingal's growing anxiety.

It started to rain. Rajan drove on, and keeping his lights off, Israel followed, leaving as much distance as he could. They reached a junction by the football ground where a group of men were standing noisily outside a small bar. Two roads led off to the left in a V. There was a sign saying *Shimmerlicious Pizza* with a big finger pointing down the right fork of the V and another sign pointing down to the left, reading *Heavy Roast Fish*. Rajan took the right-hand option and turned quickly right again, heading towards the coast. 'Perfect,' said Israel, 'he now know whey he go.'

~ CHAPTER 42 ~

THE RAIN WAS so heavy and loud they had to raise their voices to hear each other speak. It had suddenly hammered down upon the galvanised iron roof and sounded as though the devil's stable door had been breached and a herd of horses in their thousands were galloping above them. Lights flickered. Tanty Jo – wearing a stained, once-white apron adorned with the word *Cookin'* in stylised red letters – was busy grinding a mixture of ingredients in a mortar. She stopped, holding the pestle like a sword, and looked upwards. 'Yuh heavens above,' she said, 'rain down on my righteousness. Let de clouds shower it down. Let de earth open wide, and let salvation spring up. Let righteousness flourish with it.'

Lola and Camille looked at her. 'Isaiah 45,' she said, returning to her work. 'What you make?' asked Lola.

'Me grindin' worm weed. Whey yuh from is called *simen contra*.'

Lola's eyes widened. '*Un vermífugo*,' she said.

'Huh yuh know de ting? Yeah, is a vermifuge.'

Camille nodded in recognition of the word, which was the same in French. 'A purge?' she asked.

'Can be, but dis a li'l more strong. Now is jus' add some jumbie beads an' a li'l a de angel's trumpet.'

The three were sitting at Tanty Jo's large, dark wooden table. The old woman was absorbed in her grinding, perspiring with the effort. Lola walked to the window and peered out. She could see very little through the rain and so didn't notice a car pulling up at the end of the unmade track leading to their houses. As she turned around again, she saw Camille looking at her with a frightened expression.

Lola came to Camille's side and stroked her hair, then cradled her head in her arms. 'Don't worry,' she said and kissed the top of Camille's head. She switched on the little black fan.

Tanty Jo stopped grinding and looked at them. 'Nah doh worry, I eh sure anyting go happen. I jus' bein' careful, yuh know? We safe here, anyway. Nobody go come by we on a night like dis. Let we relax a li'l, but Lola, girl, doh look out de window.' She tipped the powdered mixture from the mortar into the pocket of her apron.

~ CHAPTER 43 ~

RAJAN BENT DOWN to sniff another line of cocaine that he had chopped onto a magazine he kept on the passenger seat for that very purpose. A car silently pulled up behind him. He tilted his head backwards to maximise absorption of the cocaine through the snot flowing through his nasal passages, and when he looked back to the dimly-lit house, he saw a figure looking out from one of its windows. 'It have to be she,' he thought.

The rain meant his visibility was reduced but even through the wet haze, he could make out the charms and fetishes hanging from branches of the trees in the front garden area. A painted cow's skull sat atop a pole at the head of the pathway leading from the track to the front door. It wasn't as though he was entirely dismissive of obeah – and on a night such as this, even the most sceptical person would have to be senseless not to feel a frisson of fear when faced with so much evidence of the supernatural – but he quickly rationalised any trepidation away. Fingering the gold crucifix around his neck, he whispered to himself, 'Is real dotishness. Only de old believe in dis superstition an' too many a dem obeah people jus' fakery, trickin' we for we money and makin' we scared. Is stupidness. Real stupidness. Nah, let me see if de French girl dey.'

He moved quickly, taking the gun from his waistband as he approached. He saw the petals encircling the house and hesitated. 'Shit,' he said a little too loudly. Then he saw the chalk circle with the cross and stick figures, but his momentum was too strong for him to stop, and he aimed the sole of his right foot at the latch on the door.

~ CHAPTER 44 ~

WHEN RAJAN KICKED at the front door of the house, Fingal tried to get out of the car only for Israel to pull him back. He put his finger to his mouth to say *shhhh*. Fingal started to protest, but Israel left him with no doubt that he had to obey. 'Wait nah, man. Soon come.'

Israel checked in the rear-view mirror, and after what felt to Fingal like an age but in reality was only a couple of minutes, they saw the Hummer pull up in the shadows behind them. Without telling Fingal what he had been waiting for, Israel said in a voice so calm and hushed he could have been putting a child to bed: 'We go now. I go first. Give me a minute. Count it slowly, more slow dan yuh heartbeat, den yuh go in carryin' yuh gun. Let everybody see yuh holdin' it. If I in trouble, den act how yuh tink best. But doh worry nah, everyting irie.' And with that, he was out of the car and halfway down the pathway to the house in seconds.

Now, it was happening. Now, the crescendo was building to its climax like a rushing river headed for a waterfall. Now was the culmination of every second of his previous life. Now, the past and the future ceased to exist. And now, as the icy cold reality of the present consumed him wholly, Fingal felt a calm he had never experienced before. It was the most serene and peaceful few seconds of his life.

He watched Israel through the rain, haloed by the warm glow of light emanating from the open doorway and began to count more slowly than his heartbeat.

~ CHAPTER 45 ~

TANTY JO SPOKE to the dog that wasn't there. 'Rocky, why yuh bark so?' just as the crash of wood made all three women look up in alarm to see Rajan standing there, his eyes wide, red, and aroused and a gun in his hand. Camille screamed. Lola gasped and put her hand to her mouth as he approached the table they were all sitting at.

'Shut yuh damn mouth,' he said, looking at Camille.

'Boy, yuh doh know wha – ' started Tanty Jo.

'An' *you* shut yours!' he spat, moving closer to them and pointing the gun at Camille.

'You...bitch...stand up!'

She hesitated.

'Now!' he shouted.

She started to move.

Lola put a hand on her forearm.

Rajan pointed the gun at Lola. 'Leave she! Less yuh wah some a wha' she go get.'

With a grace of movement belying both her age and size, Tanty Jo reached into her apron pocket, stood up, and threw the powdered mixture into Rajan's eyes. As he raised his hands to his face, Lola, in an unpremeditated but swift, flowing action, grabbed the small black fan from behind her, pulling it from its socket, and ran at Rajan, striking him across the face with it.

He fell to the ground. She then kicked the gun from his hand as blood trickled from his head, sticking to the powder all over his face.

Camille, having grabbed Lola's cutlass, stood over him like an executioner poised to deliver the final blow.

They looked up, aware of another presence in the room. In astonishment, they all stared at the tall, rain-spattered Rasta standing just inside the doorway holding a gun with both his hands, pointing it downwards towards Rajan. He looked as surprised as they did.

He raised his left hand in a gesture of reassurance. 'I come for he,' he said, jerking his head towards Rajan, who was now looking up at him in horror. Looking at Camille, he added, 'An' I bring a friend for yuh. He come to rescue yuh.'

The three women continued to stare in silence at Israel as they tried to organise their thoughts and understand what was happening. Where de damn hell is he? wondered Israel. A few seconds later, not quite on cue and looking as tentative as a mouse in a room full of cats, Fingal appeared.

'Oh, my God!' exclaimed Camille.

'Everything okay?' he asked, his apparent equanimity hiding his abject horror at the scene before his eyes.

Israel acted quickly and decisively, taking hold of Rajan's arms and asking Tanty Jo where the back door was. She pointed it out to him, and he dragged Rajan towards it. Rajan didn't resist.

Fingal went to Camille and tried to take her in his arms. She drew back and asked him, 'Fingal...what are you doing here? How did you know where?'

'Long story,' he said, 'but it looks like you didn't need me.'

She yielded and allowed him to hold her. They sat down at the table, their legs suddenly unable to support either of them. Lola went to Tanty Jo, who stared into space, grimly silent, and held her. They all heard the two shots coming from the back of the house – *pop! pop!* – like someone was piercing bubble-wrap.

Slowly edging its way to the fore of his thoughts, coming into focus like a bedroom at dawn as the hushed lines of the dream world sharpened and tautened into clarity, Fingal was beginning to realise an inescapable truth, that Israel, despite his easy-going, soon-come attitude, all his generosity of spirit and effort and all his genuine regard for and love of life, operated at a level Fingal was only just beginning to understand. What had just happened at the back of the house?

Israel walked back in, his presence immediately commanding and authoritative. 'I need for allyuh to listen,' he said. They all understood he was a dangerous man, but for now, he was on their side. He was their friend and protector so they would listen to him and find out what was going to happen next and how much they were still in danger, if at all. 'For a li'l while, yuh all bound to stay here. Doh go outside. It have some people go help we with tings. Doh worry, jus' stay calm an' quiet an' everyting go be cool...okay?'

Fingal started to say something, but Israel shook his head at him, telling him the relationship of near equals they had shared thus far was now on hold.

The four of them sat at the table while Israel went to the door. He flashed a few times using the torch on his phone and waited. At some point, the rain had stopped, and no one had noticed. They heard the sound of a car moving slowly over the unmade road towards them.

~ CHAPTER 46 ~

OG FLICKED HIS cigarette onto the lawn before entering, followed immediately by Ronaldo and Messi and a fair-skinned black man who waited, framed by the door as the others approached Israel, who fist-bumped all three of them. 'Done?' asked Dog. Israel nodded. Dog sighed. 'Whey?' 'De back.'

Without speaking and by gesture alone, Dog instructed Ronaldo and Messi to check. They returned in a few seconds, Messi nodding a confirmation. Dog removed his tinted spectacles and folded them into his breast pocket, his forehead jewelled with sweat. He took out a wad of US dollars and handed them to Israel, who stuffed them into his trouser pocket without counting. He showed Rajan's car key to Dog, who pointed to Ronaldo. 'Give it to he,' he said.

'De boat dey?' asked Israel, throwing the key to Ronaldo. Dog nodded, and pointing towards the man at the door, said, 'He go help yuh.' Then, turning to the four of them sitting at the table, said, 'Ladies an' gentleman...please allow me to apologise for de...er...intrusion tonight. I wah ask yuh all for a li'l more a yuh time an' patience. We almost get through here. Jus' a few li'l ting to attend to, an' den we gone, an' yuh wouldn' have to worry no more. Yuh safe.' He looked at them with an expression of chilling disdain before adding, 'I eh interested in any a yuh.'

Israel and the doorman left the room via the back door, Israel calling out, 'Fingal, wait here for me nah. I go be a li'l while. I go call yuh.'

Dog tapped in a number on his cell phone. 'Now good,' was all he said before turning it off again. He pulled up a chair to sit at the table with his audience, all of whom were silent and tried to avoid eye contact. Lola gripped Camille's hand as though she were about to fall off a cliff edge.

Dog linked his pudgy fingers, rested them on his belly, and sighed once more. 'Madam,' he said, addressing Tanty Jo, 'yuh have sweet drink?'

She got up without responding and fetched a bottle of bright red liquid with a glass.

'Ice,' said Dog, and Tanty Jo filled a cereal bowl with ice cubes from a plastic bag in her freezer. He put three cubes of ice in the glass, one by one, then poured a glassful of the drink over them. Every move was watched intently by everyone else in the room.

'What is this?' he asked.

'Sorrel,' she answered.

'Yuh add any a yuh...special ingredient?'

She shook her head.

Dog pushed the glass towards Lola. 'Drink some,' he commanded.

Lola looked up at Tanty Jo who nodded. She took a gulp and pushed the glass back towards Dog. As he sipped the drink, he sucked his teeth, making a series of tuts as though he were scolding them all.

The sound of an outboard motor broke the silence.

A half-hour had passed before another car pulled up. Adding to their already stretched sense of incredulity and surreality, the four captives saw two policemen walk through the door. Tanty Jo recognised them as the two officers who had brought a drugged and distressed Camille to her house barely a week before. One of them, an olive-skinned man with shiny, close-cropped Afro-hair and sergeant stripes on his sleeve, smiled at everyone there. 'Goodnight,' he said with a smile as though he had arrived for a dinner party.

Dog stood up with a grunt and addressed them. 'Took yuh time.'

'Yuh done here?'

'We done.'

'Den go.'

Dog nodded and looked at the policeman through narrowed eyes. 'We goin'.' Beckoning to Ronaldo and Messi to follow him, Dog walked out the door, a stench of menace trailing behind him.

The sergeant looked from one to the other of them and back again a few times. 'Camille Brossard,' he said, looking straight at her and using such a serious tone of voice she thought he was going to announce charges against her. She raised her hand like a child in a classroom.

'We have some tings for yuh.' With a slight movement of his head towards the door, he appeared to issue an order to his subordinate, who immediately left the house. They heard the piercing note of the car's remote key and then the opening and closing of the boot. He carried a suitcase and backpack into the room and placed them on the table in front of Camille.

The sergeant smiled at her. 'It have everyting dey,' he said, 'personal effect an' phone...yuh passport. I hope yuh enjoy de rest a yuh stay. Goodnight.'

~ CHAPTER 47 ~

N O ONE REALLY slept, and dawn arrived all too quickly, bringing with it a cloudless sky and gentle breeze that blew through the net curtains like a returning spirit casting a soothing spell, allowing them all to stir without anxiety or fear. Lola and Fingal had dozed on either side of Camille on the sofa, her head on Fingal's chest and her hand holding Lola's. Tanty Jo had slept in her rocking chair on the front gallery, if she had slept at all – such had been her need for prayer and invocation. Once the sun was high over the coconut palms lining the cane field opposite, and she heard the gentle threshing sound of the spirits moving through the branches with the wind, she stopped her calling and made herself a sweet cup of tea. As she looked out and chewed on a dry cracker, she chuckled to Rocky. 'Nah, boy, yuh cah have some. Me real hungry.'

As Lola slept on, Camille and Fingal stood awkwardly together in the kitchen. 'We need to talk,' he said.

'I know,' she replied, 'let's go down to the beach – I want to bathe and freshen up.' She looked in her suitcase for her bikini and then went into Tanty Jo's room to change.

They left through the backdoor, not noticing the brown trickle of blood on the grass that was attracting a swarm of bush flies. As they reached the bottom of the path, Fingal watched Camille throw her towel onto a tree trunk and run into the water, diving through a wave without hesitation. He stood on the shoreline, wavelets turning over his bare feet. He felt she was out of reach, and he struggled to understand why. He waded in until his shorts were covered, cupped his hands, and splashed the still, cool water over his head and into his face. He watched her swimming away from him.

Then, they walked the length of the beach, sometimes hand in hand but more often unsure of whether or not to touch, until they reached the ruined jetty where a pod of pelicans were fanning their wings to get dry, nodding their heads as though they were all in agreement, their pink throat sacs flapping like rags in the wind, their calls sounding like cars with flat batteries being goaded to start. Much of the time was spent without words. Once they had both explained how they had come to be in that place at that particular time, it was as though what remained unsaid between them was too onerous to even contemplate. Halfway back, they sat on a concrete bench under a flamboyant tree in full bloom, some of its crimson petals falling about them with each puff of breeze.

A car drove up and parked next to the tree. They turned to look at the people inside. An old black man leaned out of the window and said, 'Nah problem. Yuh okay. I jus' wah a park in de shade.'

They watched as he reversed the car into position, then opened up the boot to remove two folding chairs. The man was shirtless, thin and sinewy, the muscles of his arms and calves taut and hard. His head, bald, save for a sprinkling of cropped grey hairs, glinted in the sun as he helped a woman, presumably his wife, out of the car. He led her to one of the chairs where she, wearing a faded green dress, white cardigan, and yellow, black, and red curlers in her hair, sat her wide backside down. The thin old man went back to the front of the car, switched on the radio, and turned the volume up high. Old-school soca blared out and the old man shouted, "Bachanaaaaal!"

He returned to the boot, took a bright red, sweet drink from a cooler, and handed it to his wife before pouring himself a large rum in a Styrofoam cup and adding an ice-cube. Then, looking out to sea with his drink in one hand, he started to dance with unbridled joy, barely moving his feet but whining his hips and torso, shrugging his shoulders in time, totally at one with his surroundings, occasionally smiling at Camille and Fingal as if sharing a deep secret with them, one only known to a very select few. His lack of inhibition and sheer celebration of life there under the blue sky in front of the waves and the wide expanse of sand with his wife by his side left them awestruck.

Camille laughed in joyous recognition of the man's apparent complete peace with himself as he threw off the shackles of his life and danced. He downed his drink, laughed out loud, and threw them a smile so wide the edges of his lips could have reached his ears.

'What will you do now?' she asked Fingal, patting his arm. That she even asked that told him she was unlikely to ask him to stay. Silent for a few moments, he realised that the time when their two stars had somehow aligned had now passed. He had held onto this ideal without ever having really thought it through because the unconscious desire driving that idealised view was really about something much more mundane: his romanticised, unrealistic view of himself, his lack of self-esteem and his need for recognition. To be a musician who played in front of audiences was to be a mere actor playing a part and looking for acclaim. While he had been Camille's most sympathetic lover, he had also been playing another part, another way for him to seek acclaim and affirmation. He looked at her – beautiful, bright, soft, and wise, and he blessed the day their paths had crossed, but he now knew that whatever it was they had shared had run it's course, they were on separate paths now and it wouldn't matter if, once they had said goodbye, he never saw her again.

'I left my hat in a bar,' he said, 'I need to get it – do you want to come with me?'

She shook her head, leaned back on the seat, and said, 'I think I'll stay here for now. '

His phone buzzed, and he saw it was Israel calling. The old man was still dancing. Fingal kissed the top of her head, briefly took her hand, then let her go and walked back along the beach towards the path.

THE END

ACKNOWLEDGEMENTS

First and foremost, I offer heartfelt thanks to Daniella Blechner of Conscious Dreams Publishing for affording me the time, patience and opportunity to realise this project.

Then, I would like to thank Elise Abram for her wonderful, conscientious editing and help in getting this into shape.

Thanks and appreciation to Oksana Kosovan for her excellent and efficient work with the typesetting.

I would also like to thank Steve Gander for his generous reading, proofreading, support, and encouragement through the early drafts.

Thanks also to John Ashton for his flamboyant tree paintings.

Also, for his support, reading and encouragement, I would like to thank Adam Strange of Strange Media.

Last but by no means least, I offer loving and deep gratitude to my daughter, Katherine, for her work on dialogue and for making such insightful suggestions to the text, and to my wife, Rehanna, for her love and support, and for taking me to Trinidad in the first place.

ABOUT THE AUTHOR

Rick Tucker writes prose and poetry, draws and paints, and writes and plays music. After a spell at art school, he played in bands, then gave up being an artist to spend years working as a nurse in secure mental health units, followed by a few years of uncomfortably wearing a suit while leading national policies in relation to tackling violence in the NHS. An expert witness, investigator, educator and senior lecturer came next before he gave it all up to get back to his first loves. An outpouring of pent-up creativity ensued. Married to a Trini, he has spent much time in Trinidad and Tobago, where he has beloved and loving friends and family and from where he gained much inspiration for his writing. To unwind, he sings the blues, walks miles, and talks to the animals and trees. His first self-published novel is called *A Dog Unchained* and his music is available on the usual online platforms.

Conscious Dreams
PUBLISHING

Be the author of your own destiny

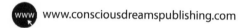
www.consciousdreamspublishing.com

info@consciousdreamspublishing.com

Let's connect